Escape From Purgatory

First Edition

Published by The Nazca Plains Corporation
Las Vegas, Nevada
2009

ISBN: 978-1-935509-39-4

Published by

The Nazca Plains Corporation ®
4640 Paradise Rd, Suite 141
Las Vegas NV 89109-8000

PUBLISHER'S NOTE
Escape From Purgatory is a work of fiction created wholly by *Mark James'* imagination. All characters are fictional and any resemblance to any persons living or deceased is purely by accident. No portion of this book reflects any real person or events.

Cover Male Photo, Vinc Trent
Art Director, Blake Stephens

Escape From Purgatory

First Edition

Mark James

In the howling storm, cruel winds whipped the sea against dark rock.

White foam crashed into jagged edges that rose up into the night like black, stone teeth. In a time before smoke stacks stained the skies, men came here and carved a prison out of the mountain. This ancient rock is the realm of men whose cries of misery are swallowed up in the dark sea. This place of the unforgiven is Purgatory Prison.

Prologue

The rapid fire clicking of a keyboard echoed in the silence of the dark basement. Kyle's fingers flew across the keys of his laptop in a fury, desperate to undo the damage he'd done. What began as a game, had blossomed into an obsession. Every night for nearly two months, Kyle rushed home from his job washing dishes and fired up his laptop.

Last night, he'd found the last piece, and crashed the Array, a weapon whose existence was categorically denied by the President. Game over, and Kyle, a nineteen year old hacker, scored the winning point.

It all went wrong when Kyle realized he couldn't bring the Array back online. Not in time to evade the Hunters who were already on his trail. He'd hidden all day, typing hundreds of lines of code, but it was no good.

Last time he'd tripped one of their systems, Homeland Security injected him with a Guardian chip. No problem. Kyle knew how to blind the Eye in the Sky, but his evasion code lasted only twenty four hours. He had to get the Array back up and running before they found him. He glanced at the tiny digital hourglass on his screen. Falling grains of virtual sand ticked away his moments of freedom.

Coppery red hair fell across his face. He bit his pink lips hard enough to leave teeth marks. His dark green eyes were narrowed in concentration. Codes flowed across his laptop screen like a red river of madness.

As a new sun shed light on a tired world, frustration lined Kyle's smooth face. Nothing he did brought the Array back online. The top half of the hour glass was empty. Time to go. He tried not to tremble when he shut his lap top. If he didn't haul ass, Homeland Security would land on him with God's vengeance.

An explosion of sound froze Kyle in the act of scooping his laptop off the floor. A brutal kick smashed the door, hurling wooden splinters through the darkness. Kyle jumped up, shielding his face. Men the size of refrigerators poured in through the dark hole that used to be a door. Kyle ran for the giant packing crates scattered around the dark corners. A soldier, who made Hercules look like a backstreet wimp, grabbed the back of Kyle's t-shirt and reeled him in.

"Where you going, kid?" the soldier said. Then he spoke into the radio on his collar. "Got him, Sir."

"Shoot him," the short command came back.

Before Kyle could beg for his life, he felt the sharp sting of a needle in the tender cheek of his backside. Blackness pulled him down into oblivion.

PART ONE
Chapter 1

Everyday for the last two weeks in the Patriot Act Homeland Security Detention Center, Kyle had waited for someone to come and ask him about the Array. Muscle bound soldiers brought him food in unbroken silence. When Kyle tried to talk to them, they looked through him, and walked around him with the same care they'd use to avoid upsetting furniture.

A week ago, Kyle blocked the way of a soldier, and asked him when he'd be able to leave. The man looked at Kyle with hard eyes for a long time before he said, "You're pretty. You're real lucky we ain't allowed to touch you, boy. Real lucky."

The animal lust that flared in the soldier's dark eyes made Kyle fall back a step. The soldier walked past him without a backward glance. After that, Kyle stopped trying to talk to the soldiers.

At night, Kyle tried not to hear the distant screams echoing down the metal corridors, like souls falling into Hell. Tonight, beyond the bars of his cell, two soldiers walked by, shadows among shadows in their black uniforms.

"Fucking Heretic's gonna get what's coming to him," a voice said out of the darkness.

"He's going straight to Redemption when he gets to Purgatory. I hear Matthew can't wait to make him scream."

Their hushed voices faded as they walked by. *Heretic.* For as long as Kyle could remember, that had been a forbidden thought. Hearing the word said so casually, with night's darkness crowding in all around, sent a cool shiver down his spine. Kyle's father was a martyred leader of the Heretics. Starving people who watched their children die from drinking dirty water, called Kyle's father a hero. Homeland Security called him an Enemy of the State.

Trapped in the belly of night, with sleep a broken promise, the vision of his father's brutal death assaulted him with unmerciful cruelty. In his mind, Kyle heard the echoing sound of the soldiers' boots. The pipes of the underground sewer caves had filled with the sound of screams and running feet.

When the soldiers took his father, Trent had looked back at his son. Kyle had seen the sure knowledge of his own death in his father's eyes. As his trembling son watched, Trent faced forward, straightened his back, and fell in step with the soldiers on either side of him.

Two days later, Kyle's father was executed at a Traitor Redemption, a version of the punishment reserved for Enemies of the State. Although his father's friends tried to stop him, Kyle watched every moment of the state sponsored torture.

Shouts of '*heretic*' and '*freedom*' rose from the throat of the live audience. Gratitude was stamped on every wildly gleeful face. Again, the state had destroyed a dangerous enemy lurking among them. The utopia of freedom and justice for all was just around the corner. They would get there one dead traitor at a time.

After the death of his father, the Heretics cared for Kyle. In the underground world of the sewers, he learned to be a sewer rat, and how to use a simple lap top to bring the government to their knees.

When Kyle hacked the banking system, and brought it crashing down, Homeland Security caught him, and tagged him with a Guardian Chip. After that, the same men who'd cared for him, kept him out of the sewers with guns aimed between his eyes. Kyle wandered the streets for weeks, hungry, dirty and scared.

He wandered into Nick's Eats, and offered to wash dishes for a meal. Nick took him in, and let Kyle stay in the spare room over the restaurant. When Nick caught Kyle sneaking into his office to use his computer, he said how a smart boy like him should have his own lap top. It wasn't long before Nick was calling Kyle into his office, or pushing him to his knees as soon as he closed up for the night.

The lap top came soon after. The horror that started with crashing the Array followed on the heels of the new lap top, like a blaring train ripping the midnight silence of tormented sleep.

Chapter 2

On the fourteenth day of detention, Kyle sat on his bunk, staring at the brick wall of his cell, wondering how much worse his life could get. When the Principal walked in, Kyle stopped wondering.

"Holy Mary, Mother of God," Kyle said. He felt like a skydiver, who'd just remembered his parachute was still on the plane.

The Principal sat on the small wooden chair that was the only furniture in Kyle's cell. His grey tailored suit would have cost most men a month's salary. Everyone in the country knew the man's face.

On holo, he was a trusted grandfather who looked straight into the cameras and told God's own truth. His reputation was impeccable, his sincerity unquestioned. It was the dark green eyes behind his round, rimless spectacles that shattered the illusion.

"Hey, kid," he said, staring at Kyle.

Kyle looked at him wide eyed, unable to make his frozen lips form words. He watched as the President's closest assistant and confidante lit a cigarette. Holo called him 'the Principal', because nobody wanted to end up in his office, not even the President. The Principal stared at Kyle through a cloud of smoke that clung to him, as if he smoked the way other people sweat.

"They been treating you okay?"

Kyle didn't bother to ask about his right to know the charges against him, his right to representation.

"Yes, Sir." His voice was a bare whisper.

"You came up in the world since last time. You got the chip that time, right?"

Kyle nodded. "Yes, Sir." They were the only two words he could bring himself to say.

The Principal looked at Kyle with expressionless eyes.

"I told you then that if you fucked with me again, I was gonna make you one sorry kid, didn't I?" His monotone voice was eerily calm. He flicked ashes onto the stone floor.

Kyle spoke in the hollow tones of a condemned man. "I didn't mean to. I'm sorry."

"You know where they're sending you, boy?"

Kyle shrugged. "Work camp, I guess."

"Guess again." Dark thoughts glittered in the Principal's dead green eyes. "You're going to Purgatory."

"What?" Kyle jumped up and paced his tiny cell. "That's a hell hole. Toughest prison in the country."

He stopped in front of the Principal, looking down into his seamed face that held not an ounce of compassion.

"I'm just some kid who fucked with your Array. Christ. I'm sorry." Kyle ran shaky fingers through his coppery hair. "Jesus."

"Bring it back online," the Principal said. He took a deep drag on his cigarette and blew smoke up to the ceiling. "Or I'll make you suffer in ways you never dreamed of, kid."

Kyle's pounding heart made his words shaky, uncertain. "I don't know how," he said in a mad rush. "I tried. I can't. I'm telling the truth. God. *Please.*" The last two words came out in a desperate plea.

The Principal looked up at Kyle with the cool eyes of a sniper honing in on his target.

"You fucking think I was born yesterday?"

Filled with the fear of a child trapped with a nightmare ogre, Kyle said, "I'm telling the truth." His voice teetered on the razor edge of hysteria.

The Principal pulled a black box from his jacket pocket. Like a demon summoned from the depths of Hell, a hologram sprang to life next to Kyle. He stared at the man, blacker than midnight. He was naked to the waist, his chest and arms were roped with muscle. He had the hard face of a hunter who stalked men to the death, and enjoyed the hunt.

————————————

"Know who that is, kid?"

"Everyone knows who he is. JT. Prisoner gladiator." Kyle looked up into the gladiator's eyes, merciless and cold.

"Know where he is?"

"Purgatory," Kyle said. His mind ticked over furiously, trying to see where this was leading.

"He's the most vicious gladiator in Purgatory," the Principal said. "Won the State Wide Championship. Brought in a lot of money. They're giving him a virgin to be his wife in there."

The Principal paused, looking into Kyle's terrified eyes. "You still a virgin, kid?"

Kyle blushed, looked down at his feet.

"There's nothing JT likes better than breaking in a pretty virgin."

Looking at the dark gladiator, all at once, Kyle knew what was coming.

The Principal bared his crooked teeth in a humorless grin. "You're JT's new cellmate." He leaned an inch closer to Kyle and said, soft and low, "His new wife."

The gladiator's image towered over Kyle. JT was a lithe sculpture of strength, built with the sleek grace of a panther. Staring at his thick arms, heavy with muscle, a terrible truth hammered through the whirlwind in Kyle's mind, *I won't be a virgin for long.*

"I don't know how to fix it. I'm telling the truth," Kyle said.

The Principal smoked in silence for a long time. "No. You're trying to lie to a man who fought in two wars before you were born." He pointed at Kyle with the two fingers holding his cigarette. "Last chance, kid."

Kyle fought a brief battle with himself that could have ended with the truth slipping from his traitorous lips. At the end, flesh had hung from his father's limp body, like delicate strips of raw meat.

"I don't know how to fix it," Kyle said. His eyes slipped away to the scarred stone floor.

"You're just like your dad, you know that, boy?"

The mention of his father made Kyle cold all over.

"I'm giving you a couple of months to be JT's punk," the Principal said thoughtfully. "I hear he likes it real rough with his punks. Maybe he'll help you remember things, so you can fix what you broke."

Kyle stared at the hologram. Words flew through his mind in a fury. He had the face of a prisoner watching men hammer his gallows together.

The man who stood beside the President when he spoke of the triumph of Democracy in foreign lands, had eyes that were windows on cold, depthless darkness.

"I signed your father's arrest warrant," the Principal said.

"Don't talk about my father," Kyle said through clenched teeth.

The Principal laughed. "You wanna come get me, boy? Come on."

Kyle flew at him in blind rage. The Principal sprang up, quick as a rattlesnake. He caught Kyle, shoved him through the hologram, and pressed him hard into the brick wall. He bent close and whispered.

"When JT fucks your ass real hard and makes you scream, remember something, kid."

"What?" Kyle said, trying to shake free.

"Purgatory isn't as bad as it can get. If you don't give me what I want, you'll end up in a room that ain't got no fucking windows. Nobody hears you scream in those back rooms, boy."

"I'll fucking *die* before I help you," Kyle said in a low whisper.

The Principal stood back, straightened his jacket, pushed his thick gray hair from his cold eyes. He gave Kyle a long look, the unfeeling gaze of a lion stalking a gazelle.

"You're real young, boy. I got a lot to teach you."

"Like what?" Kyle said.

"Like how there's worse things than dying."

The Principal dropped a card at Kyle's feet. "Don't make me wait too long. Or I'll come for you."

Chapter 3

Kyle sat behind a small metal desk in the prison's library. Today was the end of his first week in Purgatory. He slid in another blank disc and downloaded the replacement file for the damaged Book Disc. The steady boredom of downloading data lured him onto forbidden highways. Dangerous thoughts chased through his mind.

He scanned the empty aisles of neatly racked discs. No one was watching him. Kyle launched another window on his screen, and logged into the library's Card Catalog.

A question blinked across the screen – 'Search by: Author, Title, Keyword?' Kyle peeked over the top of his monitor and saw no one. He slid down on the wooden chair, leaning back and staring at the screen through half lidded eyes. Anyone looking at Kyle would have thought he was in a trance, hypnotized by his screen. It was the look that came over his face when he was in the zone, hacking, walking to nowhere.

Kyle lived to chase down the code. His fingers moved over the keys like a wizard conjuring his way to strange lands. He loved walking the dark labyrinth of numbers and symbols that programmers built. In his mind, he saw not the screen, but a dark castle; a fortress built to keep intruders out. He crept around the castle walls, looking for a chink, a crack that would let him in. He found the tiny rabbit hole, and slipped through.

JT's mug shot slid down from the top of the screen. Kyle sent a request for JT's arrest record. The answer that came back, blinking in red, was no surprise, 'Category Five – Record Secure'. Kyle didn't have time to hack past it. He didn't need to; he knew enough. Cat five killers made their victims die hard, screaming to their last breath.

Backdoors like the one Kyle had slipped through were like watchdogs. They let you in, but they kept sniffing around. Kyle had a simple code that interfaced with watchdogs and captured their alert times. He glanced down at the code that appeared on his screen as a stop watch. The digits were blinking in red. He had about three minutes before the watchdogs sent an alert to the main program.

Kyle clicked to JT's record in Purgatory Prison. He scanned through page after page. His fight or flight instinct dumped adrenaline into his bloodstream, making his heart pound in his ears. He skimmed reports of brutal assaults, shattered bones, knifings, fist fights and two suspected cases of cruel and unusual torture. Kyle closed his dark green eyes, and willed his thundering heart to slow.

He glanced at the stopwatch; minute and a half. Kyle typed steadily, scaling the castle wall to another floor. He slipped through another open window of code. When he found what he'd come for, cold sweat popped out on his pale face.

He took in every detail of the prisoner. The caption read "Jessi Sinclair", followed by his prison number. Above the words, Jessi's swollen face was distorted by a black eye and a swollen lip. Black and blue bruises decorated his smooth cheeks like strange, abstract artwork.

The stopwatch was down to '00:10'. Kyle backed out the way he'd come, smoothing over his tracks; hiding from the watchdog programs that would be on his trail.

For the first time since he'd seen the Principal, Kyle considered calling the number on the card. He'd get an offer he couldn't refuse – a job with Homeland Security, with a lifetime contract. He'd be trading Purgatory Prison for a life sentence, with the Principal as his jailer. Somehow he knew his father had turned down the same offer, and the Principal had made him pay an obscenely high price.

Kyle stared at the screen, not seeing the question, 'Search by: Author, Title, Keyword?' blinking in serene inquiry. His mind kept going back to the cast on Jessi's right arm. He tried not to think about the words above Jessi's picture.

Fear is an unrelenting predator. The five words fell through Kyle's mind like the whickering sound of the axe in a man's ears, just before his head rolls away into forever: 'Prior Cell Mate: James Tanning'.

Chapter 4

What's it worth? Kyle's secret life as a hacker always turned on that question. The answer: *what do you wanna risk?* Kyle thought that the note on the top bunk might answer at least one of the questions.

The box on the top bunk was the soft pink of a sunrise. Kyle's eyes were drawn to it because everything else in the cell was grey or black, or some other shade of hopeless.

"You want some free advice?" the guard said.

"Nothing's free," Kyle said, reading the note beside the pink box of chocolates.

Wanna be my girl? the note said.

"You ever been in a hurricane?"

Kyle shot the guard a distrustful look. Solid muscle, wrapped in a grey uniform. "What?"

There was something unyielding and stony about his crew cut, his hard grey eyes, his polished shoes. Like a gargoyle guarding Purgatory from any ray of light.

"When a hurricane hits, you get away from the windows, hunker down, and pray the roof don't get ripped off from over your head." He looked at Kyle, squinting a little. "You following me, kid?"

"No idea," Kyle said, staring at the note.

"Alright. Plain talk. If you don't wanna know how loud you can scream, don't fuck with JT."

He turned with military precision and slammed the heavy cell door behind him, leaving Kyle stranded in JT's cell. For a long moment, Kyle thought of how the guard hadn't slid the lock in place. As if no one would walk into JT's cell without his say so. Not unless they were willing to pay the price.

The painting on the wall of the cell emerged from the darkness, as if the Horsemen were riding from far off.

In the painting, a silver scythe lay in a cloud of dust left by the Horsemen of the Apocalypse. The Horsemen were hooded black figures, like shadows of doom in the shapes of men. Where their faces should have been, there was only darkness.

The things that warned of their return had been cast away in their headlong rush. The signs of their coming lay on the on the dark, twisted road behind them – scythe, sword, arrows, scales.

The time of warnings and prophecies was long gone in the world of the painting. Victory rode a white horse that sparkled beside Famine's black horse. War's stallion was the color of a sea of blood. Death rode his pale horse hard.

In the sky, a cruel scythe moon hung among the stars. Famine's shadow body hunched over his horse, urging him on. *Come on boy*, he seemed to say, *you can do it. Just a little further. Armageddon's just ahead.*

These were no messengers of the Apocalypse. They were the real thing – dark angels, come to wage ruin on the face of the world. Galloping madly, the Horsemen raced the sun, bringing night with them.

Kyle shuddered at the sight of the Horsemen racing from the wall, like the ultimate Hell Raisers. His eyes slid to the unlocked cell door. What if he slid the door back, and walked out?

His fingers were curled around the bars, ready to ease the heavy door back, when a thought hit him with the blinding terror of glaring headlights on a midnight road. *The Principal will come for me*, he thought, *and take me to room with no windows.* His hands fall away from the iron bars. He walked back to the narrow cot, not seeing the box of chocolates.

Kyle saw himself on a cold metal chair, the Principal standing there, looking down at him through a haze of smoke. And behind him, grey brick walls; no windows. Where do you go from Purgatory? Hell was the closest neighborhood.

Chapter 5

Kyle slumped down on the bottom bunk, leaned his head back against the grey brick wall. His hair fell away from his pale face. He pulled his legs close, wrapped his arms around, and sank into dark thoughts of paying for what he'd bought.

Echoing footsteps and harsh voices out in the stone corridor jolted Kyle from his gloomy thoughts. He looked up when JT slid the heavy door open with a bang. His dark face glistened with sweat. The tattoo of a screaming skull on his arm glared with malevolent red eyes.

"Somebody thinks he's fucking funny," JT said.

Gladiators didn't talk on holo. It was the first time Kyle had ever heard JT's deep voice. He watched JT crumple the note, then dump the chocolates down the toilet. The harsh sound of rushing water made Kyle jump a little.

JT took off his sleeveless t-shirt. His chest and arms rippled with sleek muscle. He soaked the faded grey shirt under the pipe, and wrung it dry.

Kyle couldn't help noticing how powerful JT's hands looked with water seeping between his thick fingers. He wiped down his body, took a fresh t-shirt from the wooden shelf behind him, and slipped it on.

"You liking the show?" JT said.

"I saw you a lot on holo," Kyle said. "You're different. I thought – "

"I know what you thought," JT said. He leaned against the wall, covering a Horseman, and pulled a pack of cigarettes from his jeans. "I got you something." His eyes shifted to the grey metal desk against the wall.

For the first time Kyle noticed the package on the desk. The wrapping was faded and dull, as if the color had worn out. He went over to the desk, feeling JT's eyes on him.

"I didn't know how many pieces you like," JT said.

Kyle tore away the dull wrapping. The antique must have cost JT enough to keep him in smokes for a year. Almost all models were virtual games.

The picture on the box showed a sleek jet, all shining silver edges against a clear, blue sky.

Kyle was running his fingers over the words stamped into the corner when JT said, "Fifteen hundred pieces too many?"

"How'd you know I like puzzles?" Kyle said.

"You broke into one to get in here, didn't you?"

A thoughtful look came over Kyle's face. "Yeah. I guess I did."

"How come you messed with their shit?" JT said.

"I like cracking code," Kyle said.

"What else you like?"

Kyle blushed, thinking of the fantasy he'd had a thousand times. JT towering over him, his bulging crotch inches from his lips. Unzipping JT's jeans, his fingers trembling with desire, then –

"Must be something you like a lot," JT said. "You got a nice smile on your face."

Kyle's cheeks flushed brilliant red.

"You still a virgin, boy?"

"I sucked dick before."

"I bet that's all you done," JT said.

He laughed soft and low. Two long steps brought him to the desk. Kyle tried to back up, but the chair was behind him. He fell onto the hard metal, making the metal feet scrape against the concrete floor. JT squatted, so he was on eye level.

"Shit, boy. You're even prettier than I heard."

Jessi's picture rose in Kyle's mind. He pressed back into the small chair.

"I'll do what you want." Kyle licked his dry lips. "You don't have to hurt me."

JT stood up, looking down at Kyle. "You think I gotta take what I want?"

"The guard said if I don't wanna scream, don't fuck with you," Kyle said.

"I can't help it if people talk shit like they got a asshole for a mouth."

Kyle's mind whirled in confusion. Was this some interrogation trick? Was the Principal listening, ready to pounce the second Kyle admitted the truth about the Array?

" – clue you in," JT was saying.

"What?" Kyle said.

"Gladiators like me get what they want in here. I could sell your virgin ass for a shit load, boy."

"Sell me?" Kyle said.

"Most men, they share a bitch between the whole gang. Eight, ten men would own your ass."

"You're selling me?" Kyle said. The words felt strange, like another language.

JT said slowly, "I didn't say that. I *said* I wasn't gonna force you." He ground his half smoked cigarette into the brick wall and tossed it into the toilet.

"You was on my bunk," JT said in a low voice. "I got a game. When I get back tonight, if I find you on my bunk, you're my girl. My property. Any questions?"

"What happened to Jessi?"

Kyle counted three hammering heartbeats before JT said, "You're real good at getting into shit that ain't your business."

Category Five.

Kyle didn't heed the warning thought. The mad need to know drove words from his lips.

"Did you beat him up like that?"

"JT, we got to go."

Beyond the cell bars, Kyle saw a man with Rastafarian dreads that fell past his shoulders.

"Coming," JT said, still looking at Kyle. "Remember what I told you, boy."

————————————

"What?" JT said the moment he was alone with Dante.

"Doc says he needs to see you."

"How come?"

Dante shrugged his broad shoulders, but there was worry in his light brown eyes. When he spoke, his voice was soft and low, with a subtle rhythm born of life on deadly streets.

"I don't know. He just said he got to see you before game time."

"Shit."

JT and Dante wound their way through the dark corridors of Purgatory Prison, on their way to see a smuggler of human cargo. For a price, Dr. Fagan smuggled prisoners out of Purgatory, no questions asked. Until tonight, JT's escape had been planned for two months from now, right after the Maze.

Chapter 6

When they walked into the back room of the infirmary, they found Dr. Fagan slouched down low behind his desk. JT's sharp eyes took in the way his dark hair clung to his head, the lines of dirt under his manicured nails, the hollow look in his haunted eyes.

"You know we ain't supposed to meet like this doc," JT said.

Dante closed the door behind them. Fluorescent lights flickered overhead, giving the infirmary the grainy look of a cheap movie.

The doctor looked JT in the eye. "I have to call it off."

JT's jaw clenched tight.

"You're hotter than the sun," Dr. Fagan said into the silence. "My people aren't willing to risk it."

"Why?"

"If they're caught, they're dead."

Fagan met JT's eyes with a level gaze, but his slender fingers trembled slightly as he reached for a dirty glass of water.

"I ain't nothing but a con with a past." JT's mild voice gave the anger in his eyes a dangerous edge. "How come I'm suddenly hotter than the sun? What the fuck doc?"

Fagan avoided JT's eyes. The doctor looked down at his fingers tapping on the desk. "Things change. I can't."

JT became perfectly still, like a panther about to pounce on his prey.

"You think that freak Matthew's gonna take no for a answer forever? He been appealing my chip for years. He wins, and every Eye in the Sky's gonna know when I take a shit. Escape won't mean nothing. I got to get out. Now, doc."

Tiny beads of sweat broke out on Dr. Fagan's forehead. "I'm sorry."

The doctor reached for the glass of water again. JT lunged across the desk and grabbed his bony wrist. His muscled body was inches away from Fagan.

"What the fuck's going on?" JT said.

Security in Purgatory Prison was notoriously slow. All three of them knew that if Fagan called for help, JT could beat him to a pulp long before the guards got there.

Dr. Fagan licked his dry lips. A distant look came into his eyes. He did the last thing JT expected. His wrist still caught in JT's cruel grip, he got to his feet.

"Go ahead," the trembling doctor said, almost lost in the dark shadow of JT towering over him. "I know you carry a knife. Cut me. Do whatever you do to men who betray you. Alexa and Siarra will live if I die in here."

JT let go of the doctor's wrist and fell back a step. He looked at Dante. A quick nod told him no one would interrupt what he might have to do next.

"Sit the fuck down and talk to me," JT said. "You got one minute to tell me why I should let you live past tonight."

Dr. Fagan sank back into his chair. His shoulders slumped. He looked down at his hands lying limp in his lap. JT thought he looked like a man beaten before the fight even started.

"Two days ago I got a phone call from a man who says he knows all about me getting men out. He gave me dates, names – all of it true. He said if I help you, he'll kill my whole family."

He paused a moment, then looked up at JT with shell shocked eyes.

"Told me what he'd do to my wife before he slit her throat, and how he'd tie my little girl to her bed so she couldn't get out when he burned my house to the ground. Said he'd do my dog first, so they could watch."

JT listened in stone silence, his heart beating too hard and fast.

From the door, Dante said, "Who called you?"

Fagan went on as if Dante hadn't spoken, talking in the steady monotone of a man caught up in a grinding nightmare.

"Siarra's two years old. I spent some of the money you gave me. If you kill me in here, I'll die knowing my wife and daughter are okay."

"I ain't making no two year old a orphan over money," JT said, trying to hide his mounting impatience. "Who called you?"

Dr Fagan spoke without looking up. "All I know is the new boy in your cell made you suddenly untouchable."

JT's voice turned deadly calm, the voice of a man fighting his hideous, darker side. "You ain't fucking with me, right, Doc?"

Dr. Fagan reached for the water, but the glass slid through his jittering fingers, and shattered on the metal desk. He didn't move when the water flowed over the edge of the desk onto his pants.

"I knew you wouldn't believe me," Fagan said. He swallowed, leaned back in his chair. "Guess I'm dead."

The lights flared bright a few seconds, then dimmed to semi darkness. The doctor's eyes flicked up to the ceiling. When JT saw the sleepless, staring terror of a hunted man in Fagan's bloodshot eyes, he knew it was all true.

"Give me another name, and I'll call it even," JT said.

"Maxell," Dr. Fagan said. "Good Samaritan type. Hates the government."

"How am I gonna find him without asking questions? They bring in a whole bunch of doctors for the Maze," JT said.

"You'll find him. Look for the doctor with the chip on his shoulder. When you find him, tell him your favorite Bible story is Samson and Delilah."

"Who?" JT said.

"I got it," Dante said, grabbing JT's thick arm. "We got to go. Time for Pre Game Check In. You're late. They'll be looking for you."

"Will he do it?" JT said, looking back at the doctor before he walked out.

Dr. Fagan looked at JT.

"I don't know. Whoever these people are, they don't fuck around."

After he slammed the door shut behind them, Dante said, "Get rid of him. Sell him."

"And start a gang war?" JT said.

"What?"

"Spector got me a virgin for a peace offering. You know what he'll do if I turn around and sell Kyle? I can't disrespect him like that."

"You got a problem."

They walked on in silence, sliding through shadows that leapt ahead of them like dark waters parting.

"No problem," JT said, staring into the darkness ahead of them. "All I gotta do is make him not wanna be in my cell no more."

Chapter 7

The harsh sound of men's laugher grated on Kyle's strained nerves. From his bunk, he watched a river of slow moving men walk by. They looked like a strange, rag tag army in their tattered prison clothes, uncombed hair, and battered, bruised faces.

Men stopped to look in at him, like Kyle was a new exhibit in a zoo. They said things he tried not to hear.

"Hope you got a tight ass, boy," one prisoner said, looking in at Kyle through the bars. "JT likes his punks real tight."

"Come on, man. You ain't never gonna find out how tight that pussy is," someone said. "Don't be worrying about it."

Kyle was staring at the Horsemen riding out of the wall opposite him, enduring the taunts about what JT would do to him when the lights went out, when a low voice said, "Hey, boy."

Something in the voice made Kyle look up. A man stood with his face pressed between the bars. His midnight black skin was shiny with beads of sweat. Short, thick Rastafarian dreads floated around his head like lazy snakes. Kyle was about to lean back into the brick wall, and let the shadows hide his face again, when the man said something that made him cold all over.

"They're watching you Nero," he said in a low whisper. "Heretics say, Trent's son can't trust nobody."

Kyle sprang off his bed and leapt to the bars, pressing his face to the exact spot where the man had been. But he was too late. The prisoner had melted into the river flowing by.

Kyle backed away on shaky legs. He'd been haunted by the same nightmare since he got to Purgatory. In his dream, Homeland Security came and dragged him out of JT's cell. They took him to a back room, without any windows.

The Principal was always there, playing a holo of his father's whipping over and over until Kyle finally screamed, promising anything if he would turn it off and silence his father's dying screams. He always woke from those dreams with the same words echoing through his mind, *nobody hears you scream in those back rooms, kid.*

"Come on, boy," a soft voice said.

Kyle pushed himself into the brick wall behind him so hard, the metal legs of the bed creaked against the concrete. He thought for a nightmarish moment it was the Principal come to get him. *Fuck Purgatory. Let's get to the part where we make you scream, boy.*

The man outside the cell bars was tall like JT, but where JT was thick and solid with hard, chiseled muscle, this man had the thick, heavy build of a wrestler and creamy skin the color of coffee with milk. Long Rastafarian dreads gave him the exotic look of a pirate on a rum runner's ship. His full lips covered even, white teeth that reminded Kyle of the wolf in grandma's bed.

"Time for dinner," the man said, his light brown eyes boring into Kyle.

"Thought JT didn't want me going anywhere." Kyle sat where he was, hearing the man slide a key into the old fashioned lock. "I don't want him mad at me."

"He ain't gonna be mad at you for being with me."

Kyle looked the man up and down. "Who are you?"

"Dante. JT's right hand."

"Great," Kyle said, quietly. "And that Heretic is his left hand, right?"

Dante's cold eyes fell on Kyle. His face had the hardened look of a natural born killer.

"Who?"

Kyle realized he'd made a bad mistake, saying that word out loud.

"Nothing. Just men saying shit. About what kind of boys JT likes." He looked down at the floor, hiding his fear, hoping Dante would think he was embarrassed. He shrugged. "No big deal."

Just someone who knows who my father is; someone who could wake up dead for knowing my secrets. Kyle thought. *No big deal.*

Dante hesitated long enough for Kyle to feel uncomfortable under his steady gaze before he said, "Get used to it. Let's go."

"How come I couldn't get out for dinner?" Kyle said, following Dante out of the cell.

Dante whirled and grabbed Kyle's arm tight.

"JT got enough trouble cause of you. Don't be going no place by yourself. You heard me, bitch?"

Dante's eyes weren't as cold and dark as the Principal's, but it was close enough. "Sure," Kyle said in a voice tense with pain. "Whatever you say."

"Good. Come on."

Kyle followed Dante down twisting, narrow stone passages in silence. Walls pressed too close. Naked light bulbs dangling from thin wires cast cones of light that made too many shadows. Every few feet, on both sides, shadowy archways opened in the stone walls. Kyle counted three turns into dark openings, before they left the noise of the prison behind. He wondered if they were heading for a room with no windows.

Chapter 8

"Seems kinda funny how we can just walk around like this," Kyle said, mostly to fill the silence.

"It do, don't it?"

"Where's the guards?" Kyle said.

"Ain't none. That's why you don't go nowhere by yourself."

Dante took them down into a mouth of darkness that became a narrow stone throat.

"You don't get lost down here?" Kyle said.

Dante stopped and turned to face Kyle. "I got radar. You got more questions to brighten my day?"

Kyle dropped his eyes, looking at the uneven cracks in the rough stone floor. "Is JT gonna rape me?"

Dante knew if Kyle was scared, it would be easier for JT to get him out of his cell without starting a gang war.

"Rape you? Yeah. You're gonna scream like a gutted pig."

Dante turned around and walked into the darkness. Behind him, Kyle pressed back against the side of the tunnel, as if he'd found a way to walk through stone walls, the way he walked through virtual walls.

"He said he wouldn't force me," Kyle said, thinking of the thick bulge between JT's legs.

"JT got a reputation in here, boy. Bitches like you squeeze through the bars trying to get away from him."

"But, he said –"

Dante had pulled far ahead into the darkness. "You better come on if you don't wanna be in the dark by yourself," he said over his shoulder.

Kyle didn't move. He tried, but he couldn't leave the strange comfort of the cool stone pressing into his back. What if JT worked for the Principal? What if he took Kyle to a room with no windows? And cuffed him to the wall and used his thick cock to rip Kyle's virgin ass wide open, and kept fucking him 'til he screamed. The white hot pain would twist through his gut and –

"What the fuck's wrong with you, boy? I said let's *go*."

Kyle ran shaky fingers through his red hair, saw that Dante was looking back at him. "What did you mean about me making trouble for JT?"

"You asked enough questions," Dante said. "Come on."

"But –"

Dante started walking again at a steady pace, leaving Kyle to follow or stay behind in the thick darkness. After living most of his life in the dark stone caves and pipes of the sewers, the twists of the underground tunnels were nearly second nature to Kyle. He wasn't afraid to get lost. He followed Dante because he was in the belly of the beast, and there was nowhere to run or hide.

Kyle's life as a hacker made him sensitive to patterns. He thought that the undertone of resentment in Dante's voice was strange. "Did I say something to piss you off?"

Dante turned and looked at Kyle, his big arms crossed over his thick chest. Standing like that in the semi darkness, he looked every inch the pirate with a foot long cutlass hidden just out of sight.

"Who the fuck are you, boy?"

Kyle fought the urge to turn and run. He wouldn't get lost. But Dante would catch him. Then the questions would really start.

"I'm – "

Dante held up a big hand, like a cop stopping traffic. "Think real hard before you lie to me, boy. Nothing pisses me off more."

Kyle's secrets weighed heavily on him. The sound of scampering claws on stone came out of the darkness behind Dante; then a low squealing that ended in a snap of broken bone. That tiny sound of a creature too slow to outrun his enemy made the truth tumble from Kyle's lips.

"I used to think I was a smart ass with a keyboard," Kyle said. "Now I know I was a dumb ass. And I'm real scared, 'cause I broke into some place I shouldn't have."

They were on the edge of a cone of dim yellow light. Dante's eyes glittered in the steady darkness. "You in here for something you stole?"

"I didn't steal it. I – " Kyle hesitated, trying to figure out how to explain hacking a Top Secret government weapons system. "I broke it."

Now Dante's coffee colored face had the look of a man solving a tricky puzzle. "You're in here just 'cause you broke somebody's shit?"

"Yeah." Kyle fell silent, looking up at Dante's rigid face, half lost in the shadows. "I know you did something really bad to end up in Purgatory. But there's lots of things you don't know."

Dante looked Kyle up and down. "Yeah, punk? Like what?"

"Like what it feels like to watch your father tortured to death," Kyle said.

The way a shadow of secret fear fell across Kyle's smooth face made Dante realize that he was looking at a kid. Just a kid caught up in something too big for him.

"They'll come get me soon," Kyle said. "Then they'll torture me, 'til I fix it for them."

"Listen up, boy," Dante said. "Just 'cause we're in here don't make us bad. You're on our turf, now. Ain't nobody coming here to torture you." He fell silent a moment, then said, "Not some dumb ass kid like you. It ain't right."

Kyle might not have heard Dante's words. He looked out into the darkness eating greedily at the cone of light. He was unaware that the haunted fear of a hunted man made his emerald eyes a little darker with each passing day.

Chapter 9

As they walked on, the passage shrank, pulling in itself, until Kyle was forced to walk directly behind Dante. Kyle followed Dante around a long, twisting bend in the narrow passageway until they passed under a thick stone archway that was carved out of the living rock. Even years of living underground didn't prepare Kyle for what he saw.

They had walked into a roughly oval cave. The walls were lumpy and rough, as if some angry beast had blasted a path through the earth's bedrock, his fury shattering her stone womb as he went.

This far below the prison, the air was cool. Long ago, shallow pits had been scooped out of the stone ground. The fires that burned in the stone craters gave the only light in the underground world. Orange flames leaped up from the shallow stone pits, casting writhing black shadows on the dark stone walls. In the orange firelight, the cave had the unearthly glow of a place for fallen men.

A boulder, nearly as high as Kyle's waist crouched just inside the archway, on his left, with magazines tossed carelessly on top. The covers showed black men fucking white boys or with their cock buried deep in a boy's stretched mouth.

Boulders were scattered all around the cave, some stacked on top of each other, as if a giant had left his toys behind. Pictures of black men fucking white boys had been taped to the stone walls here and there.

Six black men sat around a flat rock that rose up out of the floor, their shirtless bodies sculpted in hard muscle. They played a noisy game of cards. A naked slender brunette boy knelt in the middle of the table, his ass up, his head down. His round, smooth ass looked very white in the sea of dark faces surrounding him.

"You like our Clubhouse, boy?" Dante said.

Kyle looked up at him and smiled a little. "Now I know where to hide when they come looking for me."

The genuine smile that lurked around Dante's cool eyes lit a spark of hope in the darkness of Kyle's fear filled heart. He didn't dare fan the spark into a flame. Purgatory, he reminded himself, was next door to Hell.

Dante led Kyle through a group of men crowded around the holo, drinking beer, yelling slurred insults at two wrestlers. Two sleekly muscled white men, nearly naked, writhed and tumbled across the floor. It gave Kyle an eerie feeling when their solid, sweaty bodies rolled through the flames of one of the fire pits.

A black leather couch was just a couple of feet from the men watching the wrestlers. A shirtless black man with his jeans unzipped sat with his thighs spread wide. Kyle watched the slender brown haired boy between the man's legs, as he took out the man's cock, and ran his tongue slowly up and down his swollen flesh.

"Yeah, bitch," the man said softly, "that's it."

A scar twisted through his right cheek, giving him a permanent sneer. A diamond stud in his left ear caught the flickering firelight.

"Park your ass, boy," Dante said. "I'll be back."

Kyle swallowed and sank into the soft leather couch. The man's dark, greedy eyes fell on him.

"This JT's new bitch?" the man said, lifting his hips up down while the boy between his legs serviced him.

Kyle still wasn't used to men talking about him like that, but Dante didn't miss a beat.

"Kyle meet Derrick," he said. "JT got virgin pussy for winning the Championship."

Kyle felt his face turn beet red, his cheeks burning.

"Shit. Ain't had virgin pussy since before I got this bitch," Derrick said, rolling his hips a little, grinding into the boy's mouth.

"Don't go nowhere," Dante said, looking at Kyle.

Derrick rolled his head back and moaned softly, sliding his cock deep into the boy's mouth. "Oh, yeah, bitch. Fucking right. Suck me real good."

Don't leave me alone with him, Kyle thought. "Where are you going?" he said.

"You're hungry, right?" Dante said.

Kyle glanced at Derrick's muscled arms, that could snap him up in about two seconds. "I can wait."

Dante looked into Kyle's scared eyes and said, "JT owns you, boy. Ain't nobody touching you unless he says so."

Oh God, Kyle thought, feeling Derrick's eyes crawling all over him. *Unless he says so.* As Dante faded into the shifting shadows of the dark cave, Derrick moaned, grabbing the boy's hair, fucking his mouth hard and deep, choking him again and again.

"Yeah, bitch," Derrick said, panting, pumping and grinding his hips. "Here I come, boy."

He gasped in pleasure, grunting and groaning. "Fuck, yeah, take my come."

Derrick pulled the boy hard into his crotch and rammed his cock deep into his pretty mouth, his whole body tensing, a groan of pure pleasure escaping between his clenched teeth. He collapsed back onto the couch, breathing hard, pulling his dark cock out of the boy's mouth.

"Good bitch," Derrick said, running his dark fingers through the boy's hair. "I ain't gonna use your ass tonight. Lick it up."

The relief that flooded into the boy's eyes as he licked Derrick clean told Kyle everything he needed to know about his new life in Purgatory. He rested his face in his hands. Despair rose in him like a dark tide.

Chapter 10

"Ain't you a fucking ray of sunshine," a soft voice said at Kyle's shoulder.

Kyle looked up and saw the boy who'd been kneeling between Derrick's legs.

"Ryan," the boy said.

"Kyle." He looked at Ryan. "I'd say nice to meet you but – " he shrugged, looking around.

Ryan had put on black jeans and a white t-shirt. "Smoke?" he said, taking a pack of cigarettes from his back pocket.

Kyle's eyes widened. Cigarettes with filters were unreal phantoms seen on peeling billboards, hanging over dark, trash ridden alleys. The people who lived in those rat infested streets bought tobacco, gritty with dirt, and rolled their own smokes.

"Where'd you get a pack?"

Ryan laughed, a low bitter sound without joy. "If you pay, you get anything in Purgatory."

Kyle took the cigarette and let Ryan give him a light. He inhaled the smooth, menthol flavor gratefully.

They smoked in silence for a while. The Clubhouse echoed with the noise of men too full of beer, talking too loudly.

"How long have you – " Kyle stopped. He wasn't sure how to finish.

"How long have I been Derrick's wife?"

Kyle nodded, a little embarrassed. "I didn't mean it like that, but yeah."

"I was a club whore," Ryan said with a shudder. "Then Derrick bought me from JT about a year ago."

"What's JT like? Did he hurt you?" Kyle's voice was low and steady; not at all the voice of someone facing the night with a man like JT. "I keep thinking about tonight. In his cell."

"He didn't hurt me. I was for the Clubhouse, like Taylor." Ryan nodded at the boy with his ass up, where the men were still playing cards. "They're betting to see who's gonna fuck him first."

Kyle looked over at the men. They were all laughing at something. Is that what the Principal had in mind? Was he the new gang whore? He closed his eyes against the shudder of fear that ran down his spine.

"They all used to fuck me," Ryan was saying. "Then JT would send me to someone's house for the night. JT owned me, but I was the gang bitch."

Kyle's heart raced. His eyes strayed back to the table. One man rubbed his crotch, staring at Taylor's pink hole. His muscled body was tense with the need to ravage the tasty morsel before him.

"They're *all* gonna fuck him?"

Ryan nodded. "Taylor's got it pretty bad. By the end of the night, he's hurting a lot."

Kyle took a long, deep drag of his cigarette. His virgin asshole puckered at the scenes that rose in his mind; all those men fucking him night after night. Looking at Taylor's trembling ass, a terrible thought spooked Kyle. The Clubhouse was a room with no windows.

Ryan must have seen something in his face, because he said, "You okay?"

"You like being with Derrick better?" Kyle said.

Ryan met Kyle's eyes. "Derrick's a good husband. He used to cut me. But not anymore."

Kyle's gut clenched into a sickening knot. "Cut you?" he said in a thin voice. "How do you mean?"

Ryan glanced around the noisy cave. "He likes to use a knife on me, here," the boy said, touching his flat belly.

Kyle had seen something in the flickering light, but knives and cutting hadn't crossed his mind. Ryan leaned close, and lifted his t-shirt a moment. The sight of his scarred skin made the brutal horror of Purgatory rip through Kyle like an ice pick to his heart. Thin lines criss-crossed Ryan's soft belly in intricate patterns that must have taken hours to carve into his flesh.

"Why?" Kyle's voice had fallen to a low, hoarse whisper.

"He mostly did it when I used to make him real mad." Ryan paused, a haunted look in his light brown eyes. "Now, I act like his wife. Mostly he belts me or slaps me around. I live real good."

"That's living real good?"

Ryan's simple answer summed up Kyle's new life. "In here it is," he said quietly.

A tidal wave of panic sent blood rushing to Kyle's head. A swimmy, dizzy feeling of unreality washed over him. He smoked in silence, watching Taylor move his ass in little circles for the men playing cards. Firelight threw their dark faces into shadow, as they murmured low, urgent sounds of lust.

Kyle leaned close and said, "Who broke Jessi's arm?"

Ryan turned pale. Tiny beads of sweat sprang out on his forehead. "I can't," he said quietly. "Derrick would cut me."

Ryan and Kyle smoked for while, watching Taylor, until Ryan threw his cigarette into a pit. Kyle was staring off into the darkness when he felt cold, trembling fingers on his arm.

"JT broke Jessi's arm," Ryan said in a low whisper. He breathed hard, like a man confessing before an unforgiving God. "Derrick made me watch."

Kyle peered into the shadows of the Clubhouse, afraid to turn to Ryan and frighten him into silence. "I'm listening."

"He said if I wasn't a good wife, he'd break my arm the same way. Then he'd carve up my face real good."

Kyle turned to Ryan, trying not to see the same design that was on his belly carved into his soft, pretty cheeks. "Jesus," he murmured.

"It's not so bad," Ryan said. His face took on a reflective, far away look. "Before Derrick bought me, I used to get fucked real hard six, seven times a day. Derrick gives me a break and lets me suck him off sometimes, like tonight without that shit around my –"

"You ain't saying nothing you got no business saying, right, bitch?"

Derrick's harsh voice made Kyle and Ryan jump apart like thieves caught in the act.

"No. I was just telling him how JT's a good husband," Ryan said, looking up into Derrick's cold eyes.

"I better not find out you was saying nothing else," Derrick said.

He sat down and motioned Ryan to sit on the floor between his legs. Derrick stroked his soft cheeks. He didn't seem to notice the way Ryan flinched away from his touch.

When Derrick's dark eyes fell on him, Kyle thought of the scars on Ryan's belly and shrank back into the cool, soft leather.

"Dinner," Dante said, handing Kyle a sandwich and chips on a paper plate.

Food was the last thing Kyle wanted. He forced himself to take a bite. He didn't need Dante asking what Ryan had said to make him lose his appetite.

Chapter 11

JT heard Preacher's words as clearly as if his dead friend were standing next to him in the dark.

"Danger ain't just all around us. It stalks your ass. Like a wildcat. Waiting for you to make a mistake, so he can rip out your throat. Ain't no forgiveness in a jungle."

Preacher had said those words on a rainy night, on his way to meet his fate. Below the arena, the wind moaned through cracks in the stone around JT. The sound took him back to the stormy night that had blown him into the deep pit of Purgatory.

On the last night that he was a free man, Preacher, Dante and JT went to a meeting in a hollowed out building, whose guts lay all around them. Cold wind blew secretly through hidden cracks. Rat droppings, dirt and used needles skittered across the splintered wooden floor.

Ripper, the man they were meeting that night, was JT's only rival. Both men were losing soldiers on the streets in a useless gang war. That night's meeting was about a truce.

Two battery lanterns burned in the middle of the big room that used to be someone's living room, back when the moldy thing leaning in the corner had been an armchair. Now it was a rat's nest, with small black eyes gleaming at them in the darkness.

Things went bad. JT still remembered Ripper's face, lit by those electric lanterns, his eyes dark sockets, when he told JT he had a sure way to get rid of him. Before Ripper finished talking, JT knew he'd walked into a set up. He tried to turn to Preacher and Dante. Too late. Gunshots shattered the night.

Rats scampered across the rotten wood. Bullets blew out a window. A fury of wind and rain swirled in, filling the room with the stormy night. From the corner of his eye, JT saw Preacher crumple to the ground. His right eye was a bloody, ragged hole.

Even as he bent to help his friend, he felt Dante pushing him savagely to the ground, falling on top of him. Gunshots whined off the wood, peppering his face with splinters. Dante rolled off him to a dark corner.

A lantern had been shot out. The naked walls writhed with shadows. The air filled with the smell of gunpowder, fresh blood and the stench of sweating men, fighting for their lives.

Shouts echoed through the room. Rolling thunder shook the thin walls. Lightening forked across the dark skies overhead. The unforgiving blue white glare froze their faces into masks of animal fury.

JT rolled to his feet, his gun already out. He stood over Ripper, who'd fallen to the floor, his gun aimed between his eyes. The man looked up at him in an agony of fear.

"Don't!" Dante's voice screamed from the darkness. "Leave him. We can get out."

JT knew if he left, he could make it out with Dante. Cops got paid not to find men like him. But Preacher was dying, if he wasn't already dead. No way this piece of filth, begging for his life, staining his crotch with piss, was going to live with Preacher in his grave.

Looking into Ripper's eyes, JT murmured, "No forgiveness in the jungle," and squeezed the trigger.

After Ripper's face exploded in a spray of white bone and grey jelly, JT dropped his gun and slowly raised his big hands, turning to face the cops in the darkness.

Two shots rang out behind him. JT dropped and rolled across the creaking floor, dodging the bullet that flew from a dying cop's gun. Dante walked out of the darkness. He dropped his gun, stepping over the cop he'd killed. If he didn't shoot, JT would be on the floor, shot in the back.

JT and Dante stood back to back unarmed, their hands up, looking out into the shadowy darkness. As they waited for Fate to deal her hand, the indifferent storm pelted them with ice cold water.

Now, years later, JT waited on a stone platform that would lift him from the gladiator pit to the main arena. His skin glistened with the oil they made him wear for the cameras. Sleek muscle rippled under his dark skin. His tight black briefs left his muscled body nearly naked.

The lesser fights were happening in the arena above him. His fight with a gladiator from a prison down south was the main attraction tonight. He hated southerners. They were slow moving and dull. Made it hard to put on a good show.

"Final," a soft voice behind him said.

Five minutes to game time. He had to make this good. Prisoners and guards placed bets on how long it would take JT to win his games. Most of the money went into his pocket. His opponent was a known loser. The longer he made the man last, the more money he would make.

JT tried not to think about what made Fagan pull out. But that made him think of Kyle's pale, frightened face. He closed his eyes and focused his mind to the razor sharp edge he needed to control his dark side.

Chapter 12

On holo, rock and roll music blared through the arena. The live audience burst into mad applause. The men in the Clubhouse hooted and hollered. JT strutted into the arena with the cool assurance of a veteran warrior. His unforgiving eyes promised victory at the price of his enemy's blood. On the couch, next to Dante, Kyle's green eyes were fixed on the man who would soon plunder his virginity.

JT's opponent came out, a hulking man, who was as white as JT was black. His dark brown hair flowed out behind him. A dim mutter of applause rose from the audience. The man moved with slow, clumsy steps. He had the narrow, cruel eyes of a weasel.

"Damn," Derrick said, shaking his head, "Sampson's dumb and slow."

Ryan was sitting on his lap, his legs spread over Derrick's, leaning back against his barrel chest. Kyle couldn't help noticing the way Derrick's fingers moved under Ryan's t-shirt, tracing the scars he'd made on his boy's belly. He shuddered and inched closer to Dante.

On holo, the two gladiators looked close enough to touch. They circled each other in a low crouch, their knives out in front of them. The blades glinted wickedly in the arena lights.

JT struck out at Sampson. The audience gasped at the sudden move. The man's long hair flew out behind him as he jabbed at JT, but he danced away from Sampson's slow moving blade.

They circled each other again, each man looking for an opening. JT taunted Sampson with little 'come on' gestures. Sampson kicked at JT's right hand, trying to dislodge his knife. JT sidestepped him, twisting away.

"Quit fucking dancing," a voice in the Clubhouse screamed out.

On holo, JT went in fast and low, and sliced through Sampson's upper thigh.

"Why doesn't he just knock him over or something?" Kyle said. "JT's way faster than him."

Kyle saw the way Dante and Derrick looked at each other, before Derrick said, "Why don't you just sit back and watch the game, boy?"

Kyle looked at Dante, who pressed a finger to his lips. "Quiet," he said.

In the arena, a harsh drum beat backed a singer who screamed about fun and games in a jungle. The roar of the audience rose above the harsh, strident beat.

The audience cheered the gladiators, screaming the lyrics of the old song blasting from the speakers, 'Welcome to the jungle, I wanna make you scream'.

JT and Sampson danced around each other slowly, in solid holograph so real, Kyle could almost smell their sweat. JT's eyes were narrow and focused. Sampson's eyes looked everywhere at once, not sure where JT's attack would come from. They were both in a low crouch, knives ready for the attack.

"Cut his fucking balls off," one of the men in the Clubhouse yelled at the holo.

"Make that bitch bleed," someone else said.

To the savage delight of the audience, JT tossed his knife back and forth, from hand to hand, looking into Sampson's eyes, daring the other gladiator to make a move. The audience went wild, urging JT on, chanting his name. The music was a vicious back beat to their screams for blood.

'Make him bleed' they yelled; 'give it to him, JT.'

JT's knife was in mid air between his hands when Sampson swiped at him. JT grabbed his knife out of the air and avoided Sampson's blade with two quick skips back. A dark smile creased JT's lips.

"Get it over with," a voice yelled out in the audience.

JT's body relaxed, his eyes became expressionless. He weaved his knife in slow, winding patterns, like a rattle snake charming his victim.

"Here he goes," Dante muttered.

JT sprang up from his crouch and pounced on Sampson with a fury. He raked his knife in quick, vicious swipes across Sampson's chest, his arms, his back. Sampson tried to follow the rapid fire thrusts of JT's knife, but he was far too slow.

The audience jumped to their feet, roaring, jabbing their fists into the air. The Clubhouse filled with whoops and hollers of victory.

As JT came in for those vicious strikes, almost too fast to follow, Kyle felt himself grow hard. He looked into JT's black eyes as his blade danced across Sampson's flesh, leaving thin trails of blood. He wanted JT, but the controlled fury written into every line of his hard body, made Kyle very afraid. If JT worked for the Principal, Kyle was in for some real hard times in Purgatory.

Blood welled in Sampson's wounds, pouring across his white skin. The rule was ten wounds or the best out of five rounds made a victory. Kyle counted more than ten wounds before the bell finally sounded and a referee came out to separate the two gladiators. The referee raised JT's right hand, his knife dripping blood, and declared him the winner.

JT looked straight into the camera's blind eye, his face showing no emotion. Kyle met the eerie emptiness in the gladiator's dark eyes. There was no doubt in his mind that JT would have killed with equal ease. Kyle's thoughts turned to the Principal again. How many nights would he last with a gladiator who loved his work?

Chapter 13

After the fight, Dante walked Kyle back to JT's cell. It was after lights out. Night lighting filled the tier with ghostly shadow. Inside the cell, Dante leaned against the wall between Death and War. He lit a cigarette with a lighter only a little smaller than a blowtorch. Watching him in the orange glow of the fire, Kyle thought he looked like he was urging the Horsemen to ride faster.

Kyle sat on the edge of JT's bunk, thinking of the night ahead. The thought of JT's sweaty body, and the way his muscles bunched and flexed in the arena, made him so hard, it was all he could do not to squirm. He wanted JT. But he couldn't trust anyone. The more he wanted him, the more afraid Kyle became. What would JT do to him if he found out who he was, and why he was in Purgatory?

"What was you and Ryan talking about?" Dante said.

Kyle looked at the black horses, avoiding Dante's hard eyes. Thinking of the carvings in Ryan's skin he said, "Nothing. Just what it's like being a man's wife in here."

"If that's all it was, how come you look scared?"

Kyle's thoughts turned to the Principal again, and his dark promises about back rooms with no windows. "If you were me, in JT's cell, wouldn't you be scared?"

Dante looked into Kyle's frightened eyes for a long time. He leaned his head back against the wall, looking out on the tier.

"Ain't nobody that scared to get fucked. Not even a virgin bitch like you."

"I'm scared that – "

Kyle didn't know what lie was about to fall from his lips, but Dante didn't give him a chance to finish. He went on talking, as if Kyle's words had all the meaning of raindrops on the ocean.

"I'm doing you a big favor tonight, boy. Ryan and you was talking about shit he ain't got no business opening his mouth about. I ain't gonna tell JT."

"He wasn't telling me –"

Dante stopped Kyle with his palm up, like a cop halting traffic.

"You got some hard learning to do in here, bitch. Rule number one, don't fucking lie to me. That don't do nothing but piss me off."

Dante's cool gaze fell on Kyle, until he lowered his eyes, his cheeks flaming red.

"Now, was you saying something to me?"

Kyle shook his head. "No."

Dante blew smoke up to the dark ceiling, staring at Kyle. "I didn't think so."

"Is Derrick gonna beat Ryan or cut him for talking to me?"

"He can't get hurt for what Derrick don't know."

Kyle met Dante's dark eyes, unable to read his hard face.

"How come you're helping me?"

Dante shrugged his broad shoulders. "I got a soft spot for stupid people in trouble over their head."

Kyle fell silent, looking at the grime in the seam where the black wall met the stone floor. His mind hovered obsessively around the same thoughts. He wondered how many back rooms without windows were in Purgatory, not counting the cells.

"That the best you got?" Dante said, startling Kyle. "We been here ten whole minutes, and you ain't asked but three questions."

Dante's easy shift between hard edged killer and wise counselor puzzled Kyle, kept him off balance. He tried to read his dark face, but his thoughts were hidden, like a blank slate with writing on the back.

"You think JT's gonna make things bad for me?"

"You don't fuck with him, he won't make you scream. What questions you got about that?"

"None, I guess."

"Good. I got things to do," Dante said and turned to go.

Panic surged through Kyle. "You're leaving?"

Dante turned to him. "What? You scared they're gonna come get you tonight? Prison's on lock down, boy. Satan couldn't get up in here."

"Satan's boss is after me," Kyle murmured.

"What?"

Kyle didn't answer. He looked around the cell. "How come you called this JT's house?"

Dante shrugged, pushing back a few stray dreads that fell across his face. "It's just how we talk in here."

Kyle looked at Dante's body, thick with hard muscle. "Are you a gladiator too?"

"Not anymore."

"What happened?"

"I tried to escape. They got pissed."

"What did they do?"

"Gave me a chip. Took me out of the games."

"That's how come you don't have your own boy?"

Dante looked at Kyle with genuine amusement in his dark eyes. "You ain't gonna keep me talking 'til he gets here, boy."

When Dante turned to go again, Kyle leapt off the bed and grabbed his thick arm.

"Don't leave me alone in the dark." He peered into the shades of the tier. "Please."

Dante grabbed Kyle's wrist and spun him around, so his back was up against the wall. "You gonna tell me who's after you, boy?"

Mindful of what Dante had said about lying to him, Kyle let his breath out in a single word, "No."

Dante looked at him with hard, unrelenting eyes. Kyle's blood ran cold. He was sure that uncounted men, caught in that ice-cold gaze, had begged for their lives, just before they went to an early grave. But the Principal's eyes were much darker.

Dante let him go, and stepped back, so Kyle wasn't trapped between him and the wall. Kyle retreated to JT's bunk. Dante leaned up against the wall, lit another cigarette, and looked out on the dark tier.

"You ain't gonna have no secrets from JT," Dante said.

"I know," Kyle said.

Chapter 14

The harsh sound of JT sliding the cell door back broke the silence between Kyle and Dante. His black muscle shirt left JT's thick arms bare. Kyle tried not to look at JT's crotch, but he couldn't help seeing the way his faded jeans outlined the bulge between his legs. He wondered how it would feel when JT's thick cock stretched his virgin ass.

"How come you're still here?" JT said, walking into the cell.

Dante threw his cigarette between the bars. "Your new bitch's scared of the dark. I didn't him want having no nightmares."

JT started to say something else, but Dante stopped him with a glance at Kyle, shaking his head.

JT caressed Kyle's smooth face. "Ain't he pretty?"

Kyle didn't flinch from JT's touch. But he couldn't bring himself to look at him.

JT took Kyle's face in his big hand, and tilted his head back. "He's a virgin," he said, looking into Kyle's scared eyes. "But not for long."

"He's sweet," Dante said. "Like candy."

JT ran his big fingers through Kyle's silky hair. "I ever hear from Dante that you ain't done what he tells you to do, you're gonna have a world of trouble with me. Understand, boy?"

Kyle's eyes flicked to Dante, who stood off to the side, watching. JT's fingers curled into a tight fist, deep in Kyle's hair, forcing his head back.

"He says to bend your bitch ass over or open your mouth for his cock, I better not hear any shit about you giving him lip. Any questions?"

Behind JT, Dante shook his head slowly, like a helpful teacher hinting at the right answer.

"No questions," Kyle said, swallowing hard. "Whatever you say."

JT let him go and pulled Dante over to the wall. They talked in low voices for a while, then Dante left. Kyle watched JT lock the cell door, and thought, *oh God, this is it.*

"Come here, boy," JT said.

Kyle slipped to his knees, between JT's spread legs.

"No," JT said quietly. He pulled Kyle to his feet. "I wanna taste those pretty lips before you wrap them around my cock."

He pulled Kyle close, and kissed him, running his tongue into his mouth, grabbing his tight ass.

"You do what I say, boy," JT said, kissing Kyle's neck, squeezing his round ass, "and you won't have no problems."

He kissed Kyle's soft lips again, pulling him close, grinding his hard cock into him.

"Fuck baby," JT said, breathing hard. "You could drive a man crazy." He pushed Kyle. "Over there, in the corner."

Kyle reeled into the shadowy corner between the bed and the wall that smelled of piss. He slipped to his knees, his back to the wall. The feel of JT's lips was still on his mouth. He'd thought of servicing JT so many times. But this was nothing like his fantasies.

"You seen me fight tonight?" JT said, looking down at him.

Kyle nodded.

"You scared of me now?"

The truth rose to Kyle's lips before he could stop himself. "I was scared of you before I got here." He bit his lip. "Jesus. I didn't mean anything."

Kyle looked up at JT in the shadowy light. Feeling JT's thick fingers running through his hair, Kyle wondered what it would be like to feel JT's cock sliding between his lips.

Then, all at once, the Principal's warning about back rooms with no windows flashed across his mind. He couldn't keep the fear that jolted his heart out of his eyes.

"You're scared of something, boy. And it ain't just me fucking your tight little virgin ass. You keeping secrets from me?"

Secrets? Like you wouldn't believe, Kyle thought. He tried desperately to think of something to tell JT, throw him off the scent of his deepest fears. He said the first thing that came to his mind.

"How come you got mad at Jessi?"

"Who told you about him?"

Kyle shrugged, unwilling to reveal his search in the library. "I heard stuff."

"He didn't wanna be my bitch." JT ran his dark fingers along Kyle's soft pink lips. "But you ain't like that. You're gonna be a real good girl for me, right?"

"I never had a man in my ass," Kyle said. "I'm real scared."

"You plan on fucking with me?"

Kyle shook his head, looking up into JT's eyes, glittering in the darkness.

"Then you ain't got nothing to be scared about," JT said.

Kyle watched JT take off his shirt, uncovering his broad chest, sculpted in muscle. His belly was flat and hard. With a swollen hard on, Kyle watched JT undo the draw string holding up his pants. He let them slide down his hips, revealing his thick cock jutting straight up, past his navel.

"You gonna suck my dick like a good girl?" JT said, looking down at Kyle.

Oh God, yes, Kyle thought. He nodded, not taking his eyes off JT's fat cock.

"Get to it, bitch." JT pulled Kyle's silky hair, pressing the boy's face into his crotch. "Show me how good those pretty pink lips feel on a man's dick."

Chapter 15

Kyle pressed his tongue to the base of JT's thick cock, licking around his low hanging balls.

"That's it, baby, lick me real good, all up and down my dick." JT's voice was low and thick with lust.

Kyle closed his eyes, let his fear fall away. He thought of all the times he'd wanted this, to service a man like JT. Kyle ran his hot tongue up and around JT's hairy balls. Then, as JT moaned in pleasure, Kyle slid his tongue down the length of his cock, all the way to the thick head.

Kyle pressed his hands lightly against JT's muscled legs, kissing his cock softly, worshipping his black meat, looking up into his eyes. Then he swirled his tongue slowly around JT's hard flesh.

JT ran his hands through Kyle's hair. He moaned deep in the back of his throat as Kyle licked his slit. When Kyle pressed his lips to his cock head again, JT moaned. He hissed between clenched teeth as Kyle's tongue circled his thick head slowly, before sliding his hot tongue down to his heavy balls.

"You was born to suck dick, boy," JT said in a low voice.

Kyle pressed JT's hard cock up, out of his way, and slid his tongue all over JT's balls, driven by need. Then he went lower, licking the spot below his balls.

"Oh yeah," JT said. He hissed in pleasure, throwing his head back. He felt the hard inner sacs of his balls throbbing. "Suck my fucking balls."

Kyle sucked JT's ball sac gently between his lips, swirling his wet tongue around the tender flesh inside his mouth.

He licked his way down to the fat head of JT's cock again, and took the head of his throbbing cock between his pink lips and squeezed gently while his tongue probed JT's piss hole again.

"Oh fuck," JT said in a low whisper. "I can't take no more. Suck my dick, baby."

Kyle slid his hands around to JT's ass, feeling his muscles clench. He moaned softly as JT slid his fat cock in and out of his hungry mouth.

Kyle saw the dark lust in JT's eyes. He saw the way the sight of his dark cock sliding between his pink lips made JT crazy. He wanted to please JT and taste his hot come.

"Yeah, baby, that's it," JT said, pumping his hips slowly. "Suck me real good, and I'll give you what you want."

JT fucked Kyle's mouth in long, deep strokes, driving his cock deep, nearly gagging him. When Kyle's gag reflex closed his throat tight around the head of his throbbing dick, JT's hips jerked, his body shivered.

"You look so fucking hot, bitch. On your knees, my black cock in your pretty mouth," JT said.

Kyle opened his aching jaws even wider, his soft pink lips stretching tighter against JT's dark fuck meat, taking JT deep down his throat. He looked up at JT's hard body, moaning as JT slid his throbbing cock in and out of his mouth.

JT tossed his head back and pumped his hips in a more urgent rhythm. "Get ready, boy." He clenched his teeth, driving his hips into Kyle's face.

Kyle pressed his small hands to the dark skin of JT's muscled belly. He loved the way his hard muscle rippled as JT pumped his mouth.

Kyle looked up at JT, desperation in his green eyes, his cock hard and throbbing under his pants. JT twined his fingers deep into Kyle's silky red hair.

"Oh yeah, bitch. You need a load real bad, don't you?" JT grunted and groaned as he fucked Kyle's hot mouth.

The sounds of JT's pleasure echoed in Kyle's ears as JT used his mouth to pleasure his hard cock. Kyle looked up at JT, begging him with his eyes to empty his balls into his mouth. JT twined his fingers deeper into Kyle's soft hair, holding him still, pumping his face hard.

"Oh yeah," JT said, breathing hard. "Fucking suck it, bitch."

JT rammed his throbbing cock down Kyle's throat, hard and fast, moaning. He arched his back and crammed his cock deep, groaning in ecstasy.

"Take my load, bitch," JT said between clenched teeth.

His cock exploded and sent hot come shooting down Kyle's throat.

"Swallow it like a good girl," JT said, looking down at Kyle with hard eyes.

Kyle swallowed, all his fear coming back in a rush. JT pulled out of Kyle's mouth, and drew up his pants, pulling the string tight.

"You suck dick like a dream, boy," JT said. He stroked Kyle's soft cheek. "You ain't nothing like Jessie. I'm gonna like having you for my girl."

Kyle felt suddenly shy, like this was a real date. "I liked you coming in my mouth like that," he said quietly.

For the first time since Kyle had seen him, JT's voice was gentle. "Yeah. I noticed." He smiled at the light pink blush that rose to Kyle's cheeks.

"You ain't got to be all embarrassed with me. I know a bitch when I see one. Come here, baby." He pulled Kyle to his feet.

JT pressed close and cupped Kyle's crotch.

"Damn, baby," JT whispered. He massaged Kyle's dick through his jeans. "Look how hard you are after I fucked your mouth."

Kyle moaned softly.

Chapter 16

JT unzipped Kyle's jeans and slid them down the boy's slender hips. Now Kyle stood with just his t-shirt on. JT looked down at the bulge in Kyle's thin cotton briefs.

"What you got to say for yourself, boy?"

JT pressed close. He massaged Kyle's hard cock through the thin cotton, looking down into Kyle's green eyes. The way Kyle bit his lips, holding back a moan of pleasure made JT incredibly hot for the boy. JT slipped Kyle's shirt over his head and turned him to the wall.

He ran his dark fingers slowly over Kyle's smooth chest, feeling how his heart beat like a jackhammer. The way Kyle trembled with desire intoxicated JT. He slid the boy's briefs down slowly, the way a man uncovers a jewel. He passed his dark brown hands over Kyle's tight, smooth ass, caressing his creamy skin.

"You got a sweet ass," JT whispered into Kyle's ear.

JT fingered the outside of Kyle's tight hole, kissing Kyle's neck, licking and sucking the boy's tender flesh.

"I'm gonna fuck this virgin ass real hard," JT whispered.

JT heard Kyle let out a whimpering breath that sounded like a muffled scream. He savored the feel of Kyle's tight young body, pulling him close, thrilled by the feel of the boy's racing heart.

JT reached around, pulled Kyle's hard cock out of his briefs and slid his big fist up and down his cock, making Kyle moan softly and squirm in his arms.

"You know why your dick's so hard?" JT said.

"No."

"You don't know how come you're so fucking hard?" JT slid his fist up and down Kyle's cock, grinding his hard dick into Kyle, dry humping the boy's wriggling ass.

"Come on, boy, tell me how come you're all hard like this," JT whispered, working Kyle's cock.

Kyle moaned in helpless pleasure. JT kissed the side of Kyle's neck, breathing into his ear softly. His hard muscled body pressed up against Kyle, driving him crazy.

JT gripped Kyle's cock, jacking him off, making Kyle moan desperately. "Did you used to jack off, looking at me fight?" JT said.

The way Kyle stiffened in his arms told JT he was right.

"Tell me what you are, boy," JT whispered, jacking off Kyle, slowly. "Tell me how come you're all hard after you swallowed a man's come."

"Cause I'm a bitch," Kyle finally said, squirming in JT's strong arms.

JT saw the blush of desire that rose to Kyle's soft cheeks and felt the tense need in his young body, pressed hard into him. He smiled in the darkness.

"You gonna be my girl?" JT whispered, stroking the boy's cock meat.

"Yeah," Kyle said.

"Tell me."

"I'll be your girl," Kyle said, pumping his hips, sliding his cock in and out of JT's fist. "Let me come, please," he begged.

JT jacked off Kyle, grinding his thick cock against the boy's squirming ass.

"You got me all hard again," JT said, kissing Kyle's neck. "But I wanna see you come like a bitch before I fuck your virgin ass."

He spun Kyle around without warning.

"Get on your knees, jack off," JT said.

Kyle slipped to his knees, grabbed his throbbing cock and jacked off, moaning and panting softly.

"Look at me, bitch," JT said, standing over him, his legs spread.

Kyle met his dark eyes.

"You're my girl," JT said, watching Kyle jack off. He slapped Kyle's face lightly. "You got it?"

"Yeah," Kyle said, sliding his fist up and down his hard cock in a desperate rhythm.

JT grabbed Kyle's face. He loved seeing the need in his green eyes.

"You're gonna suck my fat black cock and take it up your ass. How come?"

Kyle tried to turn away, but JT slapped his face again, harder.

"How come you're gonna suck my dick and get fucked?" JT said in a hard, unyielding voice.

Kyle was panting and moaning, looking up into JT's merciless eyes.

"'Cause I'm your bitch," Kyle said. A moan of pleasure escaped him.

JT stood back, looking down at Kyle.

"Tell me you're my girl. Say it 'til you shoot."

"I'm your girl," Kyle said, jacking off wildly.

Watching Kyle make a bitch of himself, on his knees, after he'd fucked his face and come in his mouth, made JT desperate. His cock throbbed and ached. It was all he could he do to stop himself from grabbing Kyle and tearing into his virgin ass. But he didn't like it that with his girls. Not the first time.

"Louder," JT said, giving Kyle's face a rough shake. "Don't piss me off."

"I'm your girl," Kyle said, loud enough for it to echo in the cell.

"Keep saying it 'til you come." JT held Kyle's face, looking straight down into his eyes.

Kyle slid his fist up and down his slick cock madly, panting and moaning, saying over and over he was JT's girl.

"Yeah," JT said, when he saw Kyle was close. "Come for me, bitch."

Kyle tried to throw his head back, but JT held his face, looking down into Kyle's green eyes. A final groan of ecstasy escaped Kyle and he exploded all over his hand.

"Lick it up," JT said, standing back.

He watched Kyle lick the sticky mess from his hand, enjoying the way the boy met his eyes. When Kyle licked the last of his come from his fingers, he looked up at JT.

"You did real good, bitch." JT ran his fingers through Kyle's soft hair.

JT saw Kyle look at the outline of his hard cock showing through his pants. The way the boy looked up at him, desire bright in his green eyes, made JT's hard cock throb with need.

"Are you gonna –"

"You had enough. Go to sleep," JT said, interrupting him. "I'm busting your cherry tomorrow night."

JT lay in complete silence, listening to Kyle. When the boy finally fell asleep, JT slipped out of bed and lit a cigarette. He smoked, watching his new bitch sleep.

He knew Kyle had lied to him about how he found out about Jessi. Nobody was dumb enough to cross him, and talk about Jessi. The truth was, Kyle was a sweet looking boy in a world of trouble.

JT blew three perfect smoke rings up to the ceiling, unaware that he was doing it. They were his personal smoke signals that meant he was in deep thought. Thinking about the stark terror in Dr. Fagan's eyes, he blew a whole lot more smoke rings into the night before he finally slipped into bed and fell asleep. His last thought before sleep took him was, *Dante's right. I got a problem.*

Chapter 17

The next morning, Kyle sat next to JT at a table in the drafty stone room that was the prison cafeteria. Three bright hickies stood out on him, two on the right side of his neck, and one high on the left side, just below his jaw line.

Voices echoed all around them. Stark grey walls rose high to the ceiling, without the relief of windows. Fluorescent light made the dark grey stone walls harsh and unforgiving. Dull reflections shined in the heavy metal tables, that stood bolted to the stone floor. Everything about the room said, *escape is impossible, resistance is futile.*

All the men at JT's table had the lean, cruel look of men who'd spent too long in prison. Their hard bodies, bristling with muscle, spoke of a hunger for violence that gave them the look of predators on the prowl. Like JT, all of them, except Dante, wore a diamond stud in their left ears, marking them as prisoner gladiators. If they weren't in prison, they'd be rich from all the money they made for Purgatory.

"Hey JT, heard you enjoyed your new bitch last night," Terence said, looking at the bright hickies on Kyle's neck.

Terence, a black man with thick arms ridged with muscle, sat across the table from JT.

He looked at Kyle and ran his tongue across his lips.

"Yeah," Tyrone said. He sat across from JT next to Terence. He looked like he spent his life pumping iron. "I'm your girl, JT. I'm your girl," Tyrone said in a high falsetto, pumping his hips on the metal bench.

The whole table of prisoners laughed. The only one of JT's friends who didn't laugh was Dante, who sat directly across from Kyle, listening in silence. Kyle dropped his eyes to his bowl of oatmeal, his face turning a brilliant scarlet.

"Look at that bitch," Derrick said. "He's turning all red and shit. What's wrong boy, you didn't like JT's fat cock pumping your faggot ass?"

Derrick's boy, Ryan, sat next to him, eating in silence. He shot Kyle a sympathetic look, then dropped his eyes to his plate again.

Kyle felt JT's eyes on him, felt his face burning bright red, and tried to hide the tears standing in his eyes.

"Leave him alone," JT said quietly.

"Come on man, tell us," Terence said. "Did you fuck the bitch? You left fucking marks all over his neck. He got a tight ass?"

"Nah, he didn't fuck her," Tyrone said. "Ain't nobody heard no screaming."

The whole table broke into laughter again. Kyle saw Dante's jaw tighten at the harsh sound of the men's cruel laughter. To Kyle they sounded like hyenas fighting over a fresh kill. He fought back tears. He knew it would make things worse if he cried.

"I said, leave him alone." JT's voice was even quieter.

Kyle looked up at JT, surprised at the anger in his low voice. He loved the way the mood at the table changed. The other men looked afraid. Kyle saw that no one, not even his friends, wanted to make JT mad. Dante had a little smile on his face.

"Hey man," Tyrone said, "he's just a bitch. What the fuck?"

The table fell silent. All eyes turned to JT.

"You know what your problem is?" JT said to Tyrone.

"What? Bitches can't get enough of my dick?"

"No." JT looked at Tyrone mildly. "You're too stupid to know when you should shut your fucking mouth."

Tyrone opened his mouth to say something else, but Dante said, "Leave it alone Ty. Shut up."

"Stay away from my property," JT said, looking Tyrone in the eye. "Don't start no shit with me."

Tyrone looked long and hard at Kyle. His dark eyes turned vicious. The way he looked at Kyle was a clear show of disrespect. JT nearly rose to his feet. But Dante's soft voice stopped him. "He ain't worth it."

JT looked at his friend's calm face, but he spoke to Tyrone. "Don't make me do nothing you'll regret."

After that, Kyle ate his oatmeal in the new, uneasy silence at the table. In a little while, the men started talking about the coming games on holo. Soon the low, ugly sound of a buzzer filled the stone room, and all the men filed out to their work details.

Kyle sprang up from the table, rushing past JT and the other men.

"Looks like your new bitch ain't saying bye," he heard Tyrone say.

"Hey, boy." JT was nearly running to catch up with Kyle.

Kyle kept walking, pretending he'd heard nothing. He thought he'd be safe once he got to the library. Maybe.

"Get back here before I kick your bitch ass," JT said, hurrying to catch up to Kyle.

Kyle hurried on. He'd completely forgotten what Dante told him last night about not going anywhere alone.

Before Kyle knew it, JT's long strides caught up with him. He grabbed Kyle's arm, just outside the men's room. A guard stood by the door. No one was supposed to go in the bathroom before reporting for work detail.

JT walked right by the guard, dragging Kyle along as if the guard were invisible. The man in uniform watched, but said nothing. Kyle could have sworn he saw fear cross the guard's face when he met JT's dark eyes.

Inside the bathroom, JT gave Kyle a hard shove. He thumped into the wall with almost bone crushing force.

Chapter 18

JT was bearing down on Kyle before the boy could so much as clear the black spots before his eyes.

"Why you walked out on me like that? You didn't hear me calling you?"

Anger made Kyle reckless. "I didn't do anything," he said, looking up at JT. Dark rage burned in the boy's green eyes.

If fury wasn't rushing through Kyle like a black storm, he would have seen that JT was genuinely puzzled. "What the fuck's wrong with you bitch? I told them to leave you alone, didn't I?"

Kyle tried to control the storm of rage inside him, but he couldn't. All the anger, the frustration of the way JT's friends had treated him came flying out with his words.

"You *wanted* them to hear me!" Kyle yelled.

Kyle shoved at JT, and he moved, letting the boy go running past him. JT watched in puzzled silence as Kyle jumped up onto a toilet.

"I'm your girl," Kyle yelled at the top of his voice, flinging out his arms. "I'm your girl."

Looking down at JT, his green eyes flashing with rage, Kyle looked like the world's smallest avenging angel. "You want me to say it louder?"

JT looked around the grimy bathroom, hands on his hips, as if he suddenly understood nothing at all.

"What the fuck do it matter if they heard? You live in my house now. Everybody knows you're my girl."

Kyle jumped down and stood in front of JT, inches away, looking up at him.

"It matters to *me*," Kyle said in a low, choked voice. The tears he'd held back at breakfast slid down his soft cheeks.

JT had been about to take off his belt and give Kyle something to *really* scream about. But the naked sight of Kyle's tears and the pain in the boy's eyes disarmed JT completely. His hands fell away from his belt.

"Sorry." Kyle wiped angrily at his tears. "I know I'm just a bitch in here." He shrugged. "I guess you're gonna beat me up or something."

JT drew closer to Kyle. He shrank back against the wall, sure that JT was about to beat his ass.

"You're lucky I like you, boy." JT looked down at Kyle with eerily empty eyes. He ran his dark fingers slowly across Kyle's soft lips. "You're real lucky I don't take you down to the Clubhouse and share your virgin ass with my friends."

JT's cold voice chilled Kyle to the bone. Looking up into JT's black eyes, Kyle saw that same dark emptiness he'd seen last night right before he'd sliced into Sampson.

Without thinking, Kyle slipped to his knees. "I'm sorry," he said, kneading JT's crotch softly. "Don't hurt me."

Kyle ran his hands gently over JT's cock, tracing the hard outline. He pressed his soft lips to the rough fabric of his bulging jeans. "I'll be your girl. Let me show you."

JT unzipped his jeans, looking down at Kyle with that darkness in his eyes that Kyle already thought of as *dead eyes.*

Kyle reached for JT's hard cock like he was desperate to suck dick. But his trembling hands betrayed him. Kyle was sure that if he didn't suck him off real good, JT would take him to the Clubhouse, and there would be no arguing with that cold fury in his hard eyes.

JT grabbed Kyle's hair and slapped his face when the boy didn't open his mouth fast enough. His cheek stinging from JT's heavy hand, Kyle opened his mouth wide for JT's dark cock.

It was nothing like last night. JT was impatient, driving his cock hard on every stroke, choking Kyle, looking down into his wide, scared eyes.

"Don't make me mad," JT said, thrusting his hips into Kyle's face. "Or I'll make it bad for you, bitch. You'll be the gang slut."

A vivid picture rose in Kyle's mind – Taylor on the table last night, waiting to see who would win the card game, and fuck his ass first. JT twined both his powerful hands into Kyle's hair, and held him still while he pumped his dark cock in and out of his pretty pink lips.

"I'm busting your cherry tonight," JT said, riding Kyle's mouth hard.

He thrust deep into his boy's mouth, choking him again and again until the agony in Kyle's throat forced tears from his eyes.

JT's dark side rose in him. His cock surged at the sight of Kyle's tears. "Oh yeah, bitch," he said.

He dug his thick fingers deeper into Kyle's silky hair, and fucked his face in a desperate rhythm, panting and grunting. Kyle's gagging throat grabbed JT's cock head in a hot, pulsing rhythm.

JT humped Kyle's mouth, changing his rhythm to short, hard strokes, rocking his hips, grunting low in his throat.

"I'm making you my girl tonight." JT's deep voice was full of animal lust.

He rode Kyle's mouth harder and harder, holding him still in his iron grip, until his balls clenched, and his cock twitched deep down Kyle's throat.

"Oh fuck," JT said, between clenched teeth. "Take it, bitch. Take my fucking come."

JT threw his head back, thrust his hips hard and pulled Kyle's face down on his cock, moaning so low it was almost a growl of pleasure. JT's hips bucked hard against Kyle's mouth again and again as his throbbing cock jetted hot come down his boy's throat.

After Kyle swallowed JT's heavy load of thick come, he ran his tongue along JT's cock and balls, licking him clean. Jessi's face rose in his mind, both eyes blackened, his lips split, his arm in a splint.

"I'll do what you want," Kyle said, licking JT's balls, looking up into his dark eyes. "You don't have to hurt me."

JT looked down at Kyle's tear stained face. "You pissed off 'cause I fucked your mouth like that?"

Kyle tried to drop his eyes, but JT grabbed his face. "Answer me."

"I shouldn't have made you mad like that," Kyle said, his voice low and quiet.

To a man like JT, Kyle's answer made the boy irresistible. He let go, and Kyle went back to licking him clean. "After the way I fucked your bitch mouth, your tongue feels real good, boy."

JT ran his calloused fingers through his boy's soft red hair. "Next time don't leave the table before me like that."

Kyle nodded. "Are you gonna beat me up?"

Chapter 19

JT slapped Kyle's face lightly. "You fucking come to me when I call you, alright?"

"I won't mess with you," Kyle said. His pounding heart made his words jagged and uneven. "You don't have to beat me up."

A hint of a smile touched JT's hard face. "What the fuck they been telling you about me, boy?"

"I saw Jessi's picture." Kyle's voice was almost too low to be heard.

Kyle didn't see the sharp question that came and went in JT's eyes. He heard JT step back and zip his jeans.

Kyle flinched when JT bent over and took his face in his dark, deadly hands. He was sure JT was about to make him into Jessi's twin. Kyle squeezed his eyes shut, tried to be ready for the fist that would come driving into his face.

"Kyle, look at me."

Kyle's eyes flew open. JT's face loomed large over him.

"Listen to me real good. The last thing you want in this world is to be on my bad side. Jessi, he got on my bad side." To Kyle's ears, JT's low voice carried more menace than the loudest threat. "You pissed me off, but you was a real good bitch just now, so I ain't gonna beat you. I'm giving you a chance." He let go of Kyle's face, and stood up to his full height, looking down at the scared boy on his knees between his legs. "Don't be fucking with me, punk, understand?"

Kyle nodded and spoke without looking up at JT, "Do you – " Kyle swallowed, gathered his courage and forced himself to go on. "Do you rape your girls?" he said in a low, trembling voice.

"If you fight me, I'll hurt you," JT said. "If you act like a good girl, like last night, I'll make it good for you."

When Kyle looked up at JT, his green eyes sparkled with tears, like rain on emeralds.

"Your life ain't the same no more, boy," JT said in the quiet tones of a patient teacher. He stroked Kyle's cheek. "You're getting my black cock up your virgin ass tonight. Don't make it bad for yourself."

JT walked out, leaving Kyle on his knees, more scared than a man walking a high wire without a net.

Kyle got to his feet slowly, feeling dazed and somehow outside of himself. How could his life have changed so much in just one night?

The cold hardness in JT's black eyes terrified Kyle. He was sure that if he'd gone on yelling at JT, he would have taken off his belt and beat his ass 'til his screams echoed off the walls. Or worse, maybe he would have rearranged Kyle's face to look more like Jessi. Kyle shuddered at the thought.

He was about to walk out of the bathroom, when he remembered Dante's warning about not going anywhere by himself. How come JT just left him here? Kyle was about to risk going to the library alone when the door knob turned. His first instinct was to run and hide in a stall, but none of the stalls had doors.

Kyle hid in the last stall at the far end, crouching on the toilet seat, listening as footsteps drew closer and closer. Only one man. Good. Maybe he could outrun him.

Kyle didn't realize that the stalls were only six feet tall, so any man taller than six feet could see right over the metal walls.

"What the fuck you doing in there, boy?"

Kyle looked up to see Dante fighting to control himself.

"Come on," Dante said, losing the fight and laughing a little. "If you're done shitting through your pants, I got to get you to the library."

Kyle got off the white throne, feeling like a fool. He didn't mind Dante's laughter. It was good natured, not ugly and cruel like the men at breakfast. He even laughed at himself a little. It was the first time he'd even smiled in Purgatory, let alone laughed.

Dante was walking out of the bathroom when Kyle jumped in front of him and pressed his small hand to Dante's wide, muscled chest.

Dante looked down at the boy. "What?"

"Thanks for not laughing at me at breakfast, like those other men."

Dante pushed back stray dreads that had fallen across his face. "They ain't nothing but fools sometimes. Good men, except that punk Tyrone."

"Maybe they didn't mean anything. But the way you sat there, not laughing with the rest of them, means a lot to me. Thanks."

"There ain't nothing to laugh at," Dante said in his quiet way. "Just 'cause you're a bitch don't mean you got to be treated like that."

Kyle looked up at the ex-gladiator, wondering for a moment how much different things would have been if he'd landed in a cell with Dante instead of JT.

"Why you look at me like that boy?"

"Nothing." Kyle shook his head, like a man shaking off a dream. "How come JT left? Did he forget about me?"

"No." Dante headed for the door again. "He got shit to do. I'm gonna be the one walking you wherever you need to go. Remember what I told you last night?"

Kyle nodded. "Don't go anywhere by myself," he said in the sing song voice of someone repeating words for the millionth time.

"Don't say it like that. JT got to come chasing after you, it's your ass."

48

Chapter 20

When Kyle walked into to the library, he expected the guard to ask him where the fuck he'd been. Kyle had heard him say it to other prisoners who were five minutes late. But when Kyle walked in twenty minutes late, Mr. Remello, the guard on duty, nodded to him, then went back to the terminal he was reading.

Kyle worked quietly in the stacks, arranging book discs, checking for damage. He liked working in the cool, air conditioned library. It was better than working in the hot kitchen or outside in the sun.

While he worked, he thought about this morning. He didn't understand why JT changed his mind about beating him. Kyle had seen JT's big hands fall away from his belt, as if his killer hands had found better things to do than beat a boy too stupid to shut up.

Kyle was deep in these thoughts when he heard a commotion ripple through the library. He leaned over the black wrought iron railing that ran around the edge of this level. When he saw who was standing at Remello's desk, he froze, like a deer caught in headlights. Somehow he knew the gladiator was here for him. His first thought was to sneak out of the library. But where would he go?

He risked another quick look over the balcony. Tyrone, his deadly body outlined under a tight black t-shirt, was heading for the circular stone steps that led up to Kyle's floor.

Kyle ran back between the stacks, seeking out the darkest corner. He disappeared between the stacks like Alice down a rabbit hole, slipping into the darkness, willing himself to become invisible.

Kyle scampered down the aisle at the far end of the level. These stacks had old fashioned books, most of them about law. He hunkered down, pressing close to the bottom shelf, trying to squeeze himself between Procedures of Appeal and Theory of Reformation of the State, his head down, hiding his red hair from any light it might reflect. He listened for Tyrone's footsteps, but heard nothing for long minutes. He was about to breathe a sigh of relief when a deep voice floated out of the darkness.

"I smell a bitch." Tyrone's low voice came from the stack next to Kyle's hiding place. The boy held his breath, his hammering heart loud in his ears. There was silence for long minutes. Long enough for Kyle to hope Tyrone had lost his scent.

"Hey, boy," Tyrone said, standing over Kyle. He'd sniffed the boy out like an alligator scenting fresh meat.

"What you doing back here in the dark?"

Kyle shrugged, getting to his feet. He was trapped in the narrow aisle between stacks. Tyrone's thickly muscled body blocked his way. Kyle's mind raced. He felt trouble heading for him like a screaming freight train.

Tyrone came closer until he was only inches from Kyle. The diamond stud in his left ear glinted in the shadows.

"Did JT fuck your little bitch ass yet?"

Kyle swallowed, and shook his head. "No."

Tyrone pressed close to Kyle in the darkness. "When he gets a new bitch, he fucks ass the first night, to try him out. Except virgins. He likes to take his time with virgins. You been fucked up the ass before, boy?" His voice was low and intimate, like lovers having sweet talk.

"No."

Kyle was too scared to look up into Tyrone's greedy eyes. Tyrone ran his hand over Kyle's crotch, felt the growing hardness there.

"You're hard, boy. How come? You need that little virgin hole fucked real hard?"

Kyle had been hard since he swallowed JT's come in the bathroom. Now, with Tyrone's muscled body pressed so close to him, Kyle had a raging hard on.

"Please – " Kyle tried to say.

Before he could finish, Tyrone grabbed Kyle and spun him around to face the wall. He undid Kyle's jeans and pulled them down along with his cotton briefs. He clamped his big hand over Kyle's mouth, muffling the boy's cry of surprise.

"I wanna see what JT's getting," Tyrone whispered into Kyle's ear. "I'm gonna see how tight this virgin ass is."

Tyrone stuck a finger in his own mouth, then found Kyle's hole. He shoved his finger in hard, then jabbed in and out of Kyle's hole cruelly, making Kyle groan in pain.

"You're a fucking tight bitch," Tyrone said, pulling his finger out.

He ground his hips into Kyle's naked ass, dry humping the boy roughly with his hard cock. Kyle's heart beat madly.

"You're lucky you belong to JT. 'Cause if you was my bitch I would of raped your virgin ass last night and made you scream real loud."

Tyrone spun Kyle around to face him and pushed the boy to his knees. Without a word, he took out his hard cock and grabbed Kyle's hair.

"You best open your mouth, bitch. Or you want me to tell JT how you came to me and begged to suck my dick. How you think he'll like that?"

Kyle was afraid of JT, but without his protection, he'd be fresh meat in Purgatory. He thought of the men walking by at dinner time; and Taylor, with his ass up, while the men played cards for his ass. And last in his hit parade of terror, Jessi's battered face.

Kyle opened his mouth.

Chapter 21

At lunch, Kyle sat beside JT, expecting the worst. But Tyrone ignored him, as if the library had never happened. Kyle picked up a strange vibe at the table. The men talked about the gladiator games last night and coming bad weather, but they had the tense faces of soldiers poised for battle.

"Another storm's heading our way," Leon said. He was bald, like JT, but light brown like coffee with too much milk.

"You think it's gonna hit, like they say?" JT said.

He glanced up at the big clock on the wall, then met Dante's eyes for a second. Some message passed between them that Kyle didn't understand.

"We ain't nothing but sitting ducks out here on this fucking rock," Derrick said. He snapped a quick look at the clock.

"Hurricane Shira's gonna kick our ass if she comes this way," Tyrone said.

To Kyle, their conversation sounded like men marking time. They talked in circles, saying nothing, not answering each other. Everyone kept glancing at the clock overhead, like they were on some kind of weird countdown.

Kyle looked at Dante. But Dante looked right through Kyle, his dark eyes cold and hard as black marbles. Then Dante looked at the damn clock. What the hell?

"They said maybe it's gonna go right by us," Leon said. And damned if he didn't look at the clock again.

What the fu – ? Before Kyle could finish his thought, the lights went out, throwing the windowless room into pitch black chaos.

"Fuck," JT said. His low voice held no hint of surprise.

Kyle panicked when he felt strong arms close around him, and pull him up hard. His knees cracked against the table.

"I got Kyle," Dante's voice said out of the darkness. "Stay quiet. You're alright," he whispered into Kyle's ear. "Don't distract him."

Distract him from what? Kyle wanted to say.

He heard the pelting sounds of guards running in the black chaos. Curses flew across the room, radios crackled with chatter. Guards sounded off, confirming their positions in the roiling ocean of darkness. Automatic locks banged in place, locking down the cafeteria. Guards shouted orders to the prisoners.

"On the floor", a loud amplified voice said. It sounded like God talking to Moses. "On the floor. Right now. Don't move."

Sweat poured down Kyle's face, his heart knocked against his ribs, beating a staccato rhythm of pure panic.

"Shouldn't we get on the floor?" Kyle said.

"No. Shut up."

A scream rang out in the darkness. The screamer cried out desperately for help. Then his screams became wet, gurgling sounds that sent shivers down Kyle's spine.

Dante held Kyle tighter, making his big body a shield. "It's alright, boy," he said.

What's he screaming about, then? Kyle thought.

The lights shuddered, like an old man opening his eyes, then came back on. Guards ran to the far side of the cafeteria, where Kyle glimpsed a puddle of blood flowing across the stone floor.

Three men surrounded JT. Their backs were to him. He stood in the middle of the circle, a long knife in his hand, looking like the deadly gladiator that he was.

Dante let Kyle go, and sat down at the table. All the men sat down, as if nothing had happened. Kyle stood, rooted to the spot, the dying man's screams echoing in his ears.

JT glanced up at him. "Sit down and finish your lunch, boy."

Kyle sat next to JT. "Who was that screaming?"

"Don't be worried about shit that ain't your business." The hard edge in JT's voice left no room for argument.

Kyle pushed the soggy French fries and chicken nuggets around on his plate, looking around at the men at other tables. They were all talking in low voices, as if a man hadn't just died in the darkness.

"Keep your eyes to yourself, boy," Dante said quietly. He popped three of Kyle's chicken nuggets into his mouth. "Don't be looking at nobody that ain't at this table."

Guards ran back and forth in the big cafeteria. Four or five guards were gathered around a heap on the floor on the other side of the cavernous room. The automatic locks disengaged with loud clanging noises that filled the stone room.

Prisoners ignored the RATs – Rapid Assistance Teams – in black pajamas who came running in, wearing bulky flak jackets. They shouted at everyone to stay in their seat, not to move until a head count was done.

The guards shouted instructions to each other. Chaos reigned among the guards, but not the prisoners. Kyle eyed the other tables when he thought no one was looking. He was amazed. The prisoners completely ignored both the RATs and the prison guards. They stayed in their seats, and went on talking, as if nothing was happening around them.

What the hell kind of place is this? Kyle wondered.

"Does this happen all the time?" Kyle said to JT.

"Shut up, boy." JT's voice was distracted, not unkind. "Not now."

Kyle looked over at Dante, but he shook his head and pressed a finger to his lips. Guards started going from table to table, doing a head count.

I can tell you one guy who's missing, Kyle thought. He looked over at the shrouded body on the far side of the cafeteria. Red roses bloomed on the sheet covering the tangled heap on the floor.

A guard with a blonde crew cut so sharp, it bristled, came to their table. An electronic pad was in his hand. Kyle pressed closer to JT, looking at him, trying to read the expression on his dark face.

The guard counted the men at the table, then entered something on his electronic pad.

"Anybody at this table see what happened?" the guard said. He spoke in the monotone voice of someone who clearly expected no answer.

"How can anyone see in the – " *dark*, Kyle had been about to say. JT slapped Kyle's face hard.

"Shut the fuck up, bitch."

Kyle saw the anger in JT's dark eyes and shut up.

The guard ignored this and said in his monotone, "If any prisoner has any information, report it immediately."

He logged more information on his pad and walked away.

"Yeah," Derrick said, "we'll fucking come running."

JT turned to Kyle. "Learn to keep your fucking mouth shut."

Kyle touched the side of his face, looking at JT in wide eyed surprise. "Sorry," he said. "It won't happen again."

"It better not."

Kyle felt the men at the table looking at JT with grim approval, and knew this was what JT was expected to do when Kyle made a mistake.

"Everybody in here knows who done it except them," Dante said.

"Fucking idiots," Leon said.

"That shit's bad for business," Derrick said, shaking his head.

Beside Derrick, Ryan's eyes were glued to his plate, as if cold, soggy French fries were the eighth wonder of the world.

JT shrugged his big shoulders. "He shouldn't of let his bitch fuck around behind his back like that. Ain't nobody gonna respect a man who can't control his property."

Kyle paled at JT's words. He looked up at Tyrone, his green eyes tense with fear. JT sensed the change in Kyle. He gave him a sidelong look.

"What is it?" he said.

Kyle shrugged. "I got spooked." He tried to keep the tremor in his hands out of his voice. "It was so dark."

"It's over," JT said.

Thinking back to the library, Kyle drew no comfort from JT's cold voice. He looked over at Tyrone who was ignoring him. Then Kyle felt Dante's eyes on him and looked up. He saw the way Dante's eyes slid from him to Tyrone.

I'm in way over my head, Kyle thought.

Chapter 22

Kyle jumped at the sound of the alarm, expecting the lights to go out again. A loud voice boomed in the cafeteria.

"All clear. Repeat. All clear."

The prisoners slowly got up and started filing out of the cafeteria. This time, Kyle waited for JT to get up, then followed him out. JT pulled him into the bathroom again, but his mood was different this time.

"Hey, boy," JT said, once they were inside.

He pressed Kyle up against a dark brick stone wall. His palms rested against the brick, beside Kyle's head. His heavily muscled body pressed close against Kyle, making him feel like he was trapped in the shadow of a giant.

"You sucked me off real good this morning." JT rubbed his crotch against Kyle, looking down into his eyes, running his dark fingers along Kyle's pink lips.

JT's muscled body felt good pressed up against Kyle. After what he'd seen in the cafeteria, JT's big, hard body made him feel safe.

"What's wrong, boy?" JT said. "Is it what happened at lunch?"

Kyle nodded. He tried to hide the lie in his eyes by looking down at the floor, but JT didn't let him. He took Kyle's face in his big hand and made him look up at him.

"Something else happen to scare you?"

Just a bully with a thick cock in the library, Kyle thought. *Better than an assassin in the lunch room.*

Kyle licked his lips, avoiding JT's hard eyes. "Just got scared in the dark."

"Nobody said nothing to you?"

"No."

JT shook Kyle's face and looked down into the boy's startled green eyes. "I don't like it when my property lies to me," he said in a low, cold voice.

Kyle gasped, a short whimpering sound.

Quick as lightening, JT's mood changed. Instead of pressing close to Kyle, he stood back, his arms hanging at his sides, studying Kyle with hard eyes.

"Tell me what happened to you, boy."

"Don't hurt me," Kyle said in a low, unsteady voice. "He made me do it." Kyle looked at the floor, avoiding the dark emptiness in JT's black eyes.

"Who made you do what? Talk to me."

Before Kyle could stop himself, the story of what happened with Tyrone came pouring out. He told JT everything.

"After he came in my mouth, he said he'd be back whenever he wanted." Kyle finally looked up at JT. "He said if I told you, he'd say it was me who came to him. But I didn't. I swear. It happened like I told you."

For long seconds that flowed like eternity for Kyle, JT stood as still as a statue carved from ebony marble. Then, without warning, he exploded in rage. He kicked the bathroom stall behind him hard enough to dent the solid metal.

"Fucking Tyrone," he said between clenched teeth. "Should of killed him when I had the chance."

JT heaved a metal garbage barrel at the polished metal mirror that hung over the sink, scarring the metal with an ugly scratch.

"Always *fucking* with me."

JT's enraged voice filled the bathroom, echoing like heavy thunder. He knocked over two more garbage barrels and kicked them all over the bathroom, making a horrible racket that terrified Kyle.

He pressed himself up against a wall, watching JT's rampage. As JT smashed another trashcan against the wall, Kyle inched toward the bathroom door. There were no windows in the bathroom. Just lately, Kyle hated rooms without windows.

Even as JT raged against the yielding metal, Kyle sensed him holding back, not daring to let go of the monsters that lurked in the darkness inside him.

Long minutes later, long after guards should have come to see who was tearing the bathroom apart brick by brick, a smothering cloak of silence fell. The screech of metal smashing into brick echoed in Kyle's ears. The garbage barrels lay at either end of the bathroom, twisted into scrap metal. Kyle stood stone still, pressed into the wall so hard, he felt the rough bricks against his flesh.

JT stood over Kyle, breathing hard. His dark face was a mask of controlled fury.

"I'm telling the truth," Kyle said, not daring to move another inch toward the door.

"I know you are."

JT's soft voice surprised Kyle. He risked looking up into JT's furious face.

"Relax, boy. I ain't hurting you." JT stroked Kyle's soft cheek.

"You're not?"

"No," JT said in a cold flat voice. "Not you."

He pulled Kyle into his arms, and looked down into the boy's terrified eyes. "Know what happens now?"

You rain down on Tyrone like a hurricane? Kyle thought. He shook his head, looking up into JT's cold eyes.

"Now me and Tyrone are gonna duel over you. I'm fighting him for you. There's gonna be a Dark Game tonight. No lights. No cameras. Just me and that bitch."

JT's voice was even and calm, as if he were talking about the weather. But his eyes were dark and stormy with rage. "I'm gonna carve my fucking name into that punk."

JT headed for the door, kicking aside one of the garbage barrels.

"Let's go. You need to get back to the library. I got shit to do."

Kyle trailed after JT, wondering how much a gladiator had to bleed to win a Dark Game.

Chapter 23

That night, after dinner, Kyle sat on his bunk, looking out onto the empty tier. In the next cell, he heard the breathy sound of a man either fucking or getting his dick sucked. Kyle tried not to think about what would happen to him if Tyrone won the fight tonight.

JT had told Kyle that he would belong to the man who won the duel. Tyrone's words came back to Kyle with the perfect clarity of sheer terror – *if you was my bitch I would of raped your virgin ass last night and made you scream real loud*. Kyle looked at JT anxiously when he walked into their cell.

"Come on, boy," JT said. "Game time."

He grabbed a black bag and turned to go. Kyle jumped down from his bunk, and looked up at JT, uncertain.

"What is it?" JT said.

"You're gonna win, right?"

A shadow of a smile crossed JT's hard face. "Tyrone's been fucking with me for a long time. I'm getting tired of his punk ass. He's lucky I ain't in the mood to kill nobody tonight."

Before he'd heard a dying man's screams in the darkness, JT's answer would have terrified Kyle. But he realized that in a place like Purgatory, a man's mood could rip the thin veil between life and death.

———————

Kyle followed JT past guards who acted like they were both invisible. One guard nodded to JT and asked how he was doing. No one tried to stop them.

They left the tier, went down old stone steps that smelled of sweat and piss. Kyle counted two flights below the first floor before a big, black iron door blocked their way.

"Where are we?" Kyle said, looking around in the darkness. This wasn't like the part of the prison where the Clubhouse was. It seemed even older.

JT slipped a big black key from his pocket and said, "Old Purgatory."

He slid the skeleton key into the ancient looking lock. The door opened with a soft creak that spoke of well oiled hinges. The corridor beyond lay in pitch black darkness.

Kyle hung back, looking into the dark. JT switched on his powerful flashlight and took Kyle's hand again.

"Is this another way to the Clubhouse?"

"No."

JT led Kyle through dark corridors, past closed doors that hadn't been opened in over a century, deeper into the musty scent of disuse, until finally, they heard the low murmur of voices up ahead.

They turned a corner and Kyle saw a giant cage standing in the middle of the stone floor. Hurricane lanterns hung from the iron bars that formed the top of the cage, casting a shifting yellow glow all around.

No one was inside the cage yet. Men crowded around the cage made way for JT and Kyle. Dante waited near the door into the cage. A blond man with a diamond stud in his left ear, who looked as big as one of the original Vikings, headed their way. Kyle shrank back as he came up to JT and clapped him on the back hard enough to send another man sprawling.

"You show him what's what JT. He's making trouble for all of us," the Viking said.

"He won't make no more trouble after tonight, Sven," JT said quietly.

"Good." The blond man walked off, trailing a slender blonde man behind him.

"You ready?" Dante said, taking JT's bag.

"Yeah." JT looked at Kyle. "Take care of my bitch. Keep him close."

Dante pulled Kyle beside him. "Don't worry."

JT slid his t-shirt over his head. His body rippled with solid muscle in the flickering light. He took the short handled knife Dante handed him from the black bag. Dante pulled Kyle back as JT opened the door to the giant cage and stepped inside.

"Where's Tyrone?" Kyle said.

"He'll be here," Dante said.

Derrick walked through the crowd of men, with Ryan beside him. Kyle was glad to see Ryan. He thought they'd get to talk until Ryan gave him a look that warned him to silence. Derrick stood on the other side of Kyle. Both boys were in between the two men.

"You bitches don't move, hear?" Dante said.

Kyle and Ryan both nodded, looking into the cage. The crowd buzzed with excitement. Men clung to the outside of the bars, making a living wall around JT. He stood in the center of the cage, shirtless, holding his knife.

"Where's the guards?" Kyle said. "And the Referee. It's not like this on holo."

Derrick and Dante both laughed. "Those games are for show, boy. This here's the real thing," Derrick said.

Silence went through the crowd in a wave. A path cleared to let Tyrone through.

"How come he's only got two men with him?" Kyle whispered.

Derrick gave him a side long look that made Kyle inch away. Dante explained in a low voice.

The two men with Tyrone showed how powerful he was. The more men a man needed with him to feel safe walking the dark halls of the prison, he less respect he earned.

Only the most powerful men walked alone in Purgatory. Everyone knew that to attack a man powerful enough to walk alone, was a death sentence.

If a gang attacked a man walking alone, the Council branded them cowards. When the dishonorable death was avenged, the Council did nothing. The offending gang lost all respect in Purgatory.

Even Hell has rules, Kyle thought.

Tyrone took off his black t-shirt, revealing a body heavy with muscle. He took a curved knife from the man on his left.

What Tyrone did next sent a shock wave through the watching crowd. Slowly, so that every man there saw what he did, Tyrone blew Kyle a kiss.

Kyle looked from Tyrone to JT standing in the middle of the cage. He'd seen what Tyrone did, but his face showed nothing. A slight tension rippled through JT. His sculpted muscle stood out even more in the flickering golden light. It was the only sign of his fury at what Tyrone had done.

Tyrone walked into the cage, followed by the blonde Viking. When all three men were in the cage, silence fell. JT signaled to Kyle to come into the cage. Kyle looked up at Dante.

"Go on, boy," Dante said. "You'll be out before the fighting starts."

Kyle walked into the big cage, feeling the eyes of all the men on him. JT pulled him close, away from Tyrone.

"Tonight is Dark Game," the Viking said. His strong voice echoed down dark stone passages. "We come to settle a duel over property between two gladiators. We men fight our own fights."

The crowd cheered.

"This man, JT, has claimed this virgin bitch, Kyle, for his own."

The Viking fell silent, letting all the men look at Kyle and JT. Kyle's face had flushed deep crimson at the word 'virgin'. *God, can it get any worse than this?* Kyle thought, looking at the crowd of men.

"This man, Tyrone, has brought dishonor to JT by disrespecting his property behind his back. Tonight, JT will win back his honor, or Tyrone will own his virgin bitch."

The Viking looked at both men. "You both agree to be honor bound by the duel?"

Tyrone and JT both nodded. Kyle said nothing. He couldn't believe two men were about to fight to see who *owned* him. But looking into Tyrone's dark, hungry eyes, he knew this was deadly serious. The man who won tonight would own Kyle's virgin ass in Purgatory, no questions asked.

"The man who frees himself with this key, wins."

The Viking held up a large, black skeleton key, then turned and led Kyle out of the giant cage. He locked the door behind him, and hung the key beside the lock where it could be easily reached by a man standing on the other side of the bars. Kyle took up his place between Ryan and Dante, to watch the duel.

"You better hope JT wins," Ryan whispered to Kyle.

"No shit," Kyle whispered back.

Derrick's grabbed Ryan's hair, and pulled the boy's head back hard.

"What I told you about you running your mouth to JT's bitch?"

"Sorry," Ryan said, looking up into Derrick's angry eyes. "I was just telling him I hope JT wins."

"Keep your fucking mouth shut," Derrick said and let go of Ryan's hair.

"I'm sorry," Ryan said, looking up at Derrick. Quiet desperation filled his brown eyes. He rested his hands lightly on Derrick's thick arm. "I didn't say anything about anything. I swear."

Derrick shook his hands off. "Shut the fuck up," he said in a low vicious voice. "Or you want me to do you right here?"

Ryan shook his head. All of a sudden, he looked terribly afraid. He looked up at Dante with pleading eyes.

"He ain't done nothing Derrick," Dante said. "I heard him."

"I ain't JT," Derrick said. "Stay out of it."

Dante shook his head a little and gave Ryan a look that said, *sorry, I tried.*

Kyle didn't so much as look at Ryan after that. He was slowly coming to realize that Purgatory was a place of secrets, where loose lips could put your lights out forever. That was alright with Kyle. He knew all about secrets.

Chapter 24

Kyle gripped the bars so tightly, his white knuckles looked blanched against the black iron. He pressed his face between the bars, watching JT and Tyrone with unblinking attention. The way JT's muscles flexed and moved in the shadowy light reminded Kyle of last night, on his knees between JT's powerful legs.

Watching him move like a warrior in battle, knowing that JT was fighting over him, gave Kyle a raging hard on. He ached to suck JT's cock and make him groan in pleasure as he shot hot come down his throat. He'd never felt anything like the aching need in his virgin ass before. Kyle wanted to feel JT's thick cock filling his hole, taking his virginity.

Inside the cage, JT and Tyrone circled each other in a low crouch. Both held their knives easily. They were nearly matched in size and strength. JT was lithe with hard muscle, and graceful on his feet. He was only about an inch taller than Tyrone.

Tyrone didn't move with the same grace and ease as JT. Fear made his movements jittery. His eyes flicked beyond JT, distracted by noises from the crowd. JT's face was impassive, smooth, as if he were a spectator with nothing to lose. His eyes never left Tyrone.

When JT struck, no one, including Tyrone, expected it. JT's knife came in under Tyrone's extended arm in a rapid swipe. Tyrone jumped back and twisted away, but not before JT's knife left a light flesh wound.

"Next time I catch your bitch alone, I'll fuck him real hard," Tyrone said in a low hiss that only JT heard.

JT ignored Tyrone's talk. Words were for amateurs. JT's knife did all the talking in a fight. Tyrone won games because he was matched with men who were stupider than him. JT won because when he fought, the dark tide inside him brought ecstasy. In the grip of the darkness, he wanted to wreak havoc; he lived for the thrill of the kill. JT was the rarest of fighters – a warrior without fear.

JT let his mind grow still. In the stillness, he let the dark tide of fury that always flowed deep inside him rise up. JT rode the rising tide of rage – flying – like a hit of fine Bolivian flake. He saw everything with the eyes of a hawk. He smelled Tyrone's fear, saw him telegraph every move before it came.

When JT broke into a hard icy smile, Tyrone broke out in a cold sweat. Tyrone came at JT, his knife low, aiming for his belly. JT dropped into a roll, kicking out a powerful leg that nearly sent Tyrone tumbling to the stone floor.

JT came to his feet in a smooth motion, gliding his knife back and forth in a slow, hypnotic weave, smiling. JT came at Tyrone in a relentless storm of cuts and slashes. His knife struck like metal lightening, slicing through candlelight in swift arcs that drove the audience wild. They chanted JT's name, clinging to the bars, urging him on.

Again and again, JT's razor sharp knife danced through the air, harassing Tyrone with light, harmless flesh wounds. Tyrone tried to fight back, but every move was blocked or struck thin air.

JT fell back, waiting for Tyrone to come for him. The two men circled each other in a slow dance. Tyrone struck out at JT, but JT easily dodged his clumsy swipes. JT raked his knife through the air, leaving flesh wounds that stung Tyrone's pride more than his flesh.

———————

JT saw useless, uncontrolled rage running wild in Tyrone's eyes. JT was merciless. He came at Tyrone again and again, always dancing back out of reach. When Tyrone lost his temper and came charging at JT with a loud cry, his knife held high, JT let him come.

At the last second, JT stepped aside, tripping up Tyrone, letting his own weight slam him to the stone floor. JT was on him in an instant, his muscled arm wrapped tight around Tyrone's throat.

Tyrone sputtered and cursed, thrashing wildly, but JT rode his bucking back like a man riding a raging bull. The men in the audience went wild, screaming JT's name. But when JT showed no signs of releasing Tyrone from his deadly embrace, a hush fell, then deepened into uneasy silence.

In the cold silence that fell, JT said, "You even let your shadow fall on my property again, I'll kill you."

Every man watching heard JT's words, just like they'd seen Tyrone blow Kyle a kiss. JT's words proclaimed Kyle to be his property, to be touched by no man, unless they wanted to die. He gave one last squeeze, pushing Tyrone into unconsciousness, then he let him go.

Before he got up, JT used his knife to carve his initials just above Tyrone's right shoulder blade. Tyrone would have to burn the skin to erase it, unless he wanted to be someone's bitch. JT wiped his knife on his pants, and walked toward the door to the cage, where the key hung waiting for him to claim victory.

Behind JT, Tyrone rose to his feet, like a man rising from a drugged sleep. His eyes focused blearily on JT, and he came at him, gaining speed with all the grace of a charging bull.

Screams of warning came from the audience. JT whirled to face Tyrone, his knife ready. No more bullshit. If Tyrone kept coming, it'd be the last stupid thing he ever did.

"You wanna die tonight?" JT said quietly.

Tyrone stopped in his tracks, looking around the shadowy square. If JT killed him, all the men watching would be honor bound to be silent witnesses.

Tyrone held up both hands in a gesture of surrender and dropped his knife.

"I didn't think so," JT said and deliberately turned his back on Tyrone.

He reached through the bars and got the key that unlocked the cage. Dante and Derrick met him outside the door. They tried to hold Kyle back, but JT signaled to let him go. Kyle ran into JT's arms with such unexpected force that JT fell back a step.

When Kyle looked up at JT, his green eyes were dark and unreadable.

"You would have killed him for me?" Kyle said.

"You're mine, boy. Ain't nobody taking you from me."

A sudden shyness came over Kyle and he dropped his eyes. JT took the boy's face in his big hand and made Kyle look up at him.

"What?" JT said.

Seeing JT move like that, the way his muscles flexed with every move, Kyle felt something he'd never felt before. He wanted JT to take him, and make him his bitch. He wanted to feel JT's thick cock slide deep into his virgin ass, plowing into him. He ached to surrender to this dark warrior.

"I don't wanna be a virgin anymore." Kyle blushed the deepest shade of crimson. "I want it to be you."

JT chuckled. "That's the nicest thing anybody ever told me after a fight."

He kissed Kyle's soft pink lips.

Behind them, Tyrone slammed through the open door and made his way through the crowd without a backward glance. As JT turned to watch Tyrone walk away, he knew he'd made a mistake. He should have let Tyrone cut him, at least once. The fact that JT didn't have a single cut on him from Tyrone's knife completed Tyrone's humiliation. After tonight, he would be marked as a man who couldn't fight for what he wanted.

"What about him?" Dante said, looking at Tyrone's retreating back. "You want us to do anything?"

JT shook his head. "No. Not unless he fucks with us."

Dante nodded, but he gave Tyrone a side long look that JT didn't like.

"I mean it," JT said, waiting for Dante's hard eyes to focus on him. "Leave him alone. Don't make trouble where we don't need it."

Dante held up both hands. "I won't do nothing to his punk ass." He watched Tyrone's back disappearing down a dark stone tunnel. "Unless I got to."

Chapter 25

JT led Kyle down dark twisting stone corridors, guiding them with the narrow beam of the flashlight. Kyle tried not to think about what would happen if the flashlight's batteries died.

Kyle peered into the darkness that pressed all around. "We're not going back upstairs?"

"No, baby." JT pulled Kyle along. "I'm taking you on a date."

Kyle fell silent, and concentrated on following JT through the twisting darkness. A few times Kyle thought he heard far away screams. He asked JT about it, but got no answer.

When Kyle thought he couldn't stand anymore of following the flashlight beam through coal black darkness, JT said, "Stay here."

Kyle panicked, until he realized JT wasn't going far. They'd stopped in front of a cell that was three times the size of the cells in the prison above them.

JT walked into the cell, taking a lighter from his pocket. He lit fat midnight blue candles. Shadows jumped to life on the dark stone walls.

The flickering candlelight revealed a stained stone floor, and a strangely new mattress on an ancient prison cot. A wooden table that had been new when this part of the prison was built, leaned in one corner. Black handcuffs hung from the iron bars to Kyle's left, just the right height to cuff someone to the bars, standing up.

JT lay on the wide cot on his side, one leg up.

"Come here, boy," he said softly.

Kyle hesitated. Even if he was willing to brave the pitch blackness beyond the candlelight, he'd never find his way through the dark maze. He walked into the cell, stood in front of JT.

"Get naked," JT said.

JT watched Kyle undress in the candlelight. Kyle's tight young body filled him with raw animal need. He ached to cuff Kyle to the bars and snatch his virginity in one deep thrust.

JT called Kyle to him. Kyle sat on the edge, naked, as far from JT as he could.

"I ain't gonna lie to you, baby," JT said, stroking Kyle's smooth legs. His voice was soft, gentle. "You're the sweetest bitch I ever seen. I feel like raping your virgin hole and hearing you scream while I take you."

Kyle's breathing changed. He trembled like a live wire. JT didn't mind.

"But if you're a real good girl, I won't do that, hear?"

Kyle nodded, looking down at his trembling hands.

JT took off his shirt. He saw the way Kyle looked at his dark sculpted body in the candlelight. His chest and belly rippled with muscle. Beads of sweat clung to him from the fight.

He pulled Kyle close, not letting the boy think. Kyle pressed against him, and ran his tongue along his hard body, licking away his sweat. JT ran his dark hands down Kyle's smooth body, caressing his hairless chest.

"You're soft." JT slid his calloused fingers across Kyle's hard pink nipples. "I like my girls soft like you."

When JT's hands slid down, Kyle opened his legs, revealing his swollen cock. JT pushed back against the wall behind him and opened his legs. He pulled Kyle close, so the boy's head rested on his muscled chest and Kyle's naked ass pressed up against his crotch.

"I ain't had a virgin in a long time," he said into Kyle's ear.

JT found Kyle's pink nipples and twisted gently. He kissed Kyle's neck softly, his breath hot against his flesh.

"Don't fight me," JT whispered, working Kyle's nipples. "I'll make it good for you, baby."

"I used to watch your fights all the time," Kyle said.

"Yeah?" JT whispered. "What was you thinking about when you seen me fight?"

JT twisted Kyle's pink nipples gently, ran his tongue along Kyle's neck and whispered, "Tell me, boy. What was you thinking?"

"About sucking your dick," Kyle said, writhing in JT's arms. "And swallowing a load."

"That's all, baby?" JT whispered. "You didn't think about nothing else?"

"Yeah," Kyle said. "I did tonight when I watched you fight."

"Tell me," JT said softly. "I'm making you my girl tonight. Tell me everything."

JT took Kyle's swollen cock in his hand and jacked him off slowly. He kissed the side of Kyle's neck while he worked the boy's dick. Kyle rocked his hips, sliding in and out of JT's slick fist.

"I thought about bending over. Taking you in my ass." Kyle hissed in pleasure as JT worked his dick. "Even if your fat cock made me scream."

"Fuck, boy," JT said, smiling a little. "You could drive a man crazy."

JT kissed along Kyle's neck and whispered, "Before you got here, you jacked off thinking about me fucking your virgin pussy?"

Even in the dim candlelight, JT saw Kyle flush deep red. "You ain't gotta hide nothing from me," JT said, working Kyle's cock. "You wanted black dick real bad?"

"I wanted to get fucked, but I was scared," Kyle whispered.

JT's slick fist slid slowly up and down Kyle's throbbing cock, while he rested his finger against Kyle's virgin tightness. He let the boy's writhing ass push onto his finger.

Kyle moaned when JT's finger slid into him. JT could tell he'd never had anything in his ass before.

JT moved his finger slowly in and out. "You like it?"

"Yeah," Kyle said. "It feels so good."

"I'm so fucking hot for you, baby," JT whispered. "My cock's all hard and throbbing thinking about fucking your virgin pussy."

JT slid another finger into Kyle. The way his hot tight hole closed around his fingers made JT catch his breath. "What else you thought about when you watched me fight?"

"I was scared of you, but I wanted you. I got so hard, it hurt."

"You know what I'm gonna do to you tonight?"

JT felt Kyle stiffen in his arms.

"Don't make it hurt," Kyle said in a low voice. "Please. I won't fight."

"I ain't gonna hurt you, boy." JT kissed Kyle's soft skin, stroking his boy's cock. "I'm gonna fuck your virgin hole real good and make you take it like a pussy bitch."

JT pressed his two fingers deeper into Kyle's writhing ass. The way Kyle's tight ass clenched around his fingers drove him crazy.

"That's what you thought about all those nights you was jacking off, right? You ain't got to lie no more. Tell me."

Kyle nodded. "I wanted a man like you."

The utter surrender in Kyle's voice filled JT with undeniable, aching need.

"Tell me the kind of man you wanted, boy." JT fingered Kyle's hot ass.

"A man who'd fuck me hard, even if I said no; someone who'd choke me and come in my mouth; a man who'd – "

Kyle stopped, unable to go on. The hot flush of desire that rose to Kyle's cheeks made JT's throbbing cock surge.

"Tell me, boy." JT slid his fingers slowly in and out of Kyle's ass. "Don't hold back. You're gonna be my girl. I'll give you everything you need."

"A man who'd slap me if I pissed him off," Kyle said.

JT smiled. He'd waited a long time for a bitch like Kyle.

"Oh yeah, bitch," JT said, easing his dick into Kyle. "Here I come for your virgin ass."

Kyle gasped in pain as the thick head of JT's cock slid into his tight hole. He bit his lip, trying to hold still, trying not to make JT mad at him.

JT moved slow, feeling the way Kyle's sweet ass grabbed his cock head, pulsing around his dark meat. He looked down at his dark cock inching into the boy's virgin white ass. Kyle's moans and whimpers as JT eased his thick cock into his hot tightness drove JT crazy.

"That's it, baby," JT said inching into Kyle. "Give me that virgin pussy."

JT loved knowing he was the first man to make Kyle take a fat cock up his ass.

"Oh fuck." JT pressed his hard cock into Kyle's tight hole slowly. "I forgot how good virgin ass is."

Kyle groaned in pain as JT's thick cock stretched his virgin hole.

"Please," Kyle begged. "I can't. It hurts so bad." His voice was choked with pain.

"Easy, baby." JT caressed Kyle's trembling ass with his dark hands. "You're my girl now. Get used to my black cock stretching your little hole."

Kyle pressed his face into the mattress, groaning in pain, his body tense and trembling. The way the boy's virgin hole quivered around his throbbing cock, drove JT mad with lust.

Primitive desire stormed through him, taking him over. The urge to plunge deep into Kyle's virgin hole, and rip away his manhood was electrifying. JT grabbed Kyle's hips in his dark hands and pulled hard, driving deep into him at the same time.

Kyle cried out, and struggled, but the animal urge to fuck was too strong. JT drove into Kyle's writhing ass again and again, filled with the fierce victory of a warrior claiming his conquest. Kyle fought, bucking against JT, trying to escape.

"Fucking bitch." JT slammed into Kyle's ass over and over. "Take my cock."

JT rode Kyle hard, grunting and moaning, like a stallion breeding a mare. Kyle's groans of pain echoed in JT's ears, making his cock throb greedily with the thrill of victory.

"You ain't no virgin no more." JT pounded into the boy's quivering ass. "You're my pussy bitch now."

JT fucked Kyle hard, grunting, his balls slamming into the struggling boy's ass over and over. Sweat slid down JT's muscled chest. His dark fingers dug into Kyle's creamy white ass, leaving marks that would last for days. The muscles in his arms stood out in the candlelight, as he rode Kyle's ass hard. Kyle struggled in JT's savage grip, whimpering.

"Virgin pussy's so good and tight." JT threw his head back and let out a war cry, claiming the spoils of his victory in the Dark Game.

The stone room was full of the sounds of hard fucking. JT's low moans of animal pleasure echoed off the brick walls. Kyle's groans of pain were nearly lost under the harsh sound of JT hammering his ass. His black cock sank deep into Kyle's white virgin ass again and again.

JT's muscled body was a black sculpture of strength and power, like a dark god, taking a virgin boy's sacrificed ass. Kyle's body was smooth and creamy ivory in the flickering candlelight, as he writhed, helpless, forced to submit to JT's black cock, as JT claimed him as his property.

"Oh yeah, bitch." JT pumped Kyle's ass with a new urgency. "I made you my girl."

JT fucked Kyle's ass harder, lost in the pleasure of his sweet virgin hole pulsing around his throbbing cock. JT's whole body strained. He clenched his teeth. He was so fucking close.

"You're gonna take my load, bitch."

JT's voice was low and guttural, his breathing harsh and ragged. He dug his dark fingers deeper into Kyle's white ass, holding him tight, pumping hard into Kyle's quivering hole. JT groaned as he felt his heavy balls clench. He grabbed Kyle even tighter and jammed his thick cock hard into the boy's ass, moaning low in his throat.

"You're my girl," JT said in a strangled voice. "My fucking girl."

JT grunted and groaned as his cock twitched deep inside Kyle's hot pulsing hole, then he went rigid and jammed his hips into Kyle. He shot a load up Kyle's ass, sealing Kyle's fate as his bitch, his girl and soon, his wife.

Chapter 27

"Oh fuck," JT said, pulling out of Kyle's ass.

He collapsed on the bed beside the trembling boy, breathing hard. "Your virgin ass was a sweet fuck," JT said between breaths.

"I'm sorry," Kyle was saying over and over. "Don't beat me up. I tried, but you hurt me so bad."

Kyle was curled into a ball facing JT, shaking, begging JT not to hurt him. When JT reached out to pull Kyle close, the boy cried out and scrambled further into the corner, away from him.

"Come here, boy." JT grabbed Kyle's arm, and pulled him close.

When the terrified boy looked up at him in the candlelight, JT said, "I ain't gonna do nothing to you. It was my fault. I shouldn't of done you like that."

"Don't beat me up," Kyle kept saying, as if JT's words didn't penetrate his fear. "Please. I didn't mean to fight you."

JT pulled Kyle into his strong arms, and waited 'til he felt the boy's madly beating heart slow down.

"You ain't done nothing, baby." JT trailed his dark fingers across Kyle's creamy ass. "I ain't gonna hurt you."

When JT felt Kyle relax against him, he said, "You was a real good girl. But that virgin ass just about drove me crazy."

Kyle said nothing, still trembling in his arms. JT moved Kyle's hand to his cock, still slick with come, while he reached over and took Kyle's dick in his dark fist.

"Come on, boy," JT said, moving his fist up and down Kyle's cock, "get me hard again so I can give you what little bitches like you need – a hot load in your mouth."

Kyle's fist closed around JT's semi-hard cock and started stroking him, bringing his fuck meat back to life, while JT stroked the boy's rising cock.

"You still wanna come with my black cock in your mouth?" JT whispered into Kyle's ear.

The boy's cock was already hard in JT's fist, and Kyle had forgotten his fear.

"Yeah," Kyle said, moaning softly while they stroked each other.

"Yeah, baby?" JT stroked Kyle's cock. "After I reamed your ass, you still want a load down your throat?"

"Yeah." Kyle felt JT's cock growing rock hard in his fist.

"You're a fucking hot bitch."

Being on his knees with a thick black cock shooting hot come down his throat, sent Kyle over the edge. He groaned as his balls clenched painfully. For the first time in his life, Kyle shot a load, moaning, without touching his cock.

Coming like that, from sucking dick, without jacking off, was more satisfying than anything Kyle had ever felt. His ass throbbed in pain, his throat was in agony and he barely resisted the urge to kiss JT's feet.

With his mouth full of the bitter, salty taste of JT's come, Kyle looked up at him, his lips framed in white.

JT saw a different kind of surrender in Kyle's beautiful green eyes. It was the kind that made a boy worth keeping.

"That was sweet, seeing you come like that, baby." He caressed Kyle's cheek. "Clean me up like a good girl."

He pulled Kyle's face gently into his crotch and watched his new bitch lick his cock and balls clean.

Chapter 28

Later, they lay together on the bed, Kyle curled up beside JT, who lay quietly, looking up into the shadows, his fingers laced behind his head. He waited patiently for what he knew was coming. When Kyle tried to turn his back, JT didn't let him. Instead he pulled his boy close and held him while he cried softly.

"Ain't nothing to cry about, baby," JT said. "You're my girl now. I'm gonna take real good care of you."

"I'm just a bitch," Kyle said, through his tears. "Your friends were right."

"You're a good girl, baby, you'll – "

Kyle pushed hard at JT, going nowhere in his strong arms.

"I'm not a fucking *girl*!" Kyle screamed into JT's face.

The first time a bitch did that to him, JT nearly beat the boy senseless. Now, he knew better.

"There ain't nothing wrong with how you are Kyle. Men like me won't have nothing to do with boys who ain't like you."

Kyle, who'd been tensed for a blow, relaxed, and laid his head on JT's hard chest. "You hurt my ass real bad," he said in a low voice.

"I know." There was genuine regret in JT's voice. "I didn't mean to. Be a good girl, and you won't get it like that."

"Are you gonna hit me for yelling at you?"

JT shook his head, realized Kyle couldn't see him in the dark, and said, "No."

Kyle was quiet for a long time after that. JT reached down for the pack of cigarettes beside the bed and lit up a smoke. He blew three smoke rings up into the halo of candle light beside the bed.

"Baby?"

"Yeah?"

"Don't ever say to me again that you ain't my girl. It pisses me off."

JT felt the boy start trembling in his arms. He stroked Kyle's ass gently. "I ain't gonna beat you over it. But you watch what you say to me, hear?"

"Yeah," Kyle said, in a low, subdued voice. "Okay."

"Be a good girl." JT's voice was low and thoughtful. "Don't make me hurt you."

After that, they lay quietly for a while, then Kyle dressed when JT told him to. He followed his new lover through the dark twisting depths of Old Purgatory, up into the main prison. In their cell, Kyle hesitated, looking down at JT, who was already lying in his bottom bunk.

"What?" JT said.

Even in the dark shadows, JT saw deep red color rise to Kyle's cheeks. He sat up, and pulled Kyle close, so the boy stood between his open legs.

"Tell me, baby. You ain't got to have no shame with me."

"I wanna sleep in your bunk," Kyle said, looking down at the floor. Then he raised his green eyes to JT. "If you want me to."

JT ran his rough fingers through Kyle's silky hair. A storm of desire raged through him.

He wanted Kyle again, slow and easy this time. "Yeah. I like my girl sleeping next to me." Kyle slipped out of his clothes and slid naked into JT's bunk. JT slid into bed behind him, pulling Kyle into his arms.

"Your virgin ass was real sweet, baby," JT whispered. "You're gonna like being my girl."

Kyle was exhausted. He closed his eyes and let the darkness take him.

In just a few moments, JT felt Kyle's breathing fall into the even rhythm of deep sleep. JT lay awake, thinking. Kyle belonged to him. He'd won him in the Dark Game, taken his virginity, made him his girl. But it was more than that. The way the boy had come to sleep in his bunk; the way Kyle had looked up at him after he fucked his mouth hard in the bathroom, made JT feel things he'd never felt before.

JT couldn't stand seeing the helpless fear that came into his eyes when Kyle thought no one was looking. Feeling Kyle's weight in his arms, JT realized something.

Until this moment, he'd never known what it meant to be in love. A soft smile spread across his hard face in the darkness. In just two days, JT had decided that whatever Kyle was afraid of, whatever his boy was running from, he'd protect him. Whatever dark waters Kyle faced, he wouldn't have to face them alone anymore. JT would fight to his last breath to keep the boy in his arms safe from the dark storms of a brutal world.

JT didn't understand any of these new thoughts. He knew only one thing. He would sacrifice anything he'd ever wanted to have Kyle.

Chapter 29

"JT," Kyle whispered. He was squatting next to JT's sleeping form, shaking him. "Wake up."

Out of nowhere, a curved knife edged with tiny teeth was at Kyle's throat. JT's strong fingers were curled into Kyle's hair in a fist, pulling his head back, exposing his neck to the wicked knife's edge.

"Fuck," JT said in a low irritated voice. "What the hell you doing, boy?" He let go of Kyle, and made the knife disappear.

For a moment Kyle stared at JT in silence, pressing his fingers to his throat, making sure his head was still attached.

Kyle started to whisper. "Something's – "

"You've been called for confession and meditation."

The low words floated into JT's cell.

"Damn," JT said in a low, worried voice. He dragged Kyle back into bed.

"What's going – "

But JT pressed a big hand over Kyle's mouth and whispered urgently into his ear, "Shut up, boy. This ain't nothing you wanna know about."

Kyle looked up into JT's eyes and shut up instantly. Not because he was afraid of JT – he was; not because he was afraid JT would hurt him really bad if he pissed him off – Kyle knew he would. Kyle shut up because he saw fear running wild in JT's eyes. Anything that could make a man like JT that afraid was nothing to mess with.

JT had been looking over his shoulder, now he looked back at Kyle. The boy nodded and JT took his hand away. Kyle pressed himself into JT's strong arms, listening to the mini drama outside their cell.

"Come on Harrison, don't make it hard on yourself," a man's voice said from the cell next door.

"I ain't going," Harrison's panicked voice came back. "It ain't right. I ain't done nothing no other man in here ain't done." The words came out in a desperate rush.

"Ain't nothing personal. Your number came up," the other voice said. "Gotta keep ratings up."

There were rough sounds of a frantic struggle, then a man's muffled screams, coming from behind some kind of gag.

"You can tell it to the Father," another man's voice said.

JT and Kyle both lay in silence, listening as the man was dragged from his cell. They both saw three shadows go by, two tall shadows holding a madly writhing shadow in the middle.

"No. No. I ain't going! Let me the fuck go!"

The man's screams of bright terror echoed on the tier, like the torment of a damned soul. Kyle knew every man in every cell must be awake, but except for the man's quickly muffled screams, there was dead silence on the tier as the guards dragged him away.

"Where are they taking him?" Kyle whispered when the men had passed.

"Go to sleep, boy," JT said quietly in his deep voice. His eyes were far away, as though haunted by the memory of a lost friend. "It ain't nothing for you to worry about."

JT pulled Kyle into his arms and for just a moment Kyle felt safe surrounded by all that thick muscle.

"Why's he so scared? What's going to happen to him?" Kyle said. He couldn't let it go. Harrison's screams would haunt his nightmares forever.

JT was silent for a long time, running his thick fingers slowly through Kyle's silky hair. Kyle lay back in his arms, listening to the stealthy sounds of men awake in the darkness all around them.

Long after Kyle had given up and thought JT wasn't going to answer, he pulled Kyle close, pressed his lips to the boy's ear and spoke a single word that no man in Purgatory wanted to hear. The sound of it struck terror into Kyle's heart.

"Redemption," JT whispered.

PART TWO
Chapter 30

The naked man between the black marble Columns of Redemption trembled. His arms were raised high above his head, chained apart, as though in praise. Around his ankles were black manacles that pressed his feverish flesh to the cool, unforgiving marble. All around him, stone tiers, filled with the righteous, rose to Heaven.

Gold letters ten feet high ran down the smooth marble pillars. "GRACE" poured down the left pillar, as if from a fountain of gold. "MERCY" poured down the right pillar. Randall felt neither the grace nor mercy that was supposed to pour down on him from Heaven.

Beneath the false serenity of the drug they'd given him, Randall Harrison's thoughts ran in a deep trench of pure terror. He moved his eyes sideways, not daring to turn his head. It was a mistake.

He saw the Enforcer, naked to the waist, his upper body smooth and powerful. His black leather hood gleamed with cruel malevolence. Randall caught a glimpse of the wickedly thick leather whip in the Enforcer's clenched fist, and licked his dry lips, stifling a scream.

A surging tidal wave of primal energy rushed through the spectators in the stone tiers. Frenzied applause and roars of passion rose from the audience, sounding like a beast risen from Hell, come to wreak havoc. Randall knew what that meant. Father Matthew had taken center stage at Redemption Coliseum.

Father Matthew walked onto the floor of the Coliseum, resplendent in his black frock coat. His thick black hair hung two inches below his ears. His black eyes gleamed under the holo lights. His full lips, high cheekbones and dark, intense eyes were known all over the country. Redemptions officiated by Matthew were the highest rated shows on holovision, second only to the prisoner gladiator games.

Matthew greeted his audience with a humble smile, thinking of the boy he'd just left in his private office, chained naked to his desk. He had a bamboo cane that would leave lovely marks on the boy's pretty round ass.

"We're gathered tonight to carry on our mission," Matthew said, when the applause died down. "Our great mission began in 2002. In that year we let our enemies know that even 7,000 miles away, across oceans and continents, on mountaintops and in caves, they could not escape the justice of our great nation."

His voice, rich and deep, rolled through the Coliseum like a Pentecostal Minister calling down the Spirit. The audience cheered, roused to patriotic fervor with words full of emotion, but empty of meaning.

"We all know of the axis of great evil, aimed at threatening the peace of the world," Matthew said. His voice grew quiet, as though the weight of a great truth weighed him down. "These are dark times. The Horsemen ride the edge of the skies."

Father Matthew paused, looking at the live audience, who looked back at him with worshipful admiration.

"The duty to fight the darkness of tyranny has fallen to us, a God fearing country."

Matthew raised a hand to the black Redemption Columns behind him. "Here stands an unrepentant soul. His sin was running from his duty to serve God and country."

He looked out into the audience. They had the frenzied feel of wild beasts that scented fresh blood. Above him, his holograph image stood ten feet tall, seemingly looking every man in the eye.

"The duty to bring the light of freedom into the world falls to our great nation."

Matthew's voice rose, calling down a tide of fury on the helpless man behind him. "Make no mistake. We *must* protect our homeland. Our cause is *just*. We fight on the side of *right*."

The Coliseum echoed with cheers and shouts of 'Amen Father'.

"We seek a just and peaceful world," Matthew said. He let his voice go soft, and low. "We stand on the very brink. Rarely has the world faced a choice more clear."

The audience grew quiet with his still voice, nearly hypnotized.

"There are those who call for an end to the fighting. To them I say, this campaign of freedom may not be finished on our watch – yet it must be waged on our watch."

Men flinched as Matthew's voice roared and hammered through the Coliseum.

"And I say to you this night, my friends, this great nation is steadfast in our purpose." He pumped his right fist to the sky. "We shall press on." His voice rose to a shout that was matched with a maniacal roar from the audience of patriotic believers. "And if you are not with us, then you stand against freedom, against justice, against peace, against our great *nation*."

Father Matthew's voice fell again, the picture of a sorrowful shepherd who must lead his flock through perilous ground.

"Freedom is at risk. Yet, there are those who would turn away from their duty to bring the light of freedom into the world. How does this man stand before you?" Matthew pointed to the prisoner shackled between the black pillars.

There were cries of "lost". "forsaken" and "wandering".

"Is it not our duty to stand fast until we see freedom's victory?" Matthew cried.

The audience roared in agreement.

Matthew flung his arms out, as if in anguish. His face had gone deep red. "Does not our great nation walk in the light of freedom and justice?"

Matthew looked at his audience, many of them on their feet, red faced, shaking their fists at the man between the pillars. Every one of them had a psych profile that could be summed up in one word – zealot.

"What must be done to bring our brother back to the light?" Matthew shouted.

"Redemption", they shouted, nearly as one. "Redeem him." "Purify him."

Matthew knew that the shouts and cries of his audience were echoed all across the country. He knew that a nationwide audience was watching on holo, waiting for the first screams of the man behind him.

Redemption was the ultimate thrill for a country grown jaded with the everyday horrors of hunger, poverty and hopelessness. Patriotism offered hope. Truth offered despair.

"You speak as true shepherds of the lost," Matthew said. His voice had fallen quiet again. "Let us bow our heads in prayer, as the Saint prescribed, and offer our hearts, so that this sinner's Redemption may strengthen our walk in the light of grace."

Matthew bowed his head, but did not close his eyes. He was waiting for the right moment to call down the wrath of the ignorant on the man behind him. When he tasted the blood lust of the audience, felt it like a fever in his blood, Father Matthew, Chief Redeemer of Purgatory, raised his head.

His arms shot up over head, as though calling down God's wrath.

"Let Redemption begin!" he shouted.

Chapter 31

In the small stone chamber that served as his private office, Matthew sat back in his chair, adjusting a button on the remote control, raising the volume on the hologram he was watching. Tonight's Redemption had gone well.

He watched the man the between the pillars writhe under the Enforcer's whip. His cries of pain were matched with screams from the audience, exalting him to grace. The whip whistled through the air, and fell on the prisoner's back, leaving swollen red welts that oozed blood. He screamed in anguish, tossing his head back, pulling on the manacles that gave him not an inch of mercy.

"Do you want me to make you scream like that Jimmy?" Matthew said to the young prisoner on his knees between his legs.

The boy looked up at Matthew, horrified at the sound of the whip thudding into the man's flesh.

"N-No, Father," he said in a hoarse whisper.

Matthew passed his bamboo cane over the welts on Jimmy's back. The boy marked beautifully.

"Then suck me really good."

The naked boy on his knees with his hands cuffed behind him trembled as Matthew passed the cane back and forth across the welts on his back.

"Service me well," Matthew said, "and I'll shorten your penance next time."

The boy swallowed Matthew's cock deep, controlling his gag reflex, massaging the head of Matthew's cock deep in the back of his throat.

Matthew loved to relax like this, watching a holo of a Redemption with his cock in some trembling boy's mouth. As Matthew watched the Enforcer's whip whistle through the air again and again, he opened his legs and lifted his hips, enjoying Jimmy's talented mouth. Matthew moaned softly, watching as the prisoner in the hologram threw his head back, his eyes squeezed shut, his body writhing in agony.

Matthew was just starting to enjoy the hot feel of the boy's sweet mouth, when a low voice behind him said, "How's it hanging, Father?"

The cold voice struck Matthew like a stiletto to his heart. He pushed Jimmy back violently. The boy looked up at him, cringing.

"I'm sorry Father," he said, "I'll please you. Don't whip me anymore."

"Shut up," Matthew said in a low cruel voice. He zipped his pants.

"Get the bitch out," the man who'd walked into Matthew's office said.

Matthew used the key on his desk to undo the boy's cuffs. "Go," he said.

The boy looked from Matthew to the man standing in the shadowy corner of the Father Confessor's office, and ran out the door, naked, without a backward glance.

The man who'd walked in stood on the other side of Matthew's desk. He looked briefly at the holo of the man being whipped, then looked at Matthew with mild distaste.

Matthew turned off the holo. He didn't offer his visitor a seat.

"Mind if I sit down?" Matthew's visitor said.

He sat in the wooden chair opposite Matthew. Besides the President, the man across the table was the most trusted man in the country.

He moved with the arrogant, careless power of a man used to being obeyed without question. His round, rimless glasses sat low on his nose. On the holograph press conferences, his peppered black and grey hair and his intelligent dark green eyes gave him the distinguished look of a trusted uncle.

Here in the shadows of a stone chamber of Purgatory, he looked at home. His green eyes were cold and ruthless; the kind of eyes you might expect to see in a back room with no windows.

A tiny bead of sweat rolled down the back of Matthew's neck. He hated the cool feel of it sliding into his collar.

"You want a cigarette, Father?" the man said.

Matthew hated the way this man called him 'Father'. He hated the way he sat in his prison as if he owned it.

"You know I don't smoke."

The man lit a cigarette in the cool silence of the shady darkness. The single yellow light bulb overhead gave off light that was faded and old.

"You have a prisoner here," the man said.

The man dipped his cigarette briefly to the floor, flicking ashes carelessly to the concrete.

"I have many prisoners in my flock."

"Cut the religious bullshit," the man said in a mild, almost monotone voice.

Matthew felt another bead of sweat slide down the back of his neck with slick coolness. He waited in silence for the man to go on.

"How many times have I been here, Father?"

Matthew didn't understand why he persisted in calling him 'Father'. He wished he'd stop. It set his teeth on edge, like nails on a chalkboard.

"Twice." Matthew controlled the tremor that wanted to creep into his voice. "Including tonight."

The man nodded. "The last time I made you a rich man."

In the long silence that followed, Matthew fought to keep his fingers from tapping nervously on the thick, wooden table.

"If you do what we want this time, I'll make you a *very* rich man."

The man who'd committed more war crimes than Nazi criminals who'd been tried and sentenced to death, looked coolly at Father Matthew, with unblinking attention. He blew smoke up to the yellow light bulb where it circled lazily in the still air.

"I took a great risk last time," Matthew said.

The man gazed steadily at Matthew through remnants of smoke. For a moment he looked like a demon, surrounded by smoking brimstone. His dark green eyes were terrifying, like green marbles filled with empty nothingness. Matthew's eyes slid away from those twin depths of icy darkness.

"You have a prisoner, JT, he's a gladiator," the man said.

"What about him?"

"Give him a Guardian Chip. Make him a pirate."

"I can't. I've tried. He says no every time. I have it on appeal. But appeals are slow."

"Convince him."

"He won't do it." A note of desperation crept into Matthew's voice. It wasn't good to say no to the man sitting across from him. "It's no use. I've been trying for years."

The man smoked in silence, looking at Matthew with those horribly cold eyes. The tiny hairs on the back of Matthew's neck rose.

"How do you think your flock would like having you among them, Father?"

"I'm always among my flock."

That was true. What Matthew didn't say was that he never went anywhere in Purgatory without heavy guard.

"Maybe they'd like you better without that stupid collar, with a chip, with a prisoner ID number." The man looked into Matthew's eyes. "That way you could minister to their souls night and day."

Matthew knew exactly what his flock would do to him. This time a bead of sweat ran down the middle of his back. "What crime would you accuse me of?" he said in a breathless whisper.

"It seems there's black market activity here," the man said. He ground out his cigarette on the floor. "Carries a mandatory sentence of ten years." He looked up at Matthew. "And forty lashes, given in two weeks." He leaned across the desk, smiling at Matthew. "More humane that way."

"How long do I have?" Matthew fought to keep his fingers from twining together in his lap.

"His delivery date is in sixty days. They're growing him a Nano. Even with accelerated growth, that's as fast as we can get it. All we need from you is a consent form with a wet signature before then."

Matthew's surprise showed on his face. He couldn't help it. Nano chips were for the prison elite – serial killers. The specially grown chips, keyed to the body's DNA, stayed active even when the body they inhabited died. They were the best of the best in chip technology. And the most expensive.

"Why him? He's nobody," Matthew said. "Just a gangster who got caught."

"Don't look too deeply into things that don't concern you, Father," the man said, getting to his feet. "People get hurt that way."

He opened the door to the dark corridor and turned back to Matthew. "Sixty days. Don't make me call you."

He walked out, leaving Matthew shaken. His heart beat wildly. His mind raced. If he couldn't force JT to sign the consent form, there was no doubt in Matthew's mind that he'd spend the rest of his days in Purgatory Prison, among his flock.

Forty lashes. Holy God. The sound of the whip thudding into Harrison's flesh echoed through his mind in grim mockery. He thought frantically.

An idea came to him, so beautiful in its simplicity, that Matthew had nearly overlooked the obvious. He rose from his chair thinking, *desperate times call for desperate measures.*

Chapter 32

JT didn't know it, but he had only seven weeks left until his chip delivery date. Down in Old Purgatory, Dante and JT talked in low urgent voices in the shadowy light of the Clubhouse.

"How you doing, making him not wanna be in your cell no more?" Dante said.

A candle burned between them, casting a doubtful glow into the solid gloom. Dante waved his fingers through the flickering flame.

JT watched Dante's fingers dance in the fire. "I didn't make it bad for him," he said.

"I didn't think so." Dante got up, pacing. "Something ain't right with that boy."

"You find out anything?" JT said.

"Whoever he is, his shit is locked down tighter than Hell's gates," Dante said. "Can't nobody get to his file. He ain't even *got* a file in here."

JT smoked in silence, listening. "What else?"

Dante whirled on JT. "What the fuck else you need? He ain't just some punk that didn't wanna fight in their war. He broke into somebody's shit. He's in so deep, his fucking eyeballs float."

"You got anything else?" JT said, repeating his question calmly.

Dante told him about walking Kyle down to the Clubhouse; how the boy had just about fainted when Dante shoved him against the wall.

"They killed his Dad," Dante finished. "You seen how he's always looking like Satan's gonna pop up and grab his ass?"

"Find out who he is," JT said.

"*How*?" Dante said. "I told you. No file. Nothing. Like he's some ghost."

JT looked at his friend. "There's gotta be something."

"I'm telling you," Dante said, sitting down. "Far as the outside knows, there ain't no boy named Kyle Watson in Purgatory."

"Who showed him a picture of Jessi?"

Dante looked at JT in the uncertain light. "Nobody, why?"

JT shrugged. "Forget it."

"You got nothing but trouble in your house," Dante said.

"He's real pretty and he got a sweet ass." JT talked in the distracted tones of a man thinking out loud. "But it's something else."

Dante lit another cigarette. "It better be something real fucking good."

"I should of beat his ass for disrespecting me outside the mess hall," JT said.

Dante listened, watching his friend's face carefully.

"When I got in the bathroom with him, he was mad at me, 'cause men heard him when I fucked his mouth. Then he started crying 'cause that shit at breakfast got him upset."

JT sat in thoughtful silence before he went on.

"He got on his knees and started saying how sorry he was and touching my cock, and shit. I fucked his mouth real hard. He was all shaking and crying when I came down his throat."

JT sank into silence again, looking into the darkness. He remembered the way Kyle had looked up at him, afraid, but not mad at what JT had done to him. The memory sent a thrill of aching desire racing through him.

"When I seen he wasn't mad at what I done to him –" JT shrugged his big shoulders. "I felt something I ain't never felt with no bitch before."

After twenty years of friendship, Dante could read the look on his friend's face, even in the shadowy light of the candle between them.

"Fuck man. How you fell for this punk so quick?"

"I been wanting a boy like Kyle for a long time. A month, a week, a day, it don't matter how long I been with him." JT looked at Dante. "What you think about that?"

Dante shook his head, making his dreads fall over his face. "I think you're a fool."

JT looked into his friend's dark eyes. "I had a whole bunch of ass. I even had virgins before. But it ain't like that with Kyle."

Dante's face went still and dark. He suddenly understood what JT was saying.

"It ain't gonna happen," Dante said flatly.

The air in the underground cave grew still. A cool chill ran down JT's spine. "You ain't telling me something," he said.

"I searched like a bitch," Dante said, not meeting JT's eyes, "but I only found out one thing about your new boy."

"Oh shit," JT said softly. "Fuck, no."

Dante nodded. "I told you he's trouble. Ask yourself how come a nobody punk like that got a chip."

"I don't care," JT said. "I'm getting us both out."

"The doctor can't get *one* man out, how the fuck you think this other guy gonna get two people out, and one of you got a chip?"

JT shrugged. "I got to find a way. I don't want nothing bad to happen to the boy. I can't say it no better than that. Understand?"

Dante thought back to the night in JT's cell. Something in Kyle's scared eyes had touched Dante's cold heart. "That's how you want it? You both go or you both stay?" he said.

JT nodded. "Now you really think I'm acting the fool, don't you?"

"I ain't nobody to say," Dante said. "Look how I got when they took my boy."

After Dante escaped, they gave him one last night with his boy after they brought him back. Dante throttled one of the guards who came to take his boy. By the time six men pulled Dante off the guard, the man's face had already gone an ugly shade of blue.

"You know Tyrone ain't done fucking with you, right?"

JT ran his fingers over his bald head in a strangely delicate gesture. "That punk ain't gonna stop 'til he makes me do some evil shit to him."

"You should of took him out when you had a chance. The whole council was behind you last time."

"I ain't about to take a man's life like that. Tyrone's a punk. He don't mean no harm. But he's dangerous. He just got to be watched."

Dante shook his head. "*Now* I think you're playing the fool," he said quietly. "That punk's got to go."

"I don't like mysteries," JT said, ignoring his friend's advice. "I wanna know who the fuck Kyle is."

"Why you don't ask him?"

"He's gonna lie, unless I beat it out of him."

"You going to?"

Dante waited patiently for JT's answer, watching his friend blow three perfect smoke rings up into the darkness.

"No," JT said. "Not yet."

Chapter 33

With the passing of the Monastic Reform Law, and the merging of church and state, prisons became places of penance, not rehabilitation. Through their corporate arm, the Church bought up and privatized every prison in the country.

The Prisoner Gladiator Games were the most brutal Reality Holovision ever broadcast. It had the highest ratings in history, and generated more income than all of holovision put together. Bringing wayward souls to the light was very profitable business for the Church.

Before the Monastic Reform Law, Father Confessor Matthew would have been called a Warden. Matthew's office where he did the daily business of running the prison was a small stone chamber, with a low ceiling, sparsely decorated. The dark stone walls absorbed light, creating a den of shadows.

Standing next to a small window that let in a thick bar of yellow sunlight, Matthew thought of the men throughout history who'd refused to sell their souls. The most famous one died on a cross for his mistake.

Matthew had along ago sold his soul to the highest bidder. And he served his Master well. JT was about to learn that every man's soul had a price. Fortunately for JT, Matthew was an excellent teacher in matters of the soul.

The door opened behind him.

"Undo his cuffs," Matthew said without turning around.

"But Sir, I'm not supposed to – "

"Mr. Remello?" Matthew's voice was low, dangerous.

"Sir?"

Matthew turned from the window and looked the guard in the eye. "Why do you insist on speaking when you have nothing of value to say? Undo his cuffs. Now."

The guard uncuffed JT, red faced.

Matthew waved lazily. "That's all Mr. Remello. In the unlikely event that I think of something useful for you to do, I'll call for you."

Preston Remello stalked out of the Father Confessor's office.

Alone with JT, Matthew looked at the gladiator standing across his small desk. Even though JT stood three or four inches taller and Matthew knew the gladiator could throw him across the room without breaking a sweat, he smiled into JT's hard eyes.

Matthew took a red apple from a basket of fresh fruit on his desk. In an age where every migrant worker was overseas fighting the war, fresh fruit had become as impossible to find as diamonds, and nearly as expensive.

"I hear you're enjoying your new bitch," Matthew said.

JT said nothing. He looked at Matthew the way a man looks at a poisonous snake that's too close for comfort.

Matthew sat down behind his desk. "Is Kyle a good boy?" he said.

"He's a good bitch." JT talked to a spot just above Matthew's right shoulder.

Matthew saw the quizzical look on JT's face when he noticed the small glow of a hologram set to no picture in the far corner of the office.

"You know what this is?" Matthew touched the only piece of paper lying on his wooden desk.

Matthew watched JT's hard eyes change as he looked at the unmistakable red, white and blue of the consent form for the Guardian Chip. He'd said no to Matthew too many times not to recognize it.

"Yeah." JT looked past Matthew to the blank holo in the corner. "And I ain't doing it. So don't be wasting your breath."

"As you know, we can't inject you with the Guardian Chip without your consent," Matthew said as if JT had asked a question.

"Why don't you just do me and sign it?"

Matthew looked pained. "We here at Purgatory would never commit such an immoral act." He met JT's dark eyes, filled with murderous fantasies in which Matthew was sure he played a starring role. "Besides, computer analysis would reveal the signature as a fake."

JT looked steadily at Matthew. "Then we ain't got nothing to talk about. Unless you got some miracle down your pants."

"With the Guardian Chip, a whole new world would open to you."

"No."

Matthew looked thoughtful for a moment. "Men change, JT. The bible tells us that Saul was converted on the road to Damascus. The Lord opened his eyes and showed him the error of his ways."

"No."

"If you agree to the chip, you'll get a taste of freedom on the high seas. And you'll become a rich man."

"How many ways I got to say no? I ain't being no fucking pirate for you." JT's voice was cold and flat.

"With a war on so many fronts, the black market has become quite lucrative. Help me, and you'll be a rich man."

JT sighed with the air of a man who's been over the same ground too many times. "No."

In the old days, JT's answer would have infuriated Matthew. But things were different now. JT was in love. He'd given a hostage to Fortune. And she was a relentlessly cruel Goddess.

"I thought you'd say that," Matthew said calmly. "Sit down. I have something to show you."

JT looked at the chair in front of Matthew's desk, then looked at Matthew again. He stood where he was, unmoving.

"As you like," Matthew said. He was undisturbed by JT's stubborn refusal. It wouldn't last.

Matthew pressed a button on a panel built into his desk. The holo image in the corner mushroomed from a small ball to a life size picture in moments. Matthew watched JT's eyes widen with fear as the hologram came into focus a foot above the ground. A boy's frightened face looked back at JT.

"The resemblance to your boy is remarkable, isn't it?" Matthew said.

The naked boy chained to a metal table on all fours could have been Kyle's twin brother. The bright red marks of a harsh whip criss-crossed his naked back.

Matthew slid his finger across a bar on the panel of buttons on his desk. A green bar appeared across the bottom of the solid looking hologram, raising the volume.

In the hologram, that stood about five feet tall, Tyrone walked into the room, naked, his hard thick cock bobbing before him. The boy started whimpering as soon as he heard Tyrone walk in. Obviously, he knew what was coming.

Tyrone stood behind the boy and grabbed his hips. Without hesitation, he shoved his thick cock up the boy's ass. The boy in the hologram screamed into JT's face and struggled, but there was no escape. The image was so real that JT nearly moved to help the boy before he stopped himself.

Tyrone grabbed the boy's hair, pulling his head back, so his face was clearly revealed to the camera. The boy screamed into JT's face again and again while Tyrone rode his ass savagely.

Matthew let the boy's screams fill the stone room before he lowered the volume. He looked up at JT.

"You say Kyle is a good boy?"

Matthew saw understanding dawn in JT's black eyes.

"Yeah," JT said slowly, "he's a good bitch."

JT's eyes slid from Matthew to the boy in the holo. He couldn't help himself. Now the boy's face was beet red. Beads of sweat dotted his brow. Tyrone plowed his ass without mercy.

"Kyle seems so happy with his placement with you. Don't you think it would be a shame to move your boy and put him with someone like Tyrone?"

Chapter 34

Shelving book discs in the cool shadows of the library, Kyle thought back on what he'd learned in his short time in Purgatory. Before the Dark Game, there had been an uneasy peace between JT and Tyrone. Now, JT and Tyrone were like hostile Kings, each with their own territories.

Tyrone and JT bought and sold stuff inside Purgatory. Kyle wasn't exactly sure what JT sold, but JT's territory made more money than Tyrone's. There was some council who had to approve everything the gangs did.

"Hey."

Kyle nearly jumped out of his skin. His first thought was that Tyrone had come back. He turned to find Ryan standing at the end of the aisle of books.

"What are you doing here?" Kyle said. "Thought Derrick didn't want you talking to me."

Ryan shrugged. "I like living dangerous."

Kyle looked around, expecting Derrick to pop up any second. "Does he know you're here?"

Ryan shook his head. "Are you kidding?" He looked around. "Let's go."

"Where?"

When Ryan turned away without answering, Kyle followed him to the door on this level. He used a scratched disc to keep the door from locking.

Outside the library, Ryan headed around the corner, deeper into shadow. They stopped before a black iron door. Kyle knew he was heading for trouble when he saw what Ryan took out of his pocket.

"I stole this from him. He thinks he lost it," Ryan said, showing Kyle the black key.

Kyle's heart beat hard and fast. "Fuck. What are you doing? We're in deep shit if they catch us."

A thoughtful look came over Ryan's face. "I know," he said. "But I wish someone had told me what it meant to be a man's wife in here. I'm gonna show you."

Kyle shut his eyes to steady himself. The carved design on Ryan's belly floated behind his closed eyes. "If you piss off Derrick, he'll cut you. Let's go back," he said urgently. "Or tell me here."

"We're not going back," Ryan said in a low, angry voice. "You need to know what you're getting into."

"Why's it so important to you?"

"Because I wish someone had told me." Ryan turned to unlock the door.

"Tell me *here*." Kyle grew more nervous with each passing second, knowing that he was somewhere he wasn't supposed to be.

"Can't." Ryan pushed the door open. "Too dangerous. One of their men could see us talking."

Kyle looked into the dim darkness beyond the door.

"No way," he said. "I'm not pissing off JT. I'm going back."

"Don't you wanna know what he'll do to you when he makes you his wife?"

"I don't want my ass beat," Kyle said, looking back over his shoulder. "He doesn't fuck around."

"He'll never know you were gone."

Ryan beckoned Kyle to follow him into the darkness, pulling a tiny flashlight from his pocket. A razor thin ray of light shot through the darkness. He pushed the door shut behind them and led Kyle down the stone steps.

"Ok," Kyle said at the bottom of the steps. "Tell me."

"Not here."

Ryan walked past Kyle, who hurried after him. The way here was lit by dim light bulbs hanging from wires overhead.

When the screaming started, Kyle froze. The screamer stopped for a moment, then started again. The screams were full of horrible torment. JT had warned Kyle about coming down here alone. But he wasn't exactly alone was he?

Ryan looked back at Kyle. "Don't worry. That's just Tyrone's men having fun."

The darkness was alive with the sound of heavy wheels of some kind rolling along the uneven cobblestone floor.

Ryan led Kyle to a high arch in the rock. On the other side was a cavernous stone room, with a ceiling so high, it was lost in darkness. Scattered hurricane lamps filled the stone room with orange light. All the men working in the flickering light had the chiseled bodies of dangerous men trained to fight hard and nasty.

Gladiators, Kyle thought. They worked shirtless. Their hard bodies dripped sweat as they lifted heavy boxes, stacking them onto flat carts, grunting with effort. Other men rolled the carts away, making the noises Kyle had heard earlier. Ryan pulled Kyle into the dark shadows of the arched doorway.

"Pirated stuff," Ryan whispered.

Kyle's jaw just about dropped when he saw what filled the boxes on the ground. Gasoline was liquid gold on the streets. Ration cards limited how much people bought – unless they bought it on the black market. A three gallon drum of gasoline went for fifty bucks on the street. Five gallon drums were seventy five.

The boxes on the floor were filled with red three gallon containers of gasoline. Other boxes were loaded with yellow five gallon drums.

"Come *on*," Ryan whispered, startling Kyle.

For a moment, he'd forgotten Ryan was with him. Bright terror gnawed his nerve endings with sharp teeth. Kyle knew he'd been gone from the library too long.

Ryan led Kyle around a corner and pulled him into the shadows of an open doorway. The small room used to be an office about a thousand years ago. Furniture piled thick with dust lay scattered around. Ryan pulled Kyle away from the open door into the deep gloom of the ancient office.

"He's gonna make you his wife real soon," Ryan whispered.

"I'm already his bitch. He makes me act like his girl or he hits me," Kyle said, matching Ryan's whisper.

"It's gonna get worse."

Kyle felt the blood rush from his face. His pale skin went white against his copper hair. He'd heard of places where men had to get their balls cut off so they could be girls for men.

"Is he cutting off my balls?" Kyle said in a low, terrified whisper.

"Almost." Ryan unzipped his pants and motioned Kyle over.

Chapter 35

Ryan shined the pencil flashlight on his crotch. What Kyle saw between Ryan's legs filled him with horror, like seeing his name on a gravestone.

"Does it hurt?" Kyle heard himself say from far away.

"Only if I try to get hard." Ryan touched the tiny lock. "Remember I told you I'm Derrick's wife? He makes me wear it all the time."

"You weren't wearing it the first night I saw you." Kyle clung to the desperate hope that this was some kind of bad joke.

"He let me come that night. I sucked him again later, and jacked off."

Kyle looked at the ring locked around Ryan's balls, connected to a pink cage around his cock. The cage had bars at the end. The shape of the cage made his dick point down.

"How you do piss in that thing?" Kyle said, horrified.

"Like a girl. Sitting down."

Ryan zipped his pants. "I'm not supposed to tell you anything. That's why he was mad at the Dark Game. He warned me after your first night not to talk to you until after JT made you his wife."

"JT's doing that to me?" Kyle's face had gone pale with shock.

"He does it to every punk he makes his wife."

"I don't want my dick locked up. I won't let him."

Ryan looked at Kyle. A terrible, haunted look came into his eyes. "I didn't want it either. If you don't let him, he'll do something bad to you." He gazed into the darkness over Kyle's shoulder. "I fought back. Derrick made me sorry."

A terrifying thought struck Kyle. "Is that why Derrick cut up your belly like that?" he said.

Ryan nodded. "He cut on me for three nights in a row until I finally begged him to make me his wife."

Both boys hid under shelter of darkness as they heard men rolling a heavy cart past the open door. When the cart had rumbled by, Ryan grabbed Kyle's wrist.

"I'm telling you because I fought back and it cost me. Don't fight. They do what they want to us."

Kyle pulled his hand free from Ryan's sweaty grip and ran shaky fingers through his hair. His gut clenched into a tight knot. "Jesus H. Christ." His voice was a tormented whisper.

Ryan nodded. "You understand now? I *had* to risk bringing you down here. I wish someone had told me not to fight."

Kyle pressed a shaking hand to his crotch. The thought of his dick locked in a pink cage utterly terrified him. He couldn't imagine it. This couldn't be real.

"I'll tell him no. He can't beat me forever."

"Did I risk my ass for *nothing*?" Ryan shouted in a loud whisper. "No one's gonna get you out of JT's cell." Ryan looked anguished. "And if they do, you'll be worse off."

"Is that what happened to Jessi?"

Ryan snapped a quick look over Kyle's shoulder, like he'd seen something in the dark.

"JT beat the crap out of Jessi because he wouldn't wear it," Ryan said. "He kept picking the lock." Ryan swallowed. "When he was done, Jessi's face was —"

"I saw," Kyle said quietly.

"How?"

"Not now," Kyle said. "We have to get back."

"Wait. There's one more thing."

"What?"

"Taylor," Ryan said, taking Kyle completely by surprise.

"The gang whore?" Kyle said. He remembered the boy with his ass up, waiting for a gladiator to win a chance to fuck his ass first. "What about him?"

"He needs help. If we don't do something, I don't think he'll make it."

Kyle listened while Ryan talked in a low, fast whisper.

"What the hell can *I* do?" Kyle said. He glanced between Ryan's legs. "Look what's gonna happen to me."

Ryan shrugged. "Bring it up to JT. See if you can get him to at least talk to Taylor."

"Why doesn't Taylor go to him?"

Ryan shook his head. "No way. I tried. The night JT beat up Jessie, it was Taylor's first night here. They made him watch. JT told Taylor he'd get the same if he fucked with him. He's terrified of JT."

"I'll try," Kyle said.

"I'll tell Taylor. He's about to do something desperate."

They waited for a cart to go by, then crept through the shadowy darkness, back to the stone stairway.

Kyle grabbed Ryan's arm and squeezed. "Thanks."

"Don't fight him. You don't know how loud you can scream 'til a man like JT or Derrick gets mad at you." Ryan's voice was low and shaky in the darkness.

At the top of the stone stairs, Ryan whispered. "Stay here. I'm going back to the library. In about five minutes, come out. If anybody asks, you heard screaming and you went to see who was hurt."

Kyle nodded. "Five minutes."

"If anything happens, there's another door just like this one at the other end of this corridor. It's never locked."

Before Kyle could ask what could happen, Ryan stepped through the door. He left it open a crack.

Kyle heard a voice on the other side. "What the fuck you doing punk?"

"Mr. Stone," Ryan said. "Sorry, Sir. I thought I heard someone screaming."

"Only one gonna be screaming is you when I tell Derrick your punk ass was back here."

Shit, a prison guard. Kyle pressed his ear to the door, listening. "Please don't, Sir," Ryan's voice said.

The next sounds Kyle heard were right on the other side of the door. The guard was moaning softly, leaning against the door.

"Yeah. Fucking right," Stone said, breathing hard. "Suck me off real good and I'll keep my mouth shut."

His heavy weight leaning on the door pushed it all the way shut, locking it tight. Panic overtook Kyle, making it impossible to think through the whirlwind of terror that stormed through his mind.

Chapter 36

JT looked Matthew in the eye. "What do you want?"

Matthew broke into a brilliant smile that highlighted his cold eyes. "I want us all to be happy."

In the hologram, Tyrone pulled out of the boy, and reached off camera. The boy's screams began in earnest. In a moment JT saw why. Tyrone held a thick, black dildo in front of the boy's wide, terrified eyes. He started working the impossibly thick dildo slowly into the screaming boy's ass.

Matthew watched the boy in silence for a while. "Unfortunately, that boy isn't happy," he said.

"Cut the shit," JT said, losing his patience. "What the fuck do you want?"

"I want you to be reasonable, that's all." Matthew pushed the Guardian Chip consent form across his desk to JT. "Sign this. Keep Kyle happy."

"What if I get killed?"

Matthew reached out and touched a button on his desk. The word "MUTE" popped up on the holo, and the boy's screams fell mercifully silent.

"You know how this works," Matthew said. "You'll be on a stripped down speed boat with seven other men. You'll intercept boats on the way into port, and take a cut of whatever cargo they're carrying."

The boy on the holo screamed silently while Tyrone worked the thick dildo savagely in and out of his ass. Matthew let JT watch the screaming, red faced boy for a while.

"People in this country are happy when they feel they can get a little something extra on the black market in these tough times. Our government is very concerned with keeping the people happy."

"What if those captains don't wanna give up their shit?" JT said. He was stalling; buying time to think.

"Then you'll have to take drastic measures." Matthew looked up into JT's dark eyes. "You don't have a problem with that, do you?"

JT looked at the boy on the holo. Tyrone was fucking him again. His big hand was between the boy's legs, pinching and squeezing his balls while he plowed hard into his ass.

The boy cried miserably, struggling uselessly against the cuffs that held him in place. There was no doubt in JT's mind that if he didn't give Matthew what he wanted, Kyle would take the boy's place.

"Get me a fucking pen," JT said.

Matthew slid a pen across his desk, smiling up into JT's furious eyes. He watched as JT sprawled his signature at the bottom of the form with all the skill of a sixth grader.

"Good," Matthew said, beaming. "Excellent. You'll have delivery in seven weeks."

Mathew broke into a smile that had all the warmth of a grinning skull. He raised his voice and called for Remello.

JT looked past Matthew to the hologram, where Tyrone was fucking the crying boy with the thick dildo again. He felt like a man caught up in a Tsunami of rage. He would have gladly served another life sentence for the sheer pleasure of killing Matthew. Slowly.

———————————

Remello came in and escorted JT out. As soon as they had walked down the dark corridor, away from Matthew's office, Remello pulled JT aside, urgently.

What the fuck now? JT thought.

"It's your boy," Remello said.

JT was instantly on guard. "What about him?"

"He's missing from the library. Word is he's in Tyrone's territory. Dante has men out looking for him."

JT's cold face showed nothing. "Fucking day's getting better and better," he mumbled.

He moved past Remello at a fast walk. In seconds, his mind went into overdrive, the way it did when he was in the ring. In an instant he saw all the possible ways out of the latest pile of shit Kyle had brought into his life. What the fuck was it about that boy?

Chapter 37

In the near total darkness, Kyle fought panic like a drowning man fighting a storm at sea. Ryan had told him something important; something that would get him out of the basement.

If anything happens, there's another door just like this one at the other end of this corridor.

Kyle hurried to the bottom of the stone steps. The heavy sound of a rumbling cart made him jump back into the shadows. He waited for the right moment, then darted through the darkness. He stopped on the other side of the arched doorway, and looked back. None of the sweating, grunting men had seen him.

He walked down the dark corridor, remembering the sounds of Ryan taking a cock deep down his throat, to save his ass.

Following the natural bend of the twisting corridor, Kyle passed solid brick walls unbroken by doorways of any kind. The screams Kyle had heard earlier pierced the darkness again, surprisingly close this time.

Kyle rounded a hairpin twist in the stone corridor. Oh dear God. Now he knew who was screaming and why. He didn't want to know, but it was too late for that, wasn't it?

The corridor ended in an iron door that stood open. Beyond the door, Kyle saw stone steps. That was the way out. But he'd have to get past the man and the screaming boy.

A black man who had the build of a gladiator had a brunette boy about Kyle's age pinned to the wall, beside the doorway. He held him against the wall, fucking the boy's ass hard.

"Yeah, bitch," the man said, pumping the boy's ass. "Scream for me."

Kyle knew he would be in deep shit if the man turned and saw him. As quietly as he could, he backed away. If the man turned around, there was nowhere to hide. Only the bend in the corridor would hide him. Kyle moved slowly, resisting the urge to turn and run, holding his breath, wishing he could melt into the wall.

"Who the fuck are you, boy?" a deep voice said behind him.

Kyle whirled around, his heart knocking in his chest. He was trapped. Kyle tried to inch past the man, but the man's hand shot out and grabbed his thin t-shirt.

"Where the fuck you going, bitch?" the man said.

The man fucking the screaming boy, turned his head briefly, still pumping the boy's ass.

"You brought another bitch, Desmond?" he said.

"I found him." Desmond pulled Kyle's shirt harder.

The boy's screams surrounded Kyle, making him wonder if his screams would be any louder when JT found out he'd been down here.

"JT – I'm his –," Kyle's breath caught in his throat. "I'm in his cell."

The men looked at each other. For a moment, blind hope soared in Kyle. He'd count himself lucky to get out of this with a hard belting from JT.

"No you ain't, boy," Desmond said, leaning close. "You're on Tyrone's turf. That means you're *our* bitch."

Oh fuck. Kyle tried to twist away, digging his feet in, pulling as hard he could, thinking, *a belting, I don't care – anything – just don't let me end up like that boy.* Maybe, like Dante, the universe had a soft spot for stupid boys who got in over their head.

Kyle's t-shirt ripped, leaving a ragged hole across the top, and he was free. Kyle hauled ass down the dark corridor, streaking past the man holding the boy too fast for him to do anything. By the time the man let go of the boy, Kyle was halfway up the stone steps, taking them two at a time.

Kyle burst through the door at the top of the steps, hearing the men behind him hard on his heels. When he saw who was on the other side of the door, his knees went weak.

Dante grabbed Kyle and pushed the boy behind him. The two men came bursting through the door. They stopped short when they saw Dante. The man in back ran into his friend, nearly knocking him over. For a long moment, the three men stared at each other in silence.

Finally, the man who'd been fucking the boy said, "Tell JT to watch his bitch. Don't be letting him go no place where he don't belong."

"Tell him yourself," Dante said, looking Tyrone's man in the eye. "Or you wanna start some shit with me?"

"We don't want no trouble," the man said, backing toward the door, holding up his empty hands.

"Then get the fuck out. You're on JT's turf."

Both men looked at Kyle for a long moment, then they went back the way they had come, slamming the door behind them.

Dante turned and gave Kyle a puzzled look. "What the *fuck* was you doing down there?"

"I heard screaming," Kyle said, falling back on the cover story Ryan had given him. "I went to see if –"

"Shut the fuck up." Dante gave Kyle a hard shove. "Let's go."

"Does JT know?" Kyle said.

Dante looked at Kyle with stony anger in his harsh eyes.

"Every man JT could find is out looking for your punk ass."

"Is he real mad at me?"

"Yeah." Dante guided Kyle down the dark stone corridor behind the library. "And he's gonna kick your dumb bitch ass."

A single thought ran through Kyle's tormented mind – *Oh God . . . I'm fucked . . .*

Kyle recognized the opposite end of the cell block where he shared a cell with JT. He stopped, pulling away from Dante.

Dante looked back at Kyle. "What?"

"I can't." Kyle fingered his ripped t-shirt, chewed his soft lips. "He'll beat me up."

Dante crossed his thick arms across his solid chest. "You got no choice, boy. You can come with me or I can drag your bitch ass."

"I'll end up like Jessi," Kyle said, voicing his worst fear.

"I don't know who you are, boy," Dante said. "All I know is, trouble followed you in here. You in some serious shit with some bad people, ain't you?"

"Yeah," Kyle said, thinking of the Principal's empty green eyes. "I'm in pretty deep."

His knees threatened to buckle. He was the picture of a man with one foot over the edge of a roaring volcano.

"And you ain't gonna tell me shit, right?"

Kyle looked down at the floor, his heart pumping double time. His vision blurred in and out with every harsh heartbeat.

"If you don't wanna help me, it's okay." Kyle looked up past Dante's shoulder, down the dark corridor that lead to JT's cell. "I guess he'll beat me up and I'll end up in the infirmary or something."

Dante was a cold blooded killer, but that look of a lost, frightened boy in Kyle's light green eyes was no match for his stony heart.

"Do exactly what I say," Dante said. "He'll beat you. But you won't get it bad if you do what I tell you."

Chapter 38

Kyle walked into the cell, with Dante just behind him. JT was sitting on his bunk, his legs spread, his killer hands dangling between his legs. He looked up past Kyle.

"You had any trouble?" JT said, ignoring Kyle.

"Nothing I couldn't handle."

JT looked down at the floor again. "Get over here, boy."

The three steps that separated Kyle from JT were as wide as the Grand Canyon. Kyle's heart pounded painfully with every step. Every instinct shouted at him to run the other way. Kyle stood in front of JT, his hands shoved deep into the pockets of his jeans.

"Where you been, bitch?" JT was still looking down at the floor.

Kyle knew he couldn't tell the truth, or Derrick would hurt Ryan really bad. He wished he could see JT's eyes. The only sign of his anger was the barely restrained fury in his voice.

"I was in the library, then I went out for a smoke, then I heard this screaming and I thought – "

"Fuck that." JT finally looked up at Kyle. "What the fuck was you doing in the basement? Ain't I told you not to be no place by yourself?"

JT's hard eyes, filled with unborn violence, lay heavily on Kyle.

"I heard screaming," Kyle said, through numb lips.

JT shot to his feet and grabbed Kyle hard. Before he knew it, Kyle was slammed into the wall, JT's powerful hand wrapped around his throat.

"You *what*?" JT towered over Kyle, his furious eyes glaring down at him.

Kyle clung desperately to his cover story. His voice came out in a low, trembling whisper. "There was this screaming and I –"

"And what?" JT said, through clenched teeth. "You thought was gonna rescue some bitch who was getting fucked?"

"I didn't know – "

JT let go of Kyle's throat and hammered a fist into the wall next to his head. Red dust sifted to the floor. Kyle flinched, squeezing his eyes shut.

"What the *fuck* didn't you know?" JT shouted.

Kyle pressed into the cinder wall behind him, shaking badly.

"He didn't mean nothing," Dante said quietly.

JT looked at Dante as if he'd forgotten he was there.

"You know what this bitch cost me, wandering into Tyrone's territory like he ain't got no fucking sense?"

JT looked back at Kyle. "I had to call in favors. You almost started a fucking gang war."

Kyle trembled, looking up into JT's furious glare.

"I'm sorry," he said.

"Sorry?" JT shouted. "You don't know nothing about sorry, boy." He grabbed Kyle's face. "But I'm gonna teach you." His quiet voice utterly terrified Kyle.

"Come on JT," Dante said in a quiet voice. "He didn't know better."

JT looked back at Dante, letting Kyle go.

"He ain't shown you no disrespect," Dante went on, looking at his friend. "He's just a bitch. He don't think like a man."

JT turned his back on Kyle. "He's a bitch who's gonna get his fucking ass beat."

"He ain't nothing but a scared boy," Dante said, keeping his voice low and calm. "He's a good bitch for you. Why don't you go easy on him?"

JT turned back to Kyle, who was huddled against the wall, looking small and fragile in his ripped t-shirt. His face was pale with terror.

"Don't ever do something that fucking stupid again."

JT slapped Kyle's face viciously, whipping his big calloused hand hard across Kyle's soft cheek. He stormed out of the cell, stopping only long enough to say, "Take care of him," as he walked by Dante.

"How come he left?" Kyle said, rubbing his cheek. An ugly bruise was already rising there.

"Cause he's pissed off and he don't wanna hurt you."

Kyle stood against the wall for a moment, looking as if he'd been dropped into the cell out of a tornado, then he sank to JT's bunk, trembling all over.

"Thanks," Kyle said. "I thought I was dead."

"Let me tell you something, boy." Dante stood over Kyle, looking down at him. "I know you wasn't in the basement 'cause you heard some bitch screaming. You ain't dumb enough to piss off JT like that."

Kyle looked up at Dante, bright terror in his green eyes. "I went to see –"

Dante held up a big hand. "What did I tell you about lying to me, boy?"

Kyle fell silent instantly, as if the words had been cut off with a knife.

"I know another bitch who was in the basement today," Dante said. "I know why he brought you down there. There ain't nothing you can do about it. You're gonna be JT's wife."

"I don't want that cage around my dick," Kyle said in a low desperate, voice.

"You ain't got no say in that, boy."

Kyle looked up at him. "Are you telling JT?"

"I ain't telling nobody nothing."

"How come you're helping me?"

"I don't wanna see you get a bad ass whipping over this." Dante ran his fingers through Kyle's red hair. "And I didn't wanna see Ryan get his face all cut up."

Kyle looked up at Dante. "I guess I owe you."

Dante narrowed his eyes. "Yeah. You do. What secrets you brought in here with you, boy?"

Kyle sat back on the bunk, sagging against the hard brick wall. "I can't," he whispered.

Dante sat on the bunk next to Kyle, not paying attention when he inched away. "You want some advice about when he comes back?"

"Yeah," Kyle said, looking at the floor.

Dante started talking. Kyle listened in silence.

When Dante was done, Kyle said, "I'm scared."

"You should be."

Kyle didn't tell Dante what he was thinking. JT was only a shadow compared to the man who was going to come back pretty soon and drag him to a back room without any windows.

Chapter 39

When JT came back, he found Kyle on his bunk, his ass up, his legs spread, his soft cheek pressed to the mattress. The lights out buzzer had sounded ten minutes ago.

JT sat on the bunk next to Kyle and pulled the boy across his lap. He caressed Kyle's naked ass.

"You been a bad girl."

"I'm sorry." Kyle's voice trembled, his heart pounded in his chest.

"I'm gonna have to spank this pretty ass."

JT trailed his fingers gently across Kyle's smooth ass. His dark brown skin made a harsh contrast against the boy's creamy ivory skin.

Kyle said nothing. He lifted his ass to JT a little, remembering Dante's warning about making things worse. *Don't fight, don't struggle. Do what he tells you.*

When JT's big hand pressed down on the middle of Kyle's back, pinning him in place, Kyle held his breath, thinking that he knew how bad it was going to be. When JT's other hand came down hard on his naked ass, Kyle found out he was wrong. He'd had no idea.

"Didn't I tell you not to go no place by yourself?"

JT's rough, calloused hand was cruelly hard on Kyle's ass. His powerful hand slammed into Kyle's writhing ass, raining down blows. Kyle buried his face in the bunk and cried into the rough grey blanket.

When Kyle tried to crawl away and escape the relentless blows, JT said impatiently, "Lift your fucking ass."

When JT finally stopped, Kyle's breath came in short gasps that shook his whole body.

JT rubbed Kyle's bruised skin. "You gonna do what I tell you, bitch?"

"Yeah," Kyle said through his tears.

"How come?"

"'Cause I don't wanna get hit."

Kyle's cry was barely muffled by the blanket as JT's hand came down hard on his ass. His whole body jerked with the blow. In an instant Kyle realized that JT had been playing with him until now.

"How come you're gonna what I tell you, bitch?"

Kyle searched his frantic mind, desperate for the right answer, feeling JT's growing impatience.

When JT raised his hand to deliver another one of those blows that Kyle felt all the way down to his toes, he remembered what JT wanted to hear.

"'Cause I'm your girl," Kyle said low and fast.

After a while, his tears passed, and he realized he was rock hard. JT felt it.

"Look at that. See why you got to take it up the ass? You're all red and shit from me spanking your bitch ass, but your dick is all hard. You know why?"

"'Cause I'm your girl," Kyle said without hesitation.

"That's fucking right. And my girls fucking do what I say or I beat ass. Get on all fours."

Kyle slid off JT's lap, trembling as JT got to his feet. Kyle heard him unzip his jeans and step out of them. He looked back and saw with no surprise, that JT's hard cock was jutting up between his muscular legs.

JT slapped Kyle's ass lightly. "Come here, bitch."

The light slap sent shivers of pain through Kyle. As he lifted his bruised ass to JT's black cock, he felt his dick get harder. He spread his legs even wider, showing JT his pink hole.

"You want my dick up your bitch ass real hard?"

All at once, a thought hit Kyle. Dante was right. He'd end up with his dick in a pink cage.

"I ain't heard you, boy," JT said.

Kyle didn't know what he would say until he heard the words spilling from his lips. "I've been your girl since I came for you on my knees, with your cock in my throat." He bit his lip and said in a low whisper, "I'm sorry. It was stupid."

JT grabbed Kyle's hips and pressed his thick cock head to his tight hole.

"I won't do it again," Kyle said. His voice was low and pleading. "Please don't. Not without lube. It's gonna hurt so bad."

Kyle suddenly felt JT's strong fingers twine into his hair and pull his head back so far, he thought his neck would snap.

"Don't fuck with me, punk," JT whispered into Kyle's ear. He let go and shoved Kyle hard. "Next time, there ain't gonna be no begging."

Kyle sat on JT's bunk, pushing back against the wall, feeling his sore ass throbbing. His breath came in short, wheezing pants, like a man's who's won a marathon.

"Don't be pissing me off like that," JT said. "Get over here and take care of my cock."

For a few long seconds, Kyle couldn't believe his luck. Was JT playing with him?

"You heard me, bitch? Or you want my fat cock up your ass for a real long dry fuck?"

That got Kyle moving. He nearly flew off the bed and knelt between JT's legs. The blowjob went by in a blur. He felt JT's thick cock deep down his throat, choking him. Felt JT's fingers in his hair, pulling his face down; heard his animal grunts of pleasure as he used his mouth hard.

"Bitch," JT said between clenched teeth.

His fingers pulled Kyle's silky hair harder, and he pumped his hips once, twice and exploded deep in Kyle's throat. Hot come leaked from Kyle's pink lips, wrapped tight around JT's dark, pumping cock.

"Get me something to clean up with," JT said, pulling out of Kyle's mouth.

———————————

After Kyle wiped JT clean, they both slipped into JT's bunk. Kyle leaned timidly against JT's hard body, and relaxed a little when JT pulled him against him.

"I'm sorry," Kyle said, still trembling. "Are you gonna beat me up?"

"I don't how else to say it, boy," JT said, wiping Kyle's wet cheeks. "Don't fuck with me."

The horrors of this long, long day finally caught up to Kyle. He lay his head against JT's strong chest and cried miserably.

"I was so scared when those men got me. I thought something really bad was gonna happen to me. I'm sorry."

JT soothed Kyle's feverish brow, telling him to be quiet, and rest.

"I know I caused you a whole bunch of trouble. Are you gonna get rid of me? Like make me the gang slut and sell me or something? I don't wanna end up with those men, please," Kyle said.

JT lay thoughtfully in the dark, thinking of the boy in the hologram in Matthew's office. Kyle's hysterical words washed over him, leaving nearly no impression on his mind.

"Are you?" The sudden desperation in Kyle's voice called JT back from his thoughts.

"Am I what?"

"Getting rid of me?"

"Why you talk so much shit, boy?" JT wrapped a big arm around Kyle. pulling him even closer. "Don't cry no more. Go to sleep."

Little by little, Kyle's body relaxed. Exhaustion drew him away from the throbbing pain in his sore ass. In JT's strong arms, his breathing soon became slow and even.

JT lay awake, thinking. He knew he shouldn't have signed the consent form in Matthew's office. But laying here with Kyle in the dark, surrounded by the low cries and whimpers of the night, he couldn't stand to think of Matthew giving his boy to some Purgatory animal, like Tyrone.

His chip delivery date was in seven weeks.

JT untangled himself from Kyle and lit a cigarette. A sudden picture came to his mind. A man buried in sand up to his neck, watching high tide coming in. *I got to get us the fuck out,* he thought.

Chapter 40

JT started visiting Kyle in the library everyday. Kyle had the strange feeling he was checking up on him; making sure he wasn't riding the stupid train. If that's all it was, Kyle wouldn't have had a chance to find out that there's worse things than being in the basement when he shouldn't be. He wouldn't have found out what it felt like to fall through the gates of Purgatory straight into Hell.

JT seemed to know exactly what Kyle liked. He brought music, chocolates, pastries, video games, airplane model kits. The gifts came wrapped in plain brown paper with Kyle's name written across the front like a stencil drawing a six year old might make.

Today was just another day in Kyle's new life. He didn't know it, but every passing second got him one step closer to falling off the edge of a cliff into the stormy sea of JT's rage.

JT said the words Kyle dreaded to hear every afternoon.

"You know why I got to have my way with you, boy?" JT said, undoing Kyle's jeans and pulling them down the boy's narrow hips.

"Cause I'm your girl," Kyle said quickly, feeling JT's big hands caressing his soft ass. He was glad he wasn't sore anymore from his spanking.

"Yeah," JT said. He leaned close to Kyle and said softly into his ear, "Soon, I'm gonna make you my wife."

That shocked Kyle. JT had never said that before. He resisted the urge to shove JT back and beg him not to lock up his dick. But he couldn't. Purgatory was a place where secrets lived behind every closed door.

"Come here, boy," JT said.

He pulled Kyle over to the black brick wall and turned him around. He pressed into Kyle, rubbing his hard cock against Kyle's ass. Didn't matter what gift JT brought. This part was always the same. Kyle pressed into the wall, spread his legs, and lifted his round naked ass to JT's hungry eyes.

JT unzipped his jeans and spit on his dark cock. Then Kyle felt him grab his hips.

"You like being a black man's bitch?" JT said, kissing the side of Kyle's neck, rubbing his cock against the crack of Kyle's ass.

"Yeah," Kyle said, too afraid to say anything but what he knew JT wanted to hear.

"How come?" JT said.

"Cause I need to be used like a girl and get fucked," Kyle said, repeating the answer JT had taught him.

"That's right, bitch," JT said, sliding his cock slowly into Kyle's tight hole. "You're my girl." Fucking Kyle's smooth white ass harder and deeper, JT said, "And you got a nice tight bitch pussy."

Kyle squeezed his eyes shut while JT fucked him in short, hard thrusts. He hoped JT would come, so he wouldn't have to get fucked again tonight. But after only a few minutes, JT pulled his hard cock out of Kyle's ass.

All at once, Kyle had an idea. If JT came in his mouth now, he probably wouldn't get fucked tonight. He spun around, slipping to his knees in front of JT.

"Let me suck you off," Kyle said. He pressed his soft pink lips to JT's dark cock, licking and kissing. "I'll do it real good. The way you like it."

JT grabbed Kyle's slender arm in a painful grip and bent over the boy.

"Why you turned around? How you know I'm done fucking you?"

Kyle bit his lower lip, looking up into JT's hard eyes. "Sorry."

JT ran his rough, calloused fingers along Kyle's soft cheek. "Don't do that shit no more, hear?"

Kyle nodded, breathing a soft sigh of relief. For a moment, he'd seen that same dark fury he'd seen in JT's eyes the night he'd gone into the basement.

"I won't make you mad like that again," Kyle said, not sure if JT wasn't mad anymore or if he was controlling himself.

"You're a good bitch. I just got to teach you how to be a real good wife for me." JT ran his dark fingers over Kyle's pink lips.

Kyle hoped that JT didn't see the jolt of terror that ran through him, hearing that word again. *Wife. Oh my god. This can't be happening to me. It can't,* Kyle thought.

Taking a deep breath, Kyle said, "I like being your girl but – "

"But what?" JT's dark brown eyes fell on Kyle with all the weight of a man thinking thoughts too dark to see the light of day.

"I didn't mean anything," Kyle said, letting out his breath. "I was just gonna say I don't know what it's gonna be like to be your wife."

JT smiled and Kyle thought, *what would happen if I just say I don't want my dick in a pink cage?* Thinking back on his spanking, he thought he knew how bad things could get if he said something like that. He was wrong. He had no idea.

"I'm gonna fuck your hot little hole real hard tonight," JT said casually, pulling up his jeans.

This time Kyle knew JT saw the fear come into his eyes. He didn't try to hide it.

"I don't know what you get all scared about," JT said, walking past Kyle. "You know I ain't gonna do nothing bad to you." He stopped and gave Kyle a thoughtful look over his shoulder. "Unless you piss me off."

The strangest part of JT's visits to the library was that he never let Kyle come. The few times that Kyle had worked up the nerve to ask, JT slapped his ass hard and told Kyle not to worry about shit that wasn't his business.

Kyle didn't know what JT meant by that. There were a lot of things Kyle didn't know. He didn't understand why his cock throbbed and ached with need after JT used him like a girl. All he knew was that he had to have relief.

Kyle jacked off after JT left, trying not to think about what JT would do to him if he found out.

Chapter 41

At night after dinner, JT stuck an extra blanket in the top of the prison bars, giving them the illusion of privacy in the corner cell.

When they were alone, JT talked to Kyle about nearly everything. They talked in low voices while JT lay on his bunk and Kyle worked at the wooden table, usually building a model airplane. No topic was out of bounds, except what JT had done to end up in Purgatory and his business here in Purgatory.

There was a comfortable silence while JT flipped through a porn magazine from the seemingly endless supply under his bunk. The pictures showed black men fucking white boys.

JT lit a cigarette and watched his boy work. He didn't understand what Kyle got out of building those stupid planes and cars. All those little pieces would drive him batshit.

"Look, boy, " JT said.

When Kyle looked up, JT blew three perfect smoke rings up to the ceiling. For some reason, Kyle loved to see him do that. His boy smiled at him then went back to work.

Before Kyle, the only thing JT had enjoyed seeing in a boy's eyes was helpless fear when he fucked them real hard. It was different with Kyle.

"Does Purgatory sell black market stuff?" Kyle said, without looking up.

JT looked up at Kyle. "Why?"

Kyle shrugged. The sense that Kyle was hiding something was always there. JT let it go. For now.

"I thought maybe that's where your money came from," Kyle said.

"I already told you, boy. Don't be asking me about my business. I'll tell you anything you wanna know, except that, and what I done to get in here. You got me?"

"Yeah," Kyle said. He fell silent, concentrating on gluing tiny pieces in place. "How'd you learn how to fight?"

"On the street. Where I come from, you learn to fight real good, unless you want your fucking balls ripped off."

"You were in a gang?"

"I'm still 'in a gang' if that's how you wanna say it," JT said, putting emphasis on Kyle's words. "Everybody up in here is in a gang. Ain't no other way to survive."

"Why?"

"Cause you always got to have someone watch your back," JT said. "That's how life is in here."

"Is Dante in your gang too?"

"Yeah."

JT watched Kyle think it over quietly, fitting a few more pieces onto the wing of the plane.

"You must be the leader of the gang, right?"

JT gave his boy an amused look. "Why you say that?"

Kyle shrugged. "The way everyone is respectful to you and kind of scared of you. And they ask for your advice for stuff."

"Shit, boy. You don't miss nothing."

JT saw Kyle blush a little. "Yeah. I've been in trouble most of my life for being nosy."

"No shit," JT said. He ignored the way fear flashed through Kyle's green eyes. "Yeah, I'm like the leader of my gang. But then there's the council. It's kind of like a gang of gangs. We all work together. We share our territories and the profits."

"Tyrone is in another gang, right?"

"Yeah. He's in the Golds."

"What's that?"

"The gang that does the pirate work."

JT didn't expect to get away with an answer like that. Kyle's endless flow of questions was the closest thing to fun JT knew.

Kyle glanced up at JT. "There's real pirates in here?"

"Yeah," JT said.

Kyle looked up at him, expectantly. When JT was silent, looking at his magazine, pretending not to see Kyle's look of impatience, he said, "Come on. You can't leave me hanging like that. Tell."

"We ain't but twenty or thirty miles from the biggest port on the coast," JT said. "All kinds of shit got to go right by the prison, about thirty, forty miles out to get into port."

"On boats?"

"No. Big cargo ships."

"How do pirates get the stuff?"

"They pull up beside ships in these special stripped down boats. They got almost nothing on them but a engine built for speed and the lightest shell that can float on water. They go twice as fast as the coast guard. The big ships would still be churning water by the time they try to catch up with a pirate boat."

"Then what?"

JT shrugged. "They got tricks. Sometimes they pretend to be dead in the water, like something's wrong with their boat. But most captains don't stop for that no more."

"How do they get them to stop?"

"Easy," JT said. "They start shooting. Captain knows he can't outrun a pirate boat. So he got a choice. Keep going and get his ship all shot up and lose all his shit, his crew and his ship, or stop and give the pirates what they want."

"Most captains stop?"

"They got no choice. The pirates board the ship, unload what they want, then get gone."

"What if the captain gives them a hard time?"

"What the fuck you think, boy?" JT blew smoke up to the ceiling, looking at Kyle. "If they piss off the pirates real bad, all the crew gets dead, to make a example. Tyrone and them leave a gold card, so when the Golds board another boat to take their shit, don't nobody fuck with them unless they wanna suck cold water."

"That's fucked up," Kyle said in a low voice.

"Yeah" JT said. "Sometimes the ship Captains, they got their own pirates. And don't nobody know 'til it starts raining bullets and hellfire."

"Why don't the ships go around?"

"Around what?"

"You know, like around Purgatory. Go into port another way."

"Too far. With the price of gas, the trip would cost more than the shit they got on board."

"Who builds the speed boats?"

JT shrugged. "Nobody knows. They just show up. If something goes wrong, and a boat gets all shot up, another one shows up."

"Where do they get the pirates?"

"Prisoners," JT said quietly. His eyes darkened, remembering the consent form he'd signed.

Chapter 42

"They let prisoners go out on the open sea?" Kyle said in disbelief. "Why do they come back?"

"You gotta get a chip to be a pirate."

"Why would a man in prison be a pirate?" Kyle said, puzzled.

Cause sometimes a man ain't got no choice, JT thought.

"Cause when you get out, sure you got a chip, but you're a rich man. If you ain't gonna get out, then you sign a –" JT hesitated, thinking. "Like a contract for a couple years, kind of. If you survive –"

"*If* you survive?"

Sometimes JT forgot that for all his smart talk about computers, in a lot of ways Kyle was just a boy who didn't know nothing about nothing. He didn't want Kyle to find out the hard way; like the boy in the hologram found out.

Kyle looked up and saw JT staring at the wall just above his head with a distant, haunted look in his dark eyes.

"JT?"

"It ain't like your video games, boy." JT pushed back his dark thoughts. "They got real bullets out there. They tag your ass, there ain't no extra points to bring you back to life."

"Christ," Kyle said quietly.

"*If* you survive your contract, you live in the South Tower. I hear it's real nice over there. All the hot water you want, real good food. It ain't hardly like prison at all," JT said in a dreamy voice.

"*If* you survive," Kyle said, bringing JT back to stark reality.

"Yeah, boy," JT said.

"Who does Purgatory sell the gasoline to?"

"How you know it's gas?" JT said in a low voice.

Kyle froze in the act of gluing a tiny piece to a wing.

––––––––––––––

"I asked you a question, boy."

"I saw it in the basement," Kyle said quietly. "Boxes and boxes."

He looked at JT, fear bright in his green eyes.

"You ain't got to be worried. I already did what I got to do about that."

Something had been nagging at Kyle ever since he went into the basement.

"How come you didn't beat me up that night? I was scared. You were really mad."

JT was quiet for a long time. Long seconds ticked by. Kyle had time to think that maybe asking wasn't such a good idea.

"Why you always scared I'm gonna beat you up?"

Kyle knew he couldn't tell the truth about seeing Jessi's picture.

"'Cause sometimes you get really mad. You look like you feel like hurting me real bad," Kyle said in a low voice. "Like in the bathroom."

JT looked at Kyle, surprised. "That's what you think boy, that I wanna hurt you real bad?"

Kyle looked down into his lap, lacing his fingers together so JT wouldn't see him shaking.

"Sometimes," Kyle said quietly.

"Why?"

Kyle shrugged. "You get really mad and your eyes –" He bit his lip and stopped talking.

"What about my eyes?"

Kyle hesitated, weighing whether he should tell JT about that horrible darkness that came into his eyes. "I don't know. You just look really mad, that's all."

"And you think what? I'm gonna break your arm or something?"

Kyle looked sharply at JT when he said that. "I'm not sure."

JT was quiet for a long time, then he said, "Come over here, boy."

Kyle hesitated for a bare instant before he rose from his chair. JT pulled Kyle down and made him sit on his bunk.

"You ain't got to worry about me losing control and hurting you. I ain't like that with my girls. You piss me off, I'll belt your ass real bad. But I ain't trying to break no bones or nothing."

Kyle nodded, remembering the cast on Jessi's arm in the picture.

"How come you act like you don't believe me?"

Kyle shrugged. "I believe you."

"I told you," JT said in a low voice that had turned cold, "I don't like it when my girl lies to me."

Kyle swallowed. "I don't know what to say."

"Start by telling me who showed you a picture of Jessi."

"Nobody."

"Was it that bitch, Ryan?"

That was so far from the truth that a small laugh escaped Kyle. "No. He didn't show me anything."

"Where'd you get a picture?"

Kyle looked up at JT, thinking of the Principal, knowing somehow that JT had become part of the tangled maze of secrets that ruled his life.

"You said you wouldn't beat me up if I do what you say. But what if I've kept secrets from you?"

"I know you been keeping secrets, boy. I been waiting for you to come to me."

Kyle ran his fingers through his silky red hair.

"What is it, baby? Who you running from?"

"Oh God. I'm really scared, JT." Kyle's voice came out in a low trembling whisper.

"There's this man. If I tell you who he is, they'd probably kill you."

"Tell me, boy." JT took Kyle's small trembling hand. "Nothing you say is gonna make me stop wanting you with me."

"You sure?" Kyle looked up at him, searching his eyes for the truth behind his words.

JT pushed Kyle's red hair back from his pale face. "I risked everything I got for you. I never been more sure of nothing in my life."

Kyle took a deep breath. "I'm Nero," he whispered.

JT leaned close. "What you said, boy?"

That was when the lights went out.

Chapter 43

The lights blinked out to total darkness. Alarms clanged. In the cells up and down the tier a very dark night had fallen. Guards ran up and down the tier, yelling, waving flashlights that pierced the pitch blackness like daggers of light.

Kyle froze at the sound of a key turning in the lock. JT grabbed him and shoved him to the wall.

"Don't fucking move," JT murmured under his breath.

He rose from the bed. Kyle tried to reach out to him, but JT pushed his hand back.

"Stay," he whispered.

It's him, Kyle thought. *He came to get me.* Every nightmare he'd ever had about the Principal raced through his mind like a maniac whirlwind. The cell door slid open slowly. Kyle listened in terrified silence to the sounds of a scuffle near the door.

"What the *fuck*?" JT said. He sounded furious. "You fucking wanna die in this shit?"

"I was on my way to see you," Dante's calm voice said. "Then the damn lights went out. Where's Kyle?"

"On my bunk. He's alright. Where's everyone at?"

"Working," Dante said. He sank down on the bunk. "Hey, boy," he said, reaching behind him.

Kyle grabbed Dante's hand and held on tight, like a drowning man.

"Watch him," JT said. His voice came from near the door.

"Where are you going?" Kyle said in a low, urgent voice.

"Go do what you got to do," Dante said.

Kyle heard the cell door slide open, then shut.

"Lock it after me," JT's soft voice said.

JT's scuffle with Dante had torn down the blanket. Shadows holding beams of light ran in the dark. The beams of light stabbed across the painting of the Horsemen on the wall, making them look like they were galloping hell bent for leather, chasing down the light. Out on the tier the guards ran through a hail storm of things falling and bouncing off the stone floor.

"Stay here," Dante said, getting up.

"What's going on?" Kyle said, watching Dante light a candle.

"Rolling black out."

"They're supposed to tell you before it happens," Kyle said.

He felt Dante shrug in the dark shadows of the candlelight. "Send in a complaint form."

The painting on the wall seemed to shift in the flickering candlelight. The Horsemen looked like they were racing against Time and his wicked scythe. War's blood red horse looked sleek and ready to run a thousand races.

"Isn't it dangerous for him to be walking around alone in a blackout?"

"Ain't nobody gonna sneak up on him without JT knowing it. Anybody tries anything with him, they're dead."

A scream pierced the darkness. Kyle grabbed Dante's arm in a death grip.

"Oh God," Kyle said in a low anguished voice. "Not again."

"It's alright, boy."

"You *always* say that when people scream like they're dying," Kyle said in a low whisper.

To his surprise Dante laughed a little. "Come here, take my mind off things."

He pulled Kyle toward him, and pushed the boy's head down between his legs.

"Are you kidding?" Kyle pulled away. "I'm not even close to horny."

"That don't matter." Dante pulled him close again. "I'm hard. I ain't had a bitch in days. Get on your knees. Take care of my cock."

When Kyle hesitated again, Dante said, "Or you wanna tell me some secrets instead?"

Kyle knelt between Dante's legs, and reached for his fly, but Dante's big, strong hands were already there, unzipping, taking out his thick cock. Even though five seconds ago, sucking cock had been the last thing on his mind, Kyle was already hungry for the taste of Dante.

Dante spread his legs, looking down at Kyle. Out on the tier men shouted, others cried out in fear, guards ran back and forth, yelling instructions over their radios.

"I got something for you, boy," Dante said.

Kyle sensed the shift in his weight and knew that he was leaning back on his powerful arms, spreading his legs, giving Kyle his beautiful cock.

In the shadowy darkness, Kyle took the thick head of Dante's veined cock between his pink lips and squeezed rhythmically, massaging Dante's cock head. His tongue found Dante's piss hole and teased him, wriggling around.

"Fuck, nice tongue, boy," Dante said softly.

Kyle swirled his tongue slowly around his piss hole, then let the head of Dante's fat cock slip from his lips. Kyle licked up and down his hard flesh, letting his tongue linger, feeling Dante's breathing quicken as he got closer and closer to his balls.

When Kyle took his balls into his mouth, Dante gasped, and moaned. After Kyle swirled the tip of his tongue around Dante's balls, he slid his hot tongue down Dante's thick shaft, 'til he got to the head again. He opened his mouth wide and swallowed his cock, inch by inch.

Dante looked down at Kyle servicing his swollen cock. "Your lips look real pretty wrapped around my dick, boy," Dante said, thrusting his hips gently into Kyle's mouth.

Kyle moaned softly as Dante pressed his thick cock deeper into his mouth. His cheeks became hollow as he worked to please Dante, moving his head up and down, again and again, taking Dante deep.

Dante thrust his throbbing cock in and out of Kyle's mouth. As Dante grabbed Kyle's hair and held him down to fuck his mouth, Kyle surrendered himself to Dante's pleasure, moaning as his thick cock slid in and out of his willing mouth. He couldn't help wondering what Dante's thick cock would feel like up his ass.

"Oh fuck, boy," Dante said, holding Kyle's head down on his cock.

He jerked hard and shot a load down Kyle's spasming throat.

Dante's hand fell away. He relaxed, leaning back on his elbows as Kyle's soft tongue licked him clean.

"JT's right," Dante said, breathing a little hard. "You're a fucking hot bitch."

Kyle smiled in the darkness. He loved to please a man's cock.

"Come here," Dante said, reaching for Kyle in the shadows.

Even though he was rock hard, Kyle knew better than to ask Dante to let him come. If he came and JT found out, he'd beat Kyle's ass.

Kyle sat next to Dante in the darkness, hearing him zip his jeans.

"You got a sweet mouth, boy." Dante ran his thick fingers slowly across Kyle's soft lips. Kyle blushed in the candlelight. Dante stroked his smooth cheek gently.

"Sure you ain't got no secrets you wanna tell me?" Dante said.

Kyle thought about back rooms with no windows. He knew he should keep his mouth shut. But sometimes, secrets can be so heavy, they squeeze past the tightest lips.

"I can't stand being so scared," Kyle said in a low whisper. "I think – "

The lights snapped back on.

Chapter 44

"You had fun with my bitch?"

Neither of them had heard JT come back.

"He got a sweet mouth," Dante said, running his dark fingers along Kyle's soft cheeks.

JT walked into the cell. He ran his fingers through Kyle's hair, gently. "My bitch took care of you?"

Dante nodded. "He took real good care of me," he said. He looked up at JT. "You took care of shit?"

JT nodded. "It's cool. Everything was locked down."

Dante got up. "I gotta go."

"Later," JT said.

He locked the cell door, and put the blanket back up.

When he turned back to Kyle, the boy was sitting on his bunk, pressed back against the wall. The lights out warning buzzer sounded. Kyle jumped a little.

"That's kind of stupid," he said. "Why turn them back on?"

"Get naked," JT said. He was already stripping out of his clothes. "And get your ass up."

Kyle stripped out of his clothes and turned and put his ass up, scooting close to the edge of JT's bunk.

JT ran his dark fingers gently over Kyle's smooth white ass, then he slid a fat finger up and down the crack of Kyle's ass. "You got a real pretty ass, boy," he said.

JT stuck his finger in his mouth then slid his long finger into Kyle's ass. "You know what I been thinking about all day?"

"What?" Kyle said, squirming on JT's finger.

"I been thinking how good my cock's gonna feel inside your tight little bitch hole," JT said, shoving his fat finger deeper into Kyle's tight hole.

Kyle winced at the pain, but said nothing.

"You want my fat black cock up your bitch pussy?" JT said, sliding his finger in and out.

After sucking Dante's cock, Kyle was desperate to come. But not so bad that he wanted for JT to fuck him; not in the mood he was in tonight.

"Yeah," Kyle said. "I'm your girl," he added for good measure.

JT got behind Kyle and took hold of his hips. Kyle tried not to tense as he felt the head of JT's thick cock finding his sore hole.

Kyle wanted to plead with him, to please not fuck him; to *please* use his mouth. But he was too afraid of what JT would do to him. He felt JT's hand guide his thick cock to his hole.

"Spread your legs for me, boy," JT said, lubing his cock.

Kyle did it and bit his lips as the head of JT's thick cock stretched his hole, sliding into him, making him groan in pain.

"I thought about this sweet little hole all day, baby," JT said.

Kyle's cock was rock hard, but he knew he wouldn't be allowed to come. As JT inched slowly into his ass, Kyle wished he could reach between his legs and jack off. But he knew better. Kyle pushed back on JT's thick cock, knowing JT liked when he did that. Sometimes Kyle didn't get it so bad if he did that.

"That's it, bitch. Push back on my dick. Show me how much you love my black cock," JT said.

JT grabbed Kyle's hips in a tighter grip. Kyle knew JT was about to plunge into him hard and fast. He willed himself to relax. It hurt too bad if he tensed up.

JT sank hard into Kyle's trembling ass, fucking him in a hard and fast rhythm. Kyle moaned in pain as JT took him, hoping, like he did every night, that he would come fast. Kyle's ass was sore from getting fucked everyday. Every thrust into him was painful.

"You got a fucking hot pussy, baby," JT said, plowing Kyle like a machine.

JT's hips slammed into Kyle, shaking his whole body. Kyle groaned in JT's hard grip. He wanted it to be over.

"It's so fucking good, baby," JT said.

His dark, powerful body towered over Kyle as he fucked the boy's trembling white ass. His thick, black cock slid in and out of the hot tightness of Kyle's quivering hole as Kyle groaned in his grip.

"I'm almost done, boy," JT said. "Your pussy's driving me wild."

He drilled Kyle's sweet boy pussy, his teeth clenched in a grimace of pleasure, holding the bucking boy in his iron grip.

"Here's my load, bitch," JT said, and banged into Kyle hard, shoving his throbbing cock deep and filling Kyle's sweet hole with hot come.

Afterwards, they lay in JT's bunk. Kyle lay in JT's arms, his head resting on JT's broad chest. Kyle thought of the same thing he thought of every night after JT had his way with him. He wished JT wouldn't fuck him so hard or so much.

"JT?"

"What?"

"I wanna talk to you about how you fuck me," Kyle said, careful to keep his voice soft and low. "But I don't want you to get mad. I'm not being disrespectful."

Kyle held his breath, waiting for JT's answer.

"I'm listening," JT said. Kyle felt the growing tension in JT's body.

"You fuck me real hard. Most days two times. My ass really hurts."

JT said nothing, just lay still looking up into the darkness, holding Kyle close. Kyle knew he was too still, too quiet. It made him nervous.

"Maybe I could suck you off in the day sometimes. Whenever you say," Kyle said. "You'd decide," he added quickly.

"I don't let nothing happen to you in here. How come you're worried about things that ain't your business?" JT's soft voice had no hint of anger. Not yet.

Kyle was puzzled by his answer. "Not my business? What do you mean?"

"How I fuck you, when I fuck you and how hard I fuck you ain't your business. All you got to worry about is bending over and getting fucked. If I feel like coming in your mouth, then all you got to worry about is getting on your knees for me. I take care of you. That's all you got to know."

JT delivered this little speech with no anger, no sarcasm, and even a little hint of puzzlement. As if he really couldn't understand why Kyle would be questioning him about these things.

Kyle didn't know what to say to that.

"But you're hurting my ass," Kyle said, even more puzzled than when he played 3-D video riddles.

To Kyle's surprise, JT chuckled a little at that. "I know my dick hurts you. You got a tight little hole. But you're my girl. That's how it is for bitches. I feel like fucking you three, four times a day. But I'm good to you. I never make you take my dick more than two times a day. Sometimes, I even wait 'til night and I only fuck you one time."

Kyle was amazed. JT actually thought he was good to Kyle because he didn't fuck him *more*. He felt like a man walking on thin ice with spiked boots.

"But JT –"

"Don't waste time thinking about shit that ain't your business," JT said, pulling Kyle closer gently. "You know you're my girl, right?"

"Yeah, but –"

"Alright then," JT said. "Then there ain't nothing else to say. You're my bitch. You get my dick how I give it to you. All you got to worry about is bending over or getting on your knees when I say."

"So just bend over or get on my knees and shut up, is that it?" Kyle said, struggling to control his rising temper.

"Yeah, baby." JT sounded pleased that Kyle finally understood.

Kyle gave up. He was getting angry. It would be dangerous to lose his temper with JT. "Sorry if I made you mad," he said quietly.

"I ain't mad, boy." JT caressed Kyle's ass gently. "I know you bitches get confused sometimes. You're my girl." JT kissed Kyle's cheek. "It ain't your business how I fuck you. Don't be worrying about shit like that." He pulled Kyle closer and stroked his hair softly. "Go to sleep, boy."

Kyle relaxed against JT's solid chest, and fell asleep after only a few minutes. JT held Kyle close, thinking back on what Kyle had said to him just before the lights went out. He'd let the boy think he forgot, but it was heavy on his mind. Who was the boy in his bed? What would Kyle's secrets cost him?

He closed his eyes. JT's last thoughts before he fell into the abyss of sleep were, *four weeks and one day before they put that chip in me. Time's real fucking short.*

Chapter 45

Dr. Maxell, the man who would get Kyle and JT out of Purgatory, was powerfully built, but without JT's killer instinct.

"Let's get one thing straight," Dr. Maxell said. "I'm a doctor. You're a scumbag with loads of money. That's the only reason I'm even thinking about doing this."

Dante, standing next to JT in the prison infirmary, tensed at the doctor's words.

JT nodded, looking down into the man's magnified brown eyes behind his thick glasses. "We're straight on that. Can you help me and my boy or not?"

The doctor looked around the small back room of the infirmary, then he pulled a pack of cigarettes from the pocket of his dingy white coat. JT offered him a light, but Dr. Maxell lit his own cigarette, squinting into JT's dark eyes.

"You know my boy got a chip, right?"

The doctor nodded. "That's the most dangerous part."

"Tell me how it works," JT said.

Dr. Maxell talked for long minutes. Dante paced restlessly near the door, keeping watch.

"That's fucked up," Dante said when the doctor stopped talking. "What if you can't bring him back?"

Dr. Maxell shrugged. "I won't lie to you. That's a risk."

JT looked at Dante, then he looked at the doctor who was his salvation.

"How much?" JT said.

Dr. Maxell told him.

"That's everything I got," JT said.

"I know." The doctor smiled, a cold humorless twisting of his thin lips.

"How the fuck you know my business?" JT said, turning cold eyes on the doctor.

"You want my help or not?" Dr. Maxell said.

"You can get us out? Guaranteed?"

"Nothing's for sure in this life," the doctor said softly. "They could catch me tomorrow and take me to some dark corner of the basement. That bastard Matthew would probably rip off my balls with red hot pincers before he put a bullet in my head. If that doesn't happen, yeah, I can get you and the kid out."

The calm way the man talked about his own death made JT look at the doctor with new respect. Dr. Maxell met his gaze.

"Look. I don't care why you're in here. I'm a healer. I save lives. You can give me the money I need to save dying people in a world where they've become disposable, like toilet paper, " Dr. Maxell said.

JT gave him a puzzled look.

"Do you realize that murderers and cutthroats are eating three meals a day while children on the mainland, just twenty miles away, are dying of starvation? Their parents are getting cholera and typhoid from drinking dirty water. But the Americans in the Freedom Centers don't matter too much. They'll never be in anyone's army."

"But medicine's free," JT said, interested despite himself.

The doctor laughed, a low bitter sound. "Some test somewhere said they won't make good soldiers. So they live in Freedom Centers. Shipments of medicine are always late. Or they don't come at all. Distribution centers give out tainted water." Dr. Maxell stabbed a finger at JT. "You know what a Freedom Center is?"

JT shook his head, taken aback by the doctor's fury.

"Pretty words for concentration camp. American children in there are dying, and no one gives a *shit*, least of all our government."

"How come it ain't on holovision?" JT said.

Dr. Maxell laughed, a low, hollow sound. "Matthew's fucking boys and whipping them just as fast as he can find them. You seen it on holovision lately?"

Dante and JT both looked at the doctor in silence.

"So I have to turn away dying people from my clinic because they failed a test that says they'd never make a good soldier. But the people our government needs, the scumbags like you who run their pirate boats, they get aspirin for a fucking headache."

"We ain't got time to talk about how fucked up the world is," Dante said softly from his post by the door.

"I'll pay you what you want," JT said, looking the doctor in the eye. "I might even get some more before you get us out." He tilted his head, looking at the doctor. "Maybe a scumbag like me can help you keep a few people alive."

The doctor squinted at JT. Without saying it, both men understood that they were warriors in a world where good and bad had become badly confused.

"Alright." Dr. Maxell threw away his cigarette. He was all business again. "The Maze Gladiator Game is in two weeks. You have to win. Everything hangs on that."

JT listened intently while the doctor talked for another five minutes.

JT nodded. "What about Kyle?"

"Send him to the infirmary the day of the Maze. I'll make sure he stays until nightfall. He'll go out with me," Dr. Maxell said. "But if you lose the Maze, we can't get you out. Whatever it takes, you *have* to win."

JT nodded. "How you know I'll give you the money once I'm out?"

"I'm a real trusting man," Dr. Maxell said and smiled, but his eyes were ice cold. "Besides, if you fuck with me, we'll inject you with a chip. Kyle will be our price for getting you out. He'll sell for a good price on the Middle East black market."

"Thought I was the only scumbag," JT said with a half smile.

Dr. Maxell shrugged. "It's a tough old world."

JT gave the doctor a genuine smile. "You're alright, doc."

"Last question," Dr. Maxell said. "It's important."

"What?"

"I know about the kid's chip. What about you?"

JT did a quick calculation in his head. His delivery date fell just one day after the Maze. He shook his head. "No. Not yet. It's supposed to happen after the Maze."

"If you get a chip, it's over. I'm willing to risk it with the kid. But you're too high risk."

JT nodded. "I got it."

"You have to go. I've already been in here too long with you."

"Company," Dante said from the door.

Dr. Maxell turned his back on JT. When he turned around again, Mr. Remello was just in time to see him holding up a syringe to the light.

"Doc, I told you," Mr. Remello said. "Only one prisoner at a time."

"I'm scared of shots," JT said. "I needed Dante to hold my hand."

As JT hoped, the joke distracted Remello, and made him stop thinking about what the three of them were doing in here.

Dr. Maxell tied rubber tubing around JT's thick right arm and tapped the vein a few times, waiting for Remello to walk out.

"You sure you know what you're doing, doc?" JT said.

"This will fix you right up," Dr. Maxell said, and slid the needle into JT's arm. Remello watched, then left.

The doctor withdrew the needle and looked at JT.

"What the fuck was that?" JT said, rubbing his arm.

"Saline solution."

"What?"

"Water and salt. It's harmless."

JT looked at the doctor for a long moment.

"I used to think a man could only fight with a knife or a gun. But seems like you're a soldier too, in your own war."

"Win the Maze, JT," Dr. Maxell said. "If you don't, I have to take the kid anyway. He'll already be outside the main gates. I can't get him back in."

Dante came to get Kyle in the library nearly everyday. After the basement, Kyle never went anywhere by himself. During those long walks, Dante and Kyle became friends. The boy's silence tonight caught Dante's attention.

"What's on your mind, boy?"

"If I tell you something, will you tell JT I talked to you about it?"

"You know I don't tell JT nothing I ain't got to."

Kyle took a deep breath. Until the last moment, when the first words came out, he wasn't sure if he should trust Dante or not. But he couldn't keep it inside anymore.

"My ass is real sore," Kyle said. "He fucks me all the time."

Kyle told Dante everything that had been happening to him. Then he told him about the talk he'd had with JT in bed last week.

"A whole week's gone by, but he's still the same. What does he mean it's not my business?"

"Didn't you ask him?"

Kyle shook his head. "I was too scared he'd get mad. He was already pissed that I was talking about it."

"To JT, you're a girl. You shouldn't be worried about getting fucked. That's men's business."

Dante's answer did nothing to clear Kyle's confusion. "I don't get it," he said softly.

"Ain't nothing to get," Dante said. "That's just how it is with a man like JT."

"What about you?" Kyle looked up at Dante. "You think like that too?"

Dante shook his head, making his dreads falls around his face. "I don't think a bitch should say to no me if I wanna fuck him. But if they wanna talk to me about getting fucked different than how I do it, that's cool."

"It's not cool for JT," Kyle said.

Dante shook his head again. "No. It ain't. You better stop before you make him mad."

"I can't stop," Kyle said. "I'm afraid of him. But he hurts me so bad when he fucks me. I'm sore all the time. I have to make him understand that he's hurting me and it's not okay."

"How?"

Kyle briefly outlined his plan for showing JT his side of things.

"That ain't gonna get you nothing but a hard ass whipping, boy," Dante said quietly.

"But he's got to listen to reason."

"Why?"

They'd been walking back to JT's cell. Kyle stopped dead in his tracks and turned to Dante.

"What do you mean why?"

"Men like JT ain't always reasonable when it comes to how they treat a bitch," Dante said quietly.

"Well, I'm gonna have to teach him to see reason."

"The only one who's gonna be in school learning is you," Dante said. "Want my advice?"

"Yeah."

"Don't do it."

If Kyle had known his life was about to become a roller coaster ride through Hell, he might have done things differently. JT was on the first floor of the library, talking in a low voice to Mr. Remello, the guard on duty.

Kyle stiffened the moment he heard JT's voice. He knew the little courtship routine JT had going on, and Kyle had made up his mind that JT wasn't going to get what he wanted today. He was sick of his ass being sore.

He sat at the little work desk that had been set up for him. A pile of scratched book discs waited to be replaced. He took the next one from his stack, opened the online database, and searched for the book title – "The Church as Warden: Being Good For Dollars" He didn't look up from his monitor when he heard JT climb the steps.

"Hey, boy," JT said quietly.

"Hey," Kyle said.

He pretended to be caught up in his work. The truth was, his heart was pounding so badly, the words on the screen blurred in and out.

"I was working out and I got all hard thinking about your hot little ass," JT said softly. He rubbed his crotch, looking down at Kyle.

Kyle worked steadily, setting the file parameters for download to the new disc in the hard drive. He had time to think how ancient the prison's computers were. He concentrated on not letting his hands shake on the keyboard. He didn't want JT to see how scared he was.

"Come here, baby," JT said, "let's go in the back room. I'm gonna fuck your little bitch pussy."

Kyle took a breath to steady himself, then without looking up, he said softly, "No."

JT looked at Kyle for a moment, unsure of what he'd heard. He cocked his head to one side. "What you said, boy?"

Kyle had prepared his speech for this moment. But now, feeling JT glaring at him, he nearly lost his nerve. Driven by desperation, Kyle finally looked up at JT, feeling his thundering heart knocking against his ribs.

"I said no. My ass hurts. You fuck me hard in the middle of the day. You don't come. So you fuck me again at night. You never let me suck you off."

Kyle looked down at his shaking hands.

"I'm not going with you. You have to rape me here, and I'll scream real loud if you do. Or you have to drag me down to the back room. And I'll scream all the way."

Kyle knew he had JT trapped. The library was a kind of 'no combat' zone. Not even JT could get away with raping Kyle here in the stacks, in the middle of the day. He couldn't drag Kyle down to the back room either. Not with Kyle kicking and screaming all the way.

JT's reaction was nothing like the fury Kyle had expected. A strange smile surfaced on JT's hard face.

"You ain't coming with me, bitch?"

The unreadable look in JT's dark eyes sent chills down Kyle's spine. Maybe this wasn't such a good idea.

"No," Kyle said, looking up at JT. "I'm not going with you."

Now Kyle saw what he expected in JT's eyes – dark fury. His unwavering gaze made Kyle tremble.

"I'm giving you one more chance, Kyle," JT said softly. "Get your punk ass up and come with me. Now."

Kyle nearly changed his mind. He nearly decided not to mess with JT, and just make the best of things. Instead he made the incredibly stupid decision to stand his ground.

"I'm not going."

Kyle looked down at the table so he could escape JT's furious eyes. He couldn't cave in now. He'd risked too much to get this far. Maybe JT would see reason.

JT walked over to Kyle's desk and leaned on it so his face was inches away. Now JT's eyes were flat and expressionless, the way he'd looked in the Dark Game, slicing into Tyrone again and again.

There was no mercy in the arctic depths of JT's black eyes. There would be no begging or pleading later.

"You got a lot to learn, boy." JT caressed Kyle's cheek. "But that's alright. I'm a real good teacher."

That was too much for Kyle. He lost his nerve, tried to call out JT's name, but fear robbed his voice of any strength.

He tried again. "Wait," he finally said to JT's retreating back.

JT turned and looked at Kyle. "Too late," he said, and went back the way he'd come.

Kyle watched JT retreat slowly down the narrow aisle. *Too late.* JT's words rang in his mind over and over, like hell's bells calling the damned to perdition. Kyle felt a little like screaming.

Chapter 47

JT lay on his bunk like usual, flipping through a magazine. He'd put up the blanket right after dinner. Kyle sat on his top bunk, too nervous to concentrate on putting a model together. JT had been silent all evening.

Kyle had thought of a million ways to say "I'm sorry", but the wall of silence around JT might have been solid steel, ten inches thick. Now, with ten minutes to lights out, Kyle stared at the Horsemen riding out of the wall, wondering what was worse – JT or a back room with no windows?

The lights out warning buzzer sounded. JT didn't so much as look up. Ten minutes dragged by. Finally, the lights out buzzer sounded. Dim, shadowy darkness filled the cell. Kyle heard the sound of JT's magazine dropping to the floor.

"Come here, boy," JT said quietly.

Kyle slid down from his bunk and looked at JT warily. JT reached out too fast for Kyle to escape, and pulled Kyle to his knees between his open legs.

"How come you said no to me like that?" JT's deep voice was calm and even. He looked down at Kyle with genuine curiosity.

Kyle's thumping heart sped up to a fast trot. "I'm sorry."

"You know you're my girl." JT caressed Kyle's soft cheek. "Why you wanna piss me off like that?"

Kyle, who knew he was in deep shit, looked up at JT and said, "Sorry I made you mad." His voice came out in a low, unsteady whisper.

"I ain't mad, boy." JT's soft voice terrified Kyle, like a calm grey sky before a tornado. "I just got to teach you a lesson about saying no to me."

JT handed Kyle a long narrow box, the kind that a dozen long stemmed roses come in. The box was wrapped in pale pink paper covered with tiny yellow flowers.

"Open it," JT said.

Kyle reluctantly tore the wrapping away and opened the box. When he'd pushed the pink tissue aside, Kyle gasped in horror at what he'd uncovered. He looked up at JT with wide, unbelieving eyes. JT couldn't possibly be thinking of using that on him, could he?

JT held out his big hand. "Give it to me, bitch."

Kyle picked up the thick leather belt in trembling hands. The heavy weight of it nauseated him. This had to be a nightmare. He laid it in JT's waiting hand. JT wrapped the long belt twice around his big fist, looking into Kyle's green eyes.

When he spoke again, JT's voice was low and thoughtful. "You been up to some bad shit," he said.

Kyle stared at the leather wrapped around JT's big fist, unable to tear his eyes away.

"You been in the basement, when you ain't got no fucking business down there. You been telling me how you think you should get fucked. And today," JT said between clenched teeth, "you said no to my dick up your bitch ass."

"Sorry I said no," Kyle said, running the words together.

"It ain't no problem, bitch." JT grabbed the end of the belt and snapped it before Kyle's wide, terrified eyes. "I got all the answers to your problems right here."

Kyle dropped his eyes, unwilling to be tormented by the sight of the thick leather. JT laid the leather belt on the bed and went to get something. For a wild, desperate moment, Kyle thought of throwing the damn thing between the bars.

When JT came back with handcuffs, Kyle's terror, unbelievably, kicked up a notch. His heart beat a slow, hard rhythm, sending shock waves of horror through him with every steady, pounding beat. Cold sweat trickled down the middle of his back as Kyle watched JT lay the handcuffs next to the belt.

JT sat down again. "I'm gonna teach you how to be a good girl."

Kyle's eyes fell on JT's crotch. The unmistakable outline of his hard cock pressed against his pants.

JT grabbed Kyle's face and ran the belt's soft leather tip along his cheek. The cool touch of leather made the fear in Kyle's heart swell to hair raising terror.

"You know what's better than fucking a bitch when his ass is all red and welted?"

"What?" Kyle said through trembling lips.

"Nothing." JT let go and shoved Kyle back.

Kyle ran shaky fingers through his hair. "Please, I didn't mean –"

JT pressed a fat finger to Kyle's soft lips. "Shhh."

Looking up into JT's eyes, Kyle realized what a fool he'd been. A dark storm of fury and savage desire twisted through JT's black eyes. Kyle thought back on his plan to make JT listen to him. The dark hunger in JT's eyes brought Dante's words back to Kyle, *that ain't gonna get you nothing but a hard ass whipping.*

"Remember how I said today you got a lot to learn?"

Kyle nodded.

"You ready for your first lesson?"

Kyle hung his head, covered his face with his hands. "Please. I get it now. You don't have to hurt me."

"You're my girl," JT said calmly, as if Kyle had said nothing. "You don't say no to my dick up your bitch ass." JT pried Kyle's hands away, lifted the boy's face and looked into his eyes. "Any questions?"

It was always the same question – *what's it worth?* In Purgatory, JT was Kyle's only protection from being savagely raped by the highest bidder. But just like in the basement, it was too late to go back now, wasn't it? He had to pay the price.

────────────────

Kyle shook his head. "No questions. I get it now."

"Tell me what I said you was." JT looked down at the belt wrapped around his fist.

"Your girl," Kyle said right away. His eyes strayed to the thick leather belt. He couldn't help it.

"You gonna say no to my dick up your ass again?"

Kyle's eyes fell on the belt again, then he looked up into JT's black eyes. "No. Never."

He saw that JT wasn't just mad at him. He was pissed, yeah, but he was horny as hell. Too late, Kyle realized that he'd given JT a reason to show him a glimpse of his dark side.

JT grabbed Kyle's hair and shoved his face into his crotch. A low squeak of terror escaped Kyle.

"I need to fuck my girl's ass." JT rubbed Kyle's face against his hard cock, then shoved him hard to the floor. "Show me what you do when I feel like fucking your bitch pussy."

Kyle felt how much JT wanted to fuck his ass hard and deep and make him scream. He hurried to put his ass up, elbows on the floor, JT's favorite way to fuck.

JT was quiet for a long while before he grabbed Kyle by the hair and pulled him up hard. "How I'm supposed to fuck you with your pants on, bitch?" he said in a low, cruel voice.

He stroked Kyle's soft cheek with the leather belt wrapped around his fist. "Do it right."

JT threw Kyle back to the floor. Kyle picked himself up and undid his jeans with trembling fingers. Silent tears slid down his face. He bent over and offered his naked, round ass to JT. He gasped in fear when he felt the heavy leather belt running across his creamy smooth skin.

"That's better." JT sounded pleased. "What the fuck are you?"

"Your girl." Kyle's low voice trembled.

"No, baby." JT mimicked exactly the tones of a patient teacher. "I don't like it when you say it like that." He fell silent, caressing his boy's white ass with the rough leather.

────────────────

"H-how do you want me to say it?" Kyle said into the unbearable silence.

"Tell me you're my girl."

"I'm your girl," Kyle said with no hesitation. "Please, I'll do whatever you want. You don't have to – "

JT tapped Kyle's ass with the tip of the belt. The weight of the belt made the light touch sting. "Spread your legs."

Kyle slid his legs apart, and lifted his hips, showing JT his tight hole.

"Yeah, bitch." JT ran his dark fingers over Kyle's pink hole. "That's real fucking nice."

Without warning JT shoved a fat finger roughly in and out of Kyle's tight hole. Kyle cried out, but he didn't dare move his ass away.

"You got a sweet bitch pussy," JT said, sliding his finger roughly in and out of Kyle's ass. "My dick's all hard and throbbing thinking about fucking you after I mark you up."

JT slid his finger out of Kyle's hot hole. "Get over here."

Kyle knelt between JT's legs again. Terror ran through him with the raw power of high voltage electric current. He looked up into JT's hard eyes and saw no mercy, only the harsh discipline of a warrior who does what needs to be done.

JT held the belt up before Kyle's eyes. A single tear ran down Kyle's cheek.

"Please don't," Kyle begged. He knew it was no use, but he couldn't help it. "I'm sorry. I won't do it again. Never."

"You know what I'm gonna do to you tonight, boy?"

Pour the Devil's tidings out on me, Kyle thought. He shook his head. "No."

"First I'm gonna belt your bitch ass." JT held up the horrible leather before Kyle's eyes. "I'm gonna beat you 'til your ass is all welted and swelled up."

Kyle swallowed in his dry throat, dropping his eyes.

"After I'm done belting you raw, I'm gonna fuck you hard and dry." JT leaned close to whisper in Kyle's ear. "No fucking lube, bitch. I'm gonna shove my thick black cock up your welted bitch ass and make you scream."

Chapter 48

While Kyle was learning a hard lesson, Father Matthew was taking a late night call. He looked at the man's image floating just above his desk. The hologram was so solid, Matthew almost expected the ashes from the man's cigarette to fall on his stone floor.

"You've done your government a great service," the man said, surrounded in a haze of smoke. "Thanks to you, we'll move up the delivery date."

"To when?" Matthew said. Even in holo, the man in the picture made him nervous.

"Two days before the Maze Gladiator Games. It's been changed online. His chip growth was accelerated. It's complete. Shipment will arrive shortly."

Matthew had never dealt with nanos before. "What do I do when the chip arrives?"

"The chip will arrive in suspension. No one touches the shipment but you. You sign for it. You transport it. You watch over it like's it's your fucking baby. Understand?"

Matthew nodded. "Of course."

"The prison doctor will inject him. Once we receive confirmation, we'll make a deposit into your account."

Matthew's nervous smile twisted into a mask of greed. "How much?"

The man mentioned an amount that was enough for Matthew to retire five minutes from now.

"I don't know what to say."

"Don't say anything. Just get it done. Call me when he's injected."

"I won't let you down."

"You better not." The man's voice was icily calm, coldly terrifying. "Because if you do, I'll rip your fucking balls off and stuff them down your throat."

The transmission clicked off. Matthew was left staring at empty space. Something about this was too easy. He had a very bad feeling.

Chapter 49

Kyle didn't resist when JT dragged him to his feet and handcuffed him to a metal strut that held up the beds. He pressed his forehead to the cool metal, his eyes shut, his hands cuffed together up over his head. JT wadded a dirty underwear and stuffed it into Kyle's mouth.

"You're a good bitch." JT stroked Kyle's ass softly with his rough hand. "This ain't your fault. I been too easy on you."

Kyle looked for the joke in JT's dark eyes. But he saw that JT was deadly serious.

"I was too easy on you when you went in the basement like that. I should of belted your bitch ass that night, real hard." He caressed Kyle's trembling face. "But that's alright. I'm gonna teach you how to be a good girl. I'm real patient."

JT ran the strap across Kyle's naked ass. Kyle whimpered. He looked up at the ceiling with the pleading eyes of a man begging for mercy on Judgment Day.

JT leaned close and whispered, "You ready, boy?"

The first lash fell across Kyle's ass with a harsh, snapping noise, leaving an ugly red welt on his soft flesh. Kyle moaned behind the gag, and tried to jerk free of the handcuffs, but he was utterly trapped. After that, JT's blows fell on Kyle's ass like the devil's rain.

No matter which way Kyle twisted in the grip of the handcuffs, he couldn't escape the heavy leather battering his ass. JT's merciless blows fell on Kyle's writhing ass, again and again, biting into his tender flesh with stinging fury.

"You're in school now, boy." JT ran his rough hands over Kyle's welted ass. "And you best pay attention. 'Cause you do this shit again, I'll fucking belt you 'til you bleed."

JT lit a cigarette and sat on the bed, smoking, looking up into Kyle's miserable green eyes. He blew smoke rings up to the ceiling, listening to Kyle's steady tears.

"You ain't nothing but a black man's bitch up in here," JT said. "Your bitch pussy's gonna get all the dick I say you get. Me. Dante. The whole fucking Clubhouse if I say so. Understand?"

Kyle nodded slowly, tossing his hair across his sweaty red face.

"Good." JT got to his feet.

Kyle panicked, pulling at the cuffs, squealing behind the gag, shaking his head frantically back and forth.

"Last lesson for tonight, bitch," JT said. "Pay attention."

He slammed the belt hard across Kyle's ass. Kyle threw his head back, moaning in agony.

"I fuck you *when* I want," JT said.

Heavy leather slammed across Kyle's welted ass again.

"*How* I want."

JT raised his muscled arm and swung the leather belt down in a merciless arc.

"As *hard* I want."

After the last blow, Kyle felt his knees go weak. He hung limply in the cuffs, sobbing, his red hair covering his sweaty face.

When Kyle felt JT grab him around his waist, he struggled weakly, whimpering around the gag in his mouth. JT undid the cuffs, and caught Kyle easily before he slipped to the floor.

Kyle didn't resist when JT laid him on the bed. JT sat next to him, and pulled the gag from Kyle's mouth.

"Don't hurt me anymore," Kyle begged, between sobs. "I won't say no. I'll do what you say."

JT ran his fingers slowly through Kyle's hair, soothing his boy's tears. When Kyle's sobs had slowed to whimpers, JT pulled a small box out from under his bunk.

"You know what tonight is, baby?"

You mean besides the worst fucking night of my life? Kyle thought. "No."

His voice was hoarse from crying. His ass hurt so bad he wanted to sit in a tub of icy, cool water forever.

"You ain't gonna say to my cock no more, right?"

Kyle looked up at JT in a sudden panic. God. Now what?

"I'll do what you want," Kyle said, crying quietly. "I don't wanna get hit anymore."

"You know you're my girl, right?"

Kyle nodded quickly. "Yeah. I'm your girl."

Just when Kyle had made up his mind that tonight couldn't get any worse, JT's next words threw his shattered mind into chaos. "Now that you ain't got no more questions about that, I'm gonna make you my wife."

Kyle drew in a sharp breath. His conversation with Ryan came back in a rush.

"Your wife?" Kyle looked up at JT with wide green eyes.

"You wanna be my wife, right?"

Oh God, no, Kyle thought. He nodded, looking up into JT's hard eyes.

"Let me hear you say it, baby." JT caressed Kyle's tear stained face.

Kyle knew what was about to happen to him. The question flashed across his mind – w*hat's it worth?* "I wanna be your wife," he said slowly.

Kyle cringed inside when he saw JT's face break into a strange smile.

"I got you this." JT handed the small box to Kyle.

Kyle took the box. He knew what lay inside.

"It's your wedding present. Go on, boy." JT stroked Kyle's face softly. "Open it."

Kyle ripped away the neat wrapping. The look of shock on his face was genuine. He couldn't believe this was happening to him.

"I don't want my cock locked up, please?" Kyle said, looking down at the stone floor.

JT ran his fingers through Kyle's soft hair. "You'll like it, baby. You won't be worried no more about shit that ain't your business. And you won't be up to bad shit like jacking off when you ain't supposed to."

Kyle looked up at JT with hopeless eyes. "I don't want to."

JT looked steadily at Kyle. "Lay back. Spread your legs, boy."

Kyle thought of Ryan's warning about fighting back. He struggled with doubt for a long moment before he lay back and spread his legs. In a place like Purgatory, prices were real high.

JT opened the package, and took out the small pink cage that would fit around his boy's cock. Kyle couldn't bare to watch. He closed his eyes while JT imprisoned his cock.

Chapter 50

"That's beautiful," JT said when he was done. "Now when you suck cock or get it up the ass, you won't be thinking about how hard you're getting it or nothing else that ain't up to you. All you'll be thinking about is being a good wife for me."

JT got to his feet, looking at the pink cage between Kyle's legs.

"Bend over, bitch," he said. "Hands behind your back."

Kyle sat up on the edge of the bed. "You don't have to hurt me anymore." He looked up at JT earnestly. "I'll do what you say. Oh God, please. I hurt so bad."

"You best do what I say, boy." JT looked down at Kyle with hard, unforgiving eyes. He grabbed the belt and slid the leather across Kyle's shoulders. "Or you want more?"

Kyle dropped his head into his hands and cried miserably. He bent over, put his hands behind him. JT cuffed him and stepped back, looking at Kyle, bent over, his welted ass up, his dick in a pink cage.

JT undid his jeans and let them fall to the floor. His thick cock rose between his legs, swollen and pulsing with need. He grabbed Kyle's welted white ass tight in both his dark hands, pressing his hard cock to the outside of Kyle's hot little hole.

"Push back on my dick," JT said. "Show me how much you want my black cock up your bitch pussy."

Kyle hesitated, but only a moment, before he slowly pushed back onto JT's thick cock. He whimpered at the searing pain in his tight hole.

"Please," Kyle pleaded. He knew what was coming. "I'm sorry."

JT wrapped his strong, muscled arm around Kyle's waist, so the boy was trapped in the circle of his arm. He clamped his other hand tightly over Kyle's mouth.

"Here I come, bitch," JT said. "Now you'll see what happens when you says no to my cock."

He rammed savagely into Kyle's tight little hole. Kyle's scream was muffled by JT's hand over his mouth. He struggled desperately, but with his hands cuffed behind him, JT's arm around him kept Kyle pinned firmly in place. There was no escape from the cock pounding hard and fast into his ass.

JT slowed down, pulling his cock nearly all the way out before he sank into Kyle's ass again. Every time he slammed into Kyle's welted ass, JT ground his hips into the boy's sore flesh. The pain made Kyle's ass clench around JT's throbbing cock.

JT fucked Kyle in silence. His hard dick did all the talking Kyle needed to hear. The only sounds were Kyle's moans of pain and JT's hard body slamming into him, over and over. He fucked Kyle brutally, ramming his hard cock deep.

"It's so good fucking you like this, baby," JT said. "I love knowing your dick is all locked up while I'm fucking your bitch pussy."

JT was used to covering a boy's mouth when he fucked ass. He kept his hand firmly over Kyle's mouth, no matter how hard the boy struggled with him.

"You got a fucking good ass," JT said in a low, guttural voice.

JT loved the feel of Kyle's useless struggle. The sight of Kyle's welted, bruised ass writhing on his black cock, struggling against him, made JT crazy with lust. The more Kyle fought, the harder JT fucked his tight ass.

"Hurts, bitch?" JT said.

Kyle moaned in response.

"Good. Next time you feel like saying no to my dick up your bitch pussy, remember this."

He rammed his cock home with cruel lust that showed no mercy.

"Fucking bitch."

JT grabbed Kyle even harder, crushing the boy against him. He squeezed his eyes shut and groaned as his cock spasmed and filled Kyle's ass with hot come. He stroked into Kyle's trembling ass a few more times before he pulled out.

He undid the cuffs, and let Kyle roll over onto his side. JT ran cool water in the sink and cleaned Kyle's ass gently. When he was done, JT stood back, looking at Kyle, curled into a ball. His tears had slowed. He was staring at a point in space between the bed and JT's feet.

"You wanna sleep in my bunk tonight?" JT said, looking down at Kyle. "You can sleep in your bunk. I ain't gonna do nothing to you."

Kyle looked up at JT, afraid. Fresh tears came to his eyes. "I'll sleep wherever you say. I don't wanna get hurt anymore."

JT squatted, so he was on eye level with Kyle. "I ain't gonna beat you no more tonight. Tell me the truth. You wanna sleep in my bunk, yes or no?"

Kyle held JT's eyes, unflinching. Some prices were worth paying. "Yes."

That one word won JT's heart forever.

Kyle slid close to the wall, making room for JT beside him. JT slid into bed and wrapped his strong arms around Kyle, and pulled his boy close. Kyle cried quietly for a long time, resting his head against JT's wide chest.

"If I'm your girl, and I do what you say, I won't get hurt like that again, right?"

It made JT mad that Kyle would worry about what he would do to him. But he knew his bitch was scared, so he let it go.

"Be a good girl, and I won't hurt you like that."

"I'll be your wife." Kyle's hoarse voice was low and shaky.

JT held Kyle in silence for a long time, stroking the boy's hair gently.

"Kyle?"

JT felt him tense in his arms.

"Yeah?"

"Don't be worrying about shit that ain't your business no more. You heard me, boy?"

Kyle nodded in the semi-darkness. "I don't wanna get hit anymore," he said, trembling against JT.

JT smiled in the shadows. "Then don't fuck with me no more."

Kyle relaxed in JT's strong arms. His ass throbbed in pain. His throat hurt from crying. His body ached from struggling.

Laying there in the darkness, feeling JT's hard, muscled body pressed close to him, Kyle believed for a moment that he was utterly, completely safe. Then he remembered the Principal's low voice, the way he'd dropped his card at Kyle's feet and said not to make him wait.

Nagging thoughts circled in his head, barring Kyle from the comforting oblivion of sleep. What would JT do to him if he found out who Kyle was, and why he was really here in Purgatory?

Chapter 51

Kyle squirmed on the hard metal of the bench in the cafeteria, trying to get comfortable. His welted ass made it impossible. The cage felt weird around his cock. Kyle didn't know how, but somehow every man sitting at JT's table knew about last night. He even thought they knew about the pink cage between his legs.

Dante kept looking at Kyle, as if he wanted to say something. JT sat next to Kyle, eating and talking to the men across from them. Kyle kept his eyes on his plate, and lazily pushed around the brown stuff with lumps in it that was supposed to be beef stew.

"Why you ain't eating, boy?"

Kyle jumped at the sound of JT's voice. He looked up to find JT's dark eyes boring into him. His heart skipped a beat or two. Beads of sweat broke out on his forehead.

"Sorry." His voice trembled. "I'll eat. No problem."

He spooned the jelly like brown gravy into his mouth and resisted the urge to spew the disgusting mess back onto his plate.

"Congratulations, JT," a man said, walking by the table.

Something landed in front of Kyle with a solid thud. It was a box of imported chocolates. Kyle looked up at JT, puzzled.

"That's for you, baby."

Before Kyle could so much as ask why, another man walked by and threw more chocolate onto the table. This time it was a box of Belgian cookies. *What the hell?*

A steady stream of men walked by the table, dropping chocolates, gourmet pastries, cigarettes, even Marzipan. Some were gift wrapped, some weren't.

Twenty minutes later, Kyle had an embarrassingly big pile of goodies in front of him. There was barely room for his tray of food. He looked up at JT, a question in his eyes.

"Wedding presents, boy." JT stroked Kyle's face gently.

Kyle looked at Dante and the other men sitting at the table. He'd been right. They all knew about last night, and about that fucking cage around his dick. *Oh my God*, Kyle thought. *Can I just sink into the Earth now?*

"I got something for you, boy," Dante said to Kyle, "I'll give it to you later."

Kyle nodded blankly, staring at the pile of chocolates and pastries.

"They all know?" Kyle said softly.

"Course they know, boy." JT was smiling at Kyle; beaming, like a proud newlywed.

Kyle's bruised ass hurt more than ever. His eyes filled with tears. Last night had been a page out of his worse nightmare. The thought that just about every man in the prison knew what had been done to him was unbearable. Tears slipped down his cheeks as more men came by, dropping off more wedding gifts.

Looking at the pile of chocolates, feeling the bruises on his ass, made Kyle feel more trapped than any handcuffs JT could have used on him. This was what his life had become now. He'd been turned into JT's girl, his wife.

When JT wrapped his arm around Kyle and pulled him close, the boy fought to control himself. He barely resisted the urge to push JT away and scream into his face, *leave me alone! Haven't you done enough?*

"Don't cry, baby," JT said softly. "Ain't you happy to be my wife?"

Kyle looked up into JT's eyes and saw that he wasn't being malicious or playing some ugly mind game with him. He was serious.

"I wanna leave." Kyle looked down at his hands in his lap. "Please. I don't want them looking at me anymore."

JT looked at him a long time, his eyes turning hard. Although Kyle didn't know it, Dante saved him from a brutal honeymoon night.

"It ain't his fault." Dante's voice was calm, soothing. "The boy had a rough night. Let me take him to your house."

JT's dark eyes fell on Dante. Any other man would have feared for his life. But Dante held his gaze, until JT finally said, "Yeah. Take him."

Chapter 52

In JT's cell, Kyle lay on his top bunk, on his belly, playing a video game. He ignored Dante as if he didn't exist.

Dante leaned against the wall, watching Kyle. "Ain't you gonna thank me, boy?"

Kyle didn't look up at him. "For what?"

"Saving your ass. Again."

"What are you talking about?"

"JT was thinking bad things when you said that shit to him."

Kyle looked up from his game, fear coming into his eyes. "I didn't say *anything* to him." A note of desperation crept into Kyle's voice. "He wants to hurt me again? Why?"

"Take it easy, boy. He ain't gonna do nothing. You just got to learn how to be his wife, is all."

"How come he's mad?"

"Cause you didn't say you was happy to be his wife, in front of his men, like he wanted you to. You made him look bad."

Kyle turned pale. The welts on his ass hurt more than ever. "Is he gonna beat me again?"

Dante shook his head. "Not after what I said to him. If he beats you again tonight, he'll look real bad in front of his men. Honor's everything in here. It ain't honorable to beat on a bitch for fun."

Kyle ran his fingers through his hair, scattering it helter skelter. "I don't know anything anymore."

"No, you don't," Dante said. "And if you don't quit acting the fool, you're gonna be finding out some shit you wish you didn't know."

Kyle stared at the concrete floor, his game forgotten in his hands. "Does everyone know about last night?"

Dante jumped up easily onto Kyle's bunk and sat on the edge, his legs dangling down. "Yeah. Everyone knows you're JT's wife now and that he beat you real bad for fucking with him."

Dante saw the redness around Kyle's shadowed eyes. "What happened?" he said. "How come he beat you like that?"

Kyle shrugged. "JT doesn't take no for an answer."

"He made it bad for you, boy?"

Kyle nodded, unable to put last night's horror into words.

Dante leaned back on his powerful arms, looking down at Kyle. "How come you said no to him?"

Kyle wiped angrily at the tear that slid down his cheek. "Cause I was sick of my ass being sore all the time."

Dante sighed and leaned his head against the brick wall behind him. They were both silent for a while.

"You wanna tell me about it?" Dante said.

"No."

Dante shrugged. "Up to you. But sometimes talking about shit makes it better."

After a while, Kyle felt guilty. Dante was the only man in Purgatory who'd tried to help him. He turned off his game, sat up next to Dante, and started talking. He told Dante everything, starting with how he'd said no in the library.

"He treats me like I'm his property," Kyle finished. He squirmed on the bed, trying to find a spot on his ass that didn't hurt so bad.

"To JT, you *are* his property, boy. You got to get that through your head, or you're gonna get hurt real bad."

Kyle jumped down from the bunk, rubbing his ass. "I was thinking today," he said. He gave Dante a sideways glance, pacing the small cell.

"What was you thinking about?"

"Scales," Kyle said.

"What kind of scales, boy?"

Kyle held his arms out to both sides, like a man about to take flight. "The old fashioned kind, where you put something on one side, then you put something on the other side so it stays in balance."

Dante moved his big body on the bed, making it groan softly like a lost ghost.

Kyle dropped his arms. "In Purgatory, there's a price for everything. Last night I paid for not being JT's girl like he wants. You know what I'm really scared of?"

Dante saw the way Kyle's body stiffened, like a live wire with high voltage ramming through it. "What?" he said.

"I'm scared I'll piss him off so bad, he'll stop wanting me in his cell," Kyle said. "I'm young, not stupid. I saw that boy in the basement. I know how bad things could get for me."

"You got no idea, boy," Dante said. Then almost without a pause he said, "You like being JT's girl?"

Kyle leaned his head back against the cool wall. He could almost feel the Horsemen galloping behind him, chasing down a boy running away from secret things.

"He's the kind of man I always wanted," Kyle said. "It's just when I got wanted, it wasn't like how I thought it was gonna be."

"Sometimes," Dante said, "you got to pay for what you asked for."

Kyle felt the pink cage pressing against his cock. "I'm scared of him now. Real scared he'll do it again."

"He told you he was gonna do it again?"

"No. I don't know if I can be a good girl for him," Kyle said. "And even if I am, when he finds out what he bought, maybe he won't wanna pay the price."

"After last night, you know you're gonna have to give up whatever secrets you came in here with, right?"

Kyle said nothing. All at once, he found pieces of the model on his desk very interesting. Dante slid down from the bunk, and stood in front of Kyle, looking down at him.

"Let me tell you something about JT," Dante said. "Last night wasn't nothing but play time. When he wants to know, you're gonna tell him."

Kyle looked up at Dante. "You know what he put around my dick?"

Dante nodded, pretending not to notice that Kyle had changed the subject. "He does it to every punk he makes his wife."

"Is he gonna let me come?" The prospect of endless weeks ahead with his dick locked up, unable to get hard, desperate to come, was unbearable to Kyle.

"Yeah. He'll let you, sometimes. He likes you a lot."

"If he likes me so much, how come he's so bad to me in bed?"

Dante shrugged his big shoulders. "You're his girl. You should get fucked or open your mouth for his cock when he says so. There ain't no why, boy. I tried to tell you. That's just how he is."

"And he likes it to hurt when he fucks me sometimes, doesn't he?" Kyle looked down at the floor.

"Yeah, boy," Dante said softly. "But if you stop pissing him off, it ain't gonna be bad for you all the time."

"He's like a weird Dr. Jekyll and Mr. Hyde." Kyle walked past Dante to the cell bars, and looked out. "He's so different in the day time."

"Like who?"

"He's like two different men. As long as I let him treat me like a girl, he's good to me in the day time. He only fucks me for a little while. But at night, I get fucked hard sometimes, even when I do what he wants."

"Ain't there someplace where it's daytime for like, six months?"

Kyle laughed a little. "Yeah. But Alaska's cold as all shit."

"JT's the best he can be with you. Remember that. He had to try real hard not to put a serious hurting to you last night."

"But he did. What do you mean?"

"Look, boy. Me and JT been friends since before you was born. He wanted to beat the shit out of you for saying no to him."

Kyle grabbed Dante's thick arm, in a sudden agony of desperation. "What if I don't tell him what he wants to know?"

Dante pulled away and walked over to the model on Kyle's desk. He picked up a few pieces. They looked ridiculously small laying on the palm of his big hand.

"When he wants to know, you're gonna tell him, boy. JT can break you into so many pieces, ain't no doctor on Earth gonna glue you back together."

Kyle's thoughts swirled with untold secrets. He knew Dante was right. When JT found out he'd had been lying to him all along, there would be no dark corner of Purgatory where JT's fury wouldn't find him.

Chapter 53

Kyle carefully glued a piece onto the model plane's fuselage, thinking over the past two weeks. After JT belted Kyle and locked up his dick, life became simple. All his choices had been narrowed down to one: obey JT and be his wife or face another ass whipping.

On some nights he dreamed the Principal came and dragged him out of Purgatory. In his dreams, there were no choices. His screams started the second Kyle saw the locked iron door that he knew led to the back room with no windows.

"What you thinking about over there, boy?"

JT was laying on his bunk, flipping through a magazine.

Kyle shrugged. "Nothing much. How come you're always looking at those magazines? There's no words. What are you thinking about?"

"About fucking my wife's bitch pussy." JT flipped through the magazine, smoking.

"You're always thinking about that." Kyle glued another piece on place on the wing. "How come you're always looking at those?"

JT watched Kyle work for long moments before he answered. "I work real hard in here, baby. I ain't no big time international banker or nothing, but I work like a bitch all day long. Looking at this shit helps me think. Makes my mind go quiet, like."

Kyle was surprised, but he kept working. JT never talked to him about business.

"You mean working in the machine shop?"

"No. I mean deciding who's gonna die on Sunday."

Kyle looked up at JT, but he wasn't joking. He flipped through the magazine, smoking calmly.

"You have to decide that every Sunday?"

"No. Only when some fool fucks with me."

"Can I ask you something?"

JT nodded. "Anything, boy."

"Remember the Dark Game, when you said you'd kill Tyrone?"

"Yeah. Fucking punk."

"Would you really kill him if he came near me again?"

JT looked up at Kyle with narrow, suspicious eyes. "Why you asking me that shit?"

Kyle shrugged, working on the plane, keeping his hands steady. "Just wanna know, that's all. It's like another world in here."

"That ain't nothing for you to be asking me about, boy."

"Sorry. I didn't mean anything."

Kyle couldn't hide the way his hands shook. He desperately didn't want be on JT's bad side. Not this close to lights out.

"Don't be scared, boy. You ain't in no trouble with me."

The lights out warning buzzer sounded. Ten seconds later, the lights went out. That happened sometimes.

JT dropped his magazine. "Come here, baby."

Kyle slipped into bed with JT and relaxed into his lover's embrace. JT lay quietly, running his fingers through Kyle's silky hair until he felt his boy's breathing slip into the even rhythms of deep sleep.

He lay awake a long time, staring into the shadows of his cell. He knew his boy had secrets. And he knew eventually, he'd have to make Kyle tell him. Kyle turned in his sleep, and laid his head on JT's wide chest.

JT touched his boy's soft cheek, thinking about secrets. He hoped he wouldn't have to hurt Kyle too badly to get his boy to tell him the truth about why he'd landed in Purgatory.

Kyle's eyes snapped open. He lay completely still, listening for the sound that had called him back from sleep. It came again.

There was a low scratching by the bars, then, "Nero."

The secret name sounded so softly in the still darkness that it might have been the lingering thought of a dream. Kyle looked at JT. His chest rose slowly, his breathing deep and even. He slipped silently from the narrow bunk and knelt by the bars, grabbing the cold metal, looking out into the darkness.

A hand gripped his wrist. The touch was feverish and terrifying. Kyle barely bit back the scream that rose to his lips.

"No noise," a voice whispered urgently from the darkness. The man behind the voice was hidden in the shadows, against the wall beside the cell.

Kyle looked back at JT. He was still deep in the grip of sleep.

"What do you want?" Kyle whispered.

"Don't let them give JT the chip," the voice said. "You're the only one who can help him."

Kyle's heart hammered in his chest. "What are you talking about?"

"They're giving him a Nano chip. It's all set up. Don't let it happen."

Kyle's green eyes widened in surprise. "Nobody gets Nanos," he whispered. "You have to kill – like a whole army of kids or something. They're top of the line. For heavy hitters."

"Shut up and listen. And keep your voice down. Don't wake him up."

Kyle listened for something familiar in the voice, but he'd never it before.

"Tomorrow in the library," the voice whispered from the darkness, "get on a terminal, surf the waves, find him."

Surfing the waves was street talk for hacking a computer network. Who the hell was this? "I can't access –"

"Stop fucking around Nero," the voice hissed impatiently. "You and JT have to get out of Purgatory, or he's a dead man. They'll do it just to teach you a lesson."

Kyle's head was spinning. "Get out? How?"

"JT's got a plan to get out. But you can't let him get the chip. Or he's dead."

"They wouldn't kill a man just because of me."

"JT's just another con to them," the voice whispered. "They'll give him a chip, make him a pirate and get him killed the minute you say no again. You're the one they need. Tomorrow. In the library. Do it. They're waiting for you Nero. They'll get to you through JT."

"What the fuck you doing out of bed, boy?"

Kyle jumped at the sound of JT's deep voice. He froze, looking out into darkness. The hand on his wrist melted away, but Kyle heard no movement. The owner of the hand was still there, just out of sight, beside the cell.

JT sat up. "I'm talking to you, bitch."

"I had a bad dream." Kyle looked at JT.

"Who was you talking to?"

Kyle thought fast. "Mary."

JT was puzzled at hearing a woman's name. "Who?"

"I was praying." Kyle was already on his knees. He clasped his hands in the classic prayer position and bowed his head. "Hail Mary full of Grace, the Lord is with –"

"Get over here," JT said, irritated. "You can be saying that shit in bed."

Kyle rose to his feet fast, resisting the urge to look back over his shoulder. He heard tiny sounds just outside the cell, and knew the man behind the voice was escaping into the darkness.

When Kyle slipped into bed, JT wrapped his big arm around Kyle and smoothed his hair back from his sweaty brow. He felt how the boy's heart hammered in his chest.

"It was a real bad dream, boy?"

"Yeah."

"Don't let me wake up and find you out of bed like that again, hear?"

"Sorry," Kyle said, "the dream scared me."

"You got bad dreams, wake me up. Don't be up in the dark alone like that. What was you doing at the cell bars?"

"I dreamed about a monster on the tier." Kyle hoped JT wouldn't hear the lie behind his words. He shrugged. "I guess I was sort of looking to see if my dream monster was for real."

"The only monsters you got to worry about in here go on two legs."

"I know," Kyle said, almost to himself.

He closed his eyes, willing his hammering heart to slow down. Would the Principal really have JT killed, just to force to Kyle work for them? Thinking of the way the man's cold hard eyes glittered like dead marbles, with no human soul behind them, Kyle knew the answer.

Chapter 54

"Hey, bitch."

With a silent sigh, Kyle turned to face Tyrone. "What do you want?"

"I don't want nothing bitch. I'm just saying hey."

"You said it yesterday and the day before and the day before that. One day JT's gonna catch you."

Tyrone shrugged, drawing closer to Kyle. "Some things are worth fighting for." He raised a hand to touch Kyle's face, but Kyle batted his big hand away.

"Stop it. Didn't you hear him? He'll fucking kill you if he finds you near me. Leave me alone. Stop acting like an idiot."

"How come you ain't told him about me and you?"

"There's no me and you." Kyle looked up at Tyrone, frustration rising in his voice. "There's just you being stupid."

"You ain't told him nothing. You must be liking me coming around." Tyrone pressed too close to Kyle. "You need a real man to fuck that hot little hole now that you ain't a virgin no more?"

Kyle shook his head. "Go away."

Kyle turned to go, but Tyrone grabbed his arm and spun him around. "I'm gonna have your ass bitch," he said in a low vicious voice. "And you ain't gonna see it coming."

He let go and faded into the darkness of the stacks. Kyle watched him go, feeling scared for the first time since Tyrone had started sneaking into the library to see him.

Tyrone had never acted like that before. Kyle thought about telling JT, then decided against it, remembering the night he'd asked JT about it. Tyrone was just talking shit. He didn't deserve to die for being stupid.

Kyle went back to shelving book discs neatly on the towers at the ends of the stacks. While he slipped the discs back in place, he looked around, making sure this part of the library was deserted. When he didn't see or hear anyone for about five minutes, he sat at the terminal that was set up to access the library's card catalog and thousands of downloadable law books.

Kyle glanced over his shoulder, scanning the stacks one more time. No one was around. Even if someone saw him, he was just another prisoner using the library card catalog. There was no access to the internet from here. But of course, for a hacker like Kyle, the internet was always just a few keystrokes away.

Kyle's face settled into deep concentration. His fingers flew over the keys. He bypassed safeguards that would have defeated men twice his age. A few more keystrokes, and he was out of the library system. No sweat. Now the hard part – finding JT.

Kyle surfed the networks. Zeroes and ones and hundreds of unidentifiable symbols flowed across the screen in seeming gibberish. Kyle navigated the sea of encrypted data, his fingers flowing across the keys almost without thought, until finally, he found what he was looking for.

He tapped a few more keys and JT's picture came up on the screen along with his records. Kyle clicked the link called "Recent", and settled down to read.

Fifteen minutes later, Kyle backed out of the encrypted system, covering any tracks he might have made going in. In moments, his window on the world was a dull eye, staring back at Kyle with the idiot question, "More books?" blinking across the bottom of the screen. To be safe, Kyle turned off the computer and let it reboot before he left the station.

Why would JT let them give him a Guardian Chip? Kyle knew that one of the few civil rights still left was the right to say no to twenty four hour surveillance. After prisoner experiments became public knowledge, Congress passed hard laws that protected prisoners. The most dangerous elements in society were also the most protected from twenty four hour surveillance by the state. The system couldn't inject JT unless he signed a consent form. Why would he do that?

Kyle had way too many questions, and nearly no answers. How did his visitor last night know about the chip? Who the hell was he?

Later, straightening the shelves, the pieces came together in Kyle's mind. The plan to put Kyle in JT's cell had fallen through. Instead of yanking him out, they were planning to use JT to force Kyle into doing what they wanted.

Now Kyle understood the look in JT's eyes when they'd talked about the pirates. Someone had made JT an offer to be a pirate that he couldn't refuse. And after they gave him the chip, unless Kyle did exactly what he was told, JT would be a walking dead man.

PART THREE
Chapter 55

"Tonight's your big night, baby," JT said.

Kyle was sitting on JT's bunk, beside him. Dante was standing by the cell bars, waiting for them.

"If I do what you want, I won't get hurt, right?"

Dante turned around. "I'll be there, boy. I won't let him do nothing bad to you." He winked at Kyle, trying to make a bad night better.

Kyle sighed. "Can't we just send out wedding announcements or something?" He looked up at JT, and saw his patience wearing thin. "It was a joke. I'll do what you say. I just wanna ask you for one thing."

"What?"

Kyle had been thinking about Taylor since he'd talked to Ryan in the basement. Tonight would be a good night to try and help him.

"I'll tell you afterwards. But you promise you'll do it for me, if I let everyone see I'm your wife now?"

JT nodded. "I'll let you ask for a favor, if you act right."

Kyle looked down at his fingers, twisting together in his lap. He would have done anything to avoid the wedding party coming up tonight.

"Why does it have to be like this? Doesn't everyone know I'm your wife now?"

JT got up, took out his cigarettes and lit up. "Talk to him," he said to Dante. "Before I got to hurt him real bad."

Dante took JT's place next to Kyle. "Just do it, boy. Don't think about it, 'cause there ain't nothing you can do about it."

"I don't want them all looking at me like that." Kyle snapped a nervous look at JT's tense back. He whispered to Dante, "I'll be embarrassed. All those men seeing me like that."

Dante glanced up at JT. "Remember how he belted your ass?"

Kyle nodded.

"If you don't do this, he'll do it again. Only this time, in the Clubhouse, with everyone watching. You want that, boy?"

Kyle laced his trembling fingers together in his lap. "I just wanna leave when it's over. Can I at least have that much?"

Dante raised his voice, talking to JT. "He wants to leave when we're done with him."

JT nodded, not turning around. "I ain't gonna talk about it no more. He's my bitch, my wife. I ain't making him do nothing bad. I ain't gonna hurt him." He turned around and looked right at Kyle. "Unless he pisses me off."

———————————

Loud, drunken laughter echoed all around Kyle. On holo, men wrestled, but the gladiators hardly paid attention. Shadows jumped on the rough stone walls of the Clubhouse as shirtless men, thick with hard muscle, made their way through the hazy gloom.

Fat, midnight blue candles burned on beer kegs, casting uncertain light, dripping waxy tears. The sunken fire pits burned, sending orange sparks spiraling up into the depthless darkness overhead.

The low sound of men fucking came from all around in the shadowy darkness. Kyle was chained naked to a metal table near one of the beer kegs. Black metal cuffs held his hands and feet in place. Short chains ran from the cuffs to the corners of the table, forcing him to kneel on all fours with his legs spread wide.

Men came and went, filling plastic cups with beer. They leered at Kyle, rubbed their crotch, looked at his smooth, white ass in the shadowy light. Some men stopped to make bets with Dante, who was standing next to Kyle.

When nobody was close, Dante whispered things to Kyle.

"You're gonna like me fucking your pretty ass, boy," Dante said, stroking Kyle's ass. "Be a good bitch. Don't do nothing stupid, hear?"

Kyle saw JT a few feet away, in the middle of a group of laughing men. He knew what would happen if he did anything stupid.

"I just want it over," Kyle said.

Over at the card table, six gladiators – shirtless black men bulging with muscle – played Poker. Kyle saw Taylor, the gang whore, under the table, with a dark cock deep in his throat, stretching his pretty red lips.

Beyond the card table, a naked blonde boy was bent over a beer keg. A black man was sliding his thick cock slowly in and out of the moaning boy's pretty round ass. Further back in the shadows, Kyle heard soft whimpering and men grunting and groaning as they had their way with someone's bitch.

Tonight's celebration was a double honor for JT. He had been officially been awarded the Regional Championship medal just a few hours ago on holovision. In a little more than two weeks, JT and three other champion gladiators from prisons around the country would fight and bleed, in The Maze, here in Purgatory's arena. The second half of the celebration was JT's wedding night, Kyle's official introduction to JT's men as his new wife.

Chapter 56

Kyle had heard the men talking about 'Beat the Clock'. Dante was going to fuck him while Kyle sucked JT's cock. Kyle tried to shut out the sound of men betting on how long it would take him to come with two black cocks inside him.

"Look at this bitch," a deep voice said behind him. Kyle felt a finger slide into his ass. It felt so good. He couldn't help but wriggle a little. He needed to come so bad. "You feel how his ass grabs your finger. No way he's lasting fifteen minutes."

Gladiators with chiseled bodies, naked to the waist, hung around Kyle, drinking beer, fingering him. Some of them asked Dante how he was gonna like humping Kyle's sweet ass.

Low moans of pleasure made Kyle look up. Over on the couch, Derrick was naked. Ryan was on all fours between his legs, sucking his cock.

"Oh yeah, bitch," Derrick lifted his hips. "That's it. Swallow my dick. Take it deep."

Two men stood on either side of Derrick, stroking their dick, watching while Ryan choked on Derrick's cock. Even in candlelight, Kyle could see how their hard bodies rippled with muscle.

"Go on," Derrick said to them, "fuck my bitch while he's sucking me."

One of the men knelt behind Ryan and grabbed his hips in his big hands. He sank his thick cock into the boy's ass hard and fast, ramming deep into Ryan. Kyle saw his eyes squeeze shut in pain.

"Shit," the man said, fucking Ryan, grinding his hips into him. "Good tight pussy."

Derrick twisted Ryan's nipples hard, making him moan around his cock.

"Oh hell yeah," the man fucking Ryan said, "this bitch's pussy's grabbing my cock real good."

"See how hard he's getting it, boy?" Dante whispered into Kyle's ear. "You don't want nothing like to happen to you. Don't fuck with JT tonight."

Kyle tried not to show how scared he was about tonight. He didn't want JT to look over and think he wasn't acting right. He glanced over at the couch.

Ryan's head was buried in Derrick's lap, his thick cock stretching his lips to the limit. The man behind Ryan stroked into his ass a few more times, before he got up, and let the other man take his place.

More men came and went, fingering Kyle, making bets. JT hadn't let Kyle come in a long, long time. Every time a man's finger slid into his hungry ass, Kyle squirmed; sometimes he moaned a little, helpless to stop himself.

A thick finger slid into Kyle's ass. He arched his back, knowing he was lifting his ass like a bitch in heat. "With JT and Dante on him? This bitch won't last ten minutes," a man said behind Kyle.

Another gladiator fingered Kyle. His ass grasped at the thick finger inside him. Kyle felt the finger slide in and out, making his cock rock hard.

"Shit. This ass is good and ready to get fucked. Nine minutes," the man said, pulling his finger out.

With Dante up his ass and JT in his mouth, Kyle knew he would come in front of these men, and they'd all know he was JT's girl. A part of him thrilled at that feeling, remembering how JT had fought to win him in the Dark Game. Another part of him wished he could make the earth open up and swallow him after he came.

Kyle looked over at Ryan. Both men were taking turns fucking Ryan while he sucked Derrick's hard dick. Watching, Kyle hoped JT wouldn't change his mind about letting him leave when it was over.

"Watch this," a deep voice said behind Kyle.

A thick, lubed finger slid into Kyle's ass. He squirmed on the table, his face tuning bright red, knowing that anyone who saw the way he lifted his ass would know how badly he needed to be used.

"You had dogs before?" The man fingered Kyle slowly, gliding in and out of his pulsing hole while he talked. Kyle pushed his ass up and back, unable to stop himself. "See how he puts his ass up like a bitch ready to get fucked? With Dante dicking him, and JT in his mouth, ain't no way this bitch's lasting more than fifteen minutes."

Men slid their fingers in and out of Kyle, while Dante stood next to the table with a small notebook, writing down names, taking bets, taking money. Kyle hung his head, waiting for JT and Dante, knowing his swollen cock would jet hot come onto the table before the night was over.

"Time." Dante snapped the notebook shut. "No more bets."

Men gathered close around the table, eager to see the show. JT pushed through the crowd and stood in front of Kyle. A man grabbed Kyle's ass gently. That must be Dante. Kyle didn't want to lift his head and look back. He might meet the eyes of some other man. Kyle couldn't bear the thought of these men looking at him, seeing his swollen cock, how his body was tense with need.

"I'm gonna give you some real good black dick," Dante said, running his dark hands slowly over Kyle's creamy white ass.

Kyle was desperately horny. It felt good to be free of the pink cage JT kept locked around his cock nearly all the time. Kyle's dick was hard and throbbing, dripping pre-come. All the time he'd spent without coming made his cock feel like exploding. When Dante pressed the thick head of his lubed cock to Kyle's hungry hole, he couldn't help but push back on the big black dick waiting to slide into him.

"Look at that bitch," a man near Kyle said. "Told you. He won't last ten minutes."

As Dante slid into Kyle's hot ass, the men around the table made catcalls, told Kyle to move his ass and take it like a bitch.

"Ram his ass good and hard Dante."

"JT got a fucking hot wife."

JT's dark eyes watched Dante's black cock sliding into his boy's pretty white ass, stroking Kyle's face softly.

"You want my dick in your mouth, baby?" JT said, looking down into Kyle's green eyes.

Kyle pushed back so that his round ass pressed into the hardness of Dante's flat belly. His hard cock felt so good up his ass.

"Yeah," Kyle said, looking up at JT.

"Beg for it." JT looked at the men standing around, smiling. "Show everyone how you're a bitch for black cock since I made you my wife."

Kyle turned beet red. The men gathered around the table fell silent, watching him take Dante up his ass, and writhing like a bitch, waiting for him to beg for a black cock deep down his throat.

He knew if he didn't do what JT wanted, he'd end up screaming and begging for mercy in front of these men.

Chapter 57

"Please." Kyle pushed back on Dante's cock.

"Please what, baby?" JT looked around at the men watching, and laughed with them. "What you want, bitch?"

Dante was riding Kyle's ass deep and slow, driving him crazy. He pushed back to meet every stroke, feeling the eyes of all the men on him. He couldn't stop himself. Dante's dick felt so good.

"Tell me, baby." JT rubbed his hard dick along Kyle's pink lips, leaving a smear of pre-come. "Tell me what little white bitch boys like you need."

"JT's wife got a pretty mouth. Bet he sucks real good and deep," a man behind Kyle said.

Kyle licked JT's pre-come from his lips and said, "I wanna suck your cock." He dropped his head, writhing on Dante's cock, taking him deep in his ass.

"I can't hear you, boy. You wanna suck black cock like a bitch?" The men watching laughed.

The crowd of men pressed closer. Kyle could almost feel them breathing on him. A man beside him took out his dick and started jacking off next to Kyle's face. "You know you want that big black cock in your mouth, bitch," he said.

"Come on, boy." JT held his hard dick just out of reach of Kyle's lips. "Tell me what you want or we'll all fuck up your ass."

"I wanna suck black dick like a bitch. I want a load," Kyle said. He pushed back on Dante's thick cock, squirming his pretty ass.

Smiling at the men around him, JT said, "Open your mouth, baby. I'm gonna give you what little bitch boys like you need."

Kyle opened his mouth wide for JT's cock. JT slid into his boy's mouth, moaning softly.

Kyle writhed and moaned, feeling the two black cocks inside him. Pleasure roared through him every time Dante's dick slid across his pleasure spot up his ass. Kyle squirmed on the metal table, his hard dick throbbing, his balls heavy with come.

Voices came out of the shadowy darkness, urging on JT and Dante.

"Ride that bitch, Dante. Give it to him hard and deep."

"Fucking slut's loving all that black dick."

Kyle was deaf to the catcalls around him. JT was fucking his mouth just how he liked it.

He used Kyle's mouth in slow deep strokes, burying his cock nearly to the balls in his mouth, letting Kyle choke a little before he pulled out and left just the head of his cock in his mouth. Kyle ran his tongue slowly over the head of JT's cock, then pressed his head down, wanting to take him deep again.

"Seven minutes," someone called out.

"Look at that bitch suck dick."

The man jacking off next to Kyle watched JT's dark cock sink deep into the boy's pretty mouth again and again. "Bitch loves choking on black meat," he said.

Kyle writhed on the table, whimpering, his round white ass humping Dante's black cock. His felt his tight hole pulsing around Dante's hard dick.

"How you liking JT's wife?" a man called out.

"Fucking bitch got a hot pussy," Dante said, pumping Kyle's ass.

Kyle found himself caught in a desperate rhythm, pushing back to take Dante's cock deeper inside him, then pressing forward to take JT's cock down his throat. Kyle moved his ass in desperate little circles, moaning while he took JT's cock.

"Eleven minutes," a man yelled. "Looks like the bitch is real close."

JT pulled out of Kyle's mouth. "Is he fucking you real good, bitch?"

"Yeah," Kyle said, writhing on Dante's pumping cock.

JT signaled to Dante and he pulled out of Kyle's ass.

"Move that ass around, baby. Show us how bad you need black dick in your little bitch hole," JT said.

Kyle flushed deep red. "Please," he whispered. "Don't make me."

JT looked down at Kyle with pitiless eyes. "Do it, bitch. Or we'll fuck you real hard and make you scream."

"Yeah JT," a greedy voice said out of the shadows. "Make your bitch scream."

"Yeah. Even better than seeing the punk come," someone else said.

Kyle knew this could turn ugly in about two seconds. Looking up into JT's black eyes, he writhed his white ass in slow little circles, like he was humping the best cock of his life.

"That's it bitch," JT said, "show us how you love a black cock up your tight fuck hole."

Dante slapped Kyle's ass and teased him, pressing his hard cock to Kyle's hot hole, but not fucking him.

JT dug his fingers deeper into Kyle's soft, red hair. "Push back on that dick. Show my friends what a bitch I made you into." His voice was hard and unyielding. Kyle knew what would happen if he disobeyed.

As Kyle pushed back, feeling Dante's hard cock sinking into him, filling his hungry ass, JT slid his dick into Kyle's mouth. He looked up into JT's hard eyes.

"Good bitch. I'm gonna give you what you want. You're gonna get my load when you shoot. I'm waiting on you."

Kyle felt JT's cock throbbing in his mouth, and knew JT was holding back so he could give Kyle what he loved most – to take JT's load while he shot his come.

Knowing JT was going to do that made Kyle desperate. He humped Dante's cock faster, circling his narrow hips, pushing back onto Dante's driving dick.

JT moved closer, thrusting his hips in shorter, faster strokes. He twisted his powerful fingers deeper into Kyle's silky red hair, holding his face up, looking down into his bitch's eyes.

"Yeah, bitch," JT said. "You're gonna shoot your come like a girl, just from getting fucked and sucking dick."

"Fifteen minutes," a voice called out.

But Kyle was beyond hearing anything like that. The chains on the table rattled as Kyle rocked back and forth, taking Dante's black cock deep in his white ass while JT pumped his mouth hard.

JT twisted Kyle's nipples hard, making him moan in ecstasy. Dante groaned in pleasure as Kyle's ass clamped down on his cock again and again.

"Good pussy," Dante said, in a strained voice.

Dante spread his muscled legs and drove deep into Kyle's hot, quivering hole.

Dreadlocks fell across his sweaty face. Sweat dripped down his muscled chest and fell on Kyle's writhing ass. His cock throbbed and ached. His heavy balls slammed into Kyle's squirming ass on every stroke.

JT looked down at Kyle's round white ass writhing on Dante's pumping black cock.

Seeing Kyle take Dante up his ass, writhing and moaning like a bitch, while his cock was buried deep in his throat, drove JT wild.

Pleasure rocketed through Kyle. He felt Dante's thick cock swollen inside him, felt him throbbing against the walls of his ass. He knew Dante was about to come in his ass.

"Look at that bitch take it," a man said. "He's fucking hot."

Kyle bucked his hips uncontrollably. The chains rattled, Dante sank his cock deep into his throbbing, pulsing ass. JT grabbed Kyle's hair tighter, looking down into his eyes. He pulled out of Kyle's mouth.

"You know what you got to say," JT said.

"I'm your girl," Kyle said, looking up into JT's eyes. He bucked and writhed on Dante's driving cock.

JT slapped Kyle's face. "Louder, bitch."

"I'm your girl," Kyle cried out, wild with lust.

JT drove his cock deep down Kyle's throat again, while Dante fucked Kyle's writhing ass. Kyle bucked his hips again and felt his balls tighten.

"Yeah, bitch, that's it," Dante said. "Come like a girl."

"You're my fucking girl," JT said, through clenched teeth and let go his load, filling Kyle's throat with hot come. He timed it just right so Kyle took his load as he jerked his hips and shot come onto the metal table, looking up into JT's eyes. *I own you,* his eyes said.

Dante moaned and grunted in pleasure as his cock exploded and pumped hot come deep inside Kyle's pulsing ass.

"Time. Eighteen minutes," a voice called out.

The men fell away to celebrate with the winner.

Kyle knelt on the table, his mouth covered with JT's come. JT looked down into Kyle's tear filled eyes and felt his cock coming to life again. Dark desire roared through JT. His cock was half hard again. He wanted to shove Dante out of the way, grab Kyle's hips and ram his thick black cock deep into his bitch's ass.

Chapter 58

Dante saw the dark lust in his friend's eyes. "You said he could go when we was done with him," he said.

" I wanna go," Kyle said, looking down at the table, feeling come drip from his ass. "Please."

JT closed his eyes a second, regaining control of himself. He caressed Kyle's soft cheeks tenderly. "Alright, baby."

Dante helped JT undo the cuffs. JT slipped his t-shirt over Kyle. It dropped almost to the boy's knees.

JT kissed Kyle's soft cheek. "Good girl. Take him, Dante."

Dante had already slipped back into his jeans. Kyle slid off the table and let Dante take his hand.

"Where you taking that hot bitch man?" a man said to Dante.

"Past his bed time," Dante said and kept walking.

They made their way through the men. Kyle kept his eyes on the stone floor. He wished he could scream at all of them, *stop looking at me!* No one watched as Dante led Kyle out of the dark cave of the Clubhouse.

In the back of the Clubhouse, a tiny alcove had a black curtain pulled across it. A small cot had been set up in there. This was where men who wanted an hour with Taylor came to use his ass in privacy. Kyle lay down on the narrow cot and curled up into a ball.

He didn't know how he felt. He'd always wanted to be a girl for a man like JT. But sometimes when you get what you wish for, it's nothing like what you thought.

Dante sat next to the boy, saying nothing, rubbing Kyle's back gently. JT walked in and took in the scene.

"I'll stay with him a while. Thanks, man."

"He did good. Give him what he wants," Dante said quietly.

JT nodded and took Dante's place on the narrow cot beside Kyle

"Sorry I cried," Kyle said, his back to JT. "Are you mad at me?"

"You did real good, baby."

Kyle turned and faced JT. "You said if I did this for you, I could have a favor."

"Anything, baby." JT smoothed Kyle's coppery hair back from his tear stained face.

"Anything?" Kyle looked up at him.

JT nodded. "Anything. Except I ain't letting you stay with your dick hanging out. I'm locking you up again."

"It's not that."

"You don't want me to fuck you for a while? You want me to come in your mouth instead?"

Kyle shook his head. JT waited patiently.

"You promise not to beat anyone?"

JT's eyes turned narrow with suspicion. "What you up to, boy?"

"Do you?"

JT thought it over before he said, "Yeah. I promise. What is it?"

"Taylor wants to talk to you."

"Why he ain't come to me?"

"He's afraid you'll beat him up."

JT raised his voice. "Dante. Get in here."

When Dante appeared in the doorway, holding back the curtain, JT said, "Get Taylor."

JT made Kyle lay back and locked the pink cage around his cock while he waited for Taylor. By the time the boy walked in, Kyle had on his jeans. JT was standing beside him.

Taylor stood in front of JT, naked except for tight denim shorts that barely covered his round ass. His brunette hair hung down to his shoulders. In the stuttering candlelight, his red lips were full and inviting.

"You wanted to see me?" Taylor said quietly, his eyes on the floor.

"No, bitch. You wanted to see me," JT said.

The boy paled at JT's words. Taylor glanced at Kyle. "I didn't complain about nothing, Sir. I do what you tell me."

"It's okay," Kyle said. "Tell him. He said he won't hit you."

Taylor looked up at JT, and took a couple of steps backward, shaking his head. "I got nothing to say."

JT looked at Kyle, impatience in his dark eyes.

"Could you give us a minute?" Kyle said. JT said nothing. "Please?"

JT rolled his eyes. "Five minutes. I ain't got all night for this bitch bullshit."

He stalked out of the small alcove. Taylor nearly tripped over his own feet getting out of JT's way.

———————————

"Didn't Ryan tell you I'd get him to talk to you?"

Taylor nodded.

"Why didn't you tell him?"

"I can't."

"What do you mean, you can't? I got him to say he wouldn't hit you. Just tell him. All he can do is say no."

"Can't you tell him for me?"

Kyle shook his head. "I can't. He'll beat me. I can't get involved in business. He only let me do this 'cause he promised me a favor after I let him and Dante fuck me like that."

Taylor looked at Kyle, desperation in his brown eyes. He bit his lip before he said, "What if I end up like Jessi?"

"You won't. He keeps his word," Kyle said. "But when he gets back, you gotta tell him. He's getting pissed. He'll just send you back out there."

JT walked in and leaned against the alcove wall, looking at Taylor. "I'm waiting, bitch."

"I wanted to ask you if –" Taylor stopped. He seemed to be choking. Beads of sweat popped out on his face and trickled down his cheeks.

JT walked by him, ignoring the way the boy skittered out of his way, and sat on the cot, next to Kyle.

"Whatever it is, boy, I ain't gonna beat you. Yes or no. That's all you gonna get."

Taylor looked at JT, uncertainty written all over his pale, sweaty face.

"I don't wanna be the gang slut anymore. Please." Tears stood in his eyes. "It's real bad for me. They fuck me real hard and hurt me."

JT looked at Kyle with cold eyes. "What the fuck you doing in my business, boy?"

"You said I could ask for anything." Kyle looked down at his trembling hands. "All I asked is if you would see him."

JT stood up and looked down at Kyle and Taylor, both silent and afraid. They both jumped when JT raised his voice and called for Dante again.

"When's fresh meat coming in?" JT said to Dante when he pushed past the curtain.

"Two weeks," Dante said.

"You sure?"

Dante nodded. "A real pretty blonde bitch's coming."

"Three weeks," JT said to Taylor. "After that, you get sold."

"There's something else," Taylor said.

JT saw the boy's hands shaking. "What?"

Taylor fell to his knees at JT's feet.

"You ain't got to do that with me, boy," JT said quietly.

"There's a gladiator I don't want to be sold to." Taylor looked up at JT. "Please?"

"Who?"

Taylor bit his lip, unable to find the courage to go on. He turned so pale, JT thought the boy was going to faint.

JT crouched down so he was nearly on eye level with Taylor. "Talk to me, boy. Who is it?"

"Derrick," Taylor said in a low whisper. The tears he'd been holding back slipped down his cheeks. "Anybody but him."

JT got up and pulled the trembling boy to his feet. "Stop crying, bitch. You ain't gonna end up with him, alright?"

Taylor nodded. He looked at Kyle. "I don't know what to say. Thanks."

JT looked at Dante with mild disbelief on his dark face. "What you thanking him for? He ain't done nothing."

"If it wasn't for Kyle, I would have killed myself. I wouldn't have had the guts to come to you."

The quiet certainty in Taylor's calm voice shocked JT. He knew the boy wasn't bluffing.

"You ain't got to be scared to come to me, boy. I ain't gonna beat you just 'cause I don't like what you ask me for. Understand?"

Taylor nodded, but he wouldn't look at JT.

"Three weeks," JT said. "You can wait that long?"

Taylor nodded again, looking down at the stone floor. "Thanks for listening to me."

"Go on," JT said to the boy, but there was no threat in his voice. "Go make me some money."

Dante followed Taylor out.

JT turned on Kyle. "You ever get in my business again, I'll belt your bitch ass real bad. Got me?"

Kyle nodded. JT reached for Kyle, but he shrank back against the stone wall.

"I ain't mad at you, boy. You wanna see what the roof looks like?"

Chapter 59

Purgatory was carved out of a massive cliff that overlooked the ocean. The roof of the prison was the plateau of the great stone that had been carved away to make Purgatory.

Kyle loved it up here. He felt free. He felt like he could outrun the terrible shadow that was falling across his life. Up here, he could believe that the Principal might not come for him. Was being JT's girl all that bad? Another question, the same question, followed on the heels of that. *What's it worth?*

The light of a full moon beat a silver path across the restless waves that crashed far, far below.

"You like it up here, baby?" JT said.

"It's awesome." Kyle said. He looked around uneasily. "You sure they won't shoot us or something?"

"I wouldn't bring you up here if it wasn't safe."

JT was leaning back against a stone wall, looking out at the silvery water. Kyle sat between JT's legs, nestled close to him. JT's thick arms were wrapped around his slender body.

"You don't get sick eating all this shit, boy?"

Kyle shook his head, and opened his mouth to take another pastry.

"You know how come I brought you up here?" JT said.

Kyle shook his head. "'Cause I'm in trouble?" he said uncertainly. "Because of Taylor?"

"No. You got something to tell me."

All at once Kyle felt like he'd been turned to stone, and any second JT's fury would come crashing into him like a wrecking ball. "What do you mean?" he said in a low voice.

"You know what I mean, baby," JT said. "I been waiting for you to come to me on your own. But I can't wait no more. You came in here with secrets. You're my wife now. I wanna know what you was gonna tell me the night of the blackout."

"What if I don't want to tell you?" Kyle's heart thumped hard and fast, banging against his ribs.

"Then I'll take you down in the basement and beat you and rape you 'til you tell me what I wanna know." JT's voice was eerily calm. He kissed the side of Kyle's neck gently. "Don't make me hurt you like that, boy."

Kyle was quiet for a long time. He looked out over the water, watching the rise and fall of the moonlit waves. JT waited in silence.

Kyle took a deep breath, and said, "They put me in here because I'm Nero."

"Who?"

"Not who," Kyle said, "what."

JT ran his fingers through Kyle's hair, slowly. "You talking in riddles, boy. What's Nero?"

"Remember three years ago when all the banks went down, nobody could get money out of machines or buy stuff at the stores, 'cause the terminals were all down?"

JT nodded. "Yeah." A hint of a smile touched his hard face. "That was pretty sweet."

"Nero was the virus that brought the government to its knees," Kyle said. "I designed the program that did it, sent it out on the 'net, and gave it my online name: Nero."

"Shit, boy, you couldn't have been more than a baby."

"They got pretty mad. When they found me, they injected me with a Guardian Chip."

"How you do that, boy? How you make all them computers stop like that?"

Kyle shrugged. "I like solving puzzles. Like how I build the models. It's fun for me. Anyway, the government, they wanted me to work for them. I told them to fuck off."

"How come?"

"They want me to do bad things," Kyle said in a low frightened voice. He leaned back against JT's solid chest, feeling like a man hiding from a hurricane behind a paper wall.

"Like what?"

"Fix HAARP."

"A harp?" JT said, puzzled. "Like what angels play?"

"No. Angels don't play this harp." Kyle spelled it out for JT.

"What the fuck is that?"

"A giant array of about a hundred and eighty antennas on around thirty three acres of land up on top of the world in Gakona, Alaska."

"What's it for?"

"Supposed to be for communication, in case the satellites that link all the countries go down."

JT looked down at the top of Kyle's head. "You fucking with me, boy? They put you in here 'cause you won't fix a giant cell phone?"

"No," Kyle said. "It's *not* a cell phone. That's the cover story the government puts out. It's a weapon."

"What can it do?"

"It's unconventional. It can damp all the energy fields over a widely dispersed area."

"What?"

"Blackouts. It can black out a whole country. No electricity anywhere, all at the same time."

"What the fuck kind of weapon is that?"

"Imagine a whole country goes dark, all at the same time. People in hospitals on equipment – dead. No traffic lights. No alarms. No phones."

"Holy shit," JT said.

"No communications. No electricity to pump water. And it's not just electricity. It damps *energy* fields. No cars, no cell phones, no electrical anything. It spells instant chaos."

"You mean over there, in the war?"

Kyle nodded. "Yeah. It would cripple a country instantly. Thousands would die in riots, burnings. Cops wouldn't be able to help anyone with phones down, their cars standing still, and no radios to talk to each other. It's serious shit."

"Why they don't just do it, then? Zap it, and get it done."

"Our country doesn't own the array. It's owned by us and a whole bunch of other countries in the UN. We would need permission from the other countries in the UN, or we'll be in the war by ourselves."

"What's the UN?"

Until tonight, Kyle didn't realize how little JT knew about world politics. "It's kind of like your council in here."

"A gang of gangs?"

Kyle laughed a little. "Close enough."

"What do they want with you?"

"They want me to use HAARP to do something horrible. Probably a blackout over there in the war. Or whoever pissed them off this time. If they get some hacker kid like me to do it, they can say they don't know who did it. Then I'd have to work for them forever or they'd suddenly discover I did it and put me in prison the rest of my life."

"Damn. That's fucked up."

"It gets worse."

"How?"

"They want me to fix HAARP 'cause I'm the one who broke it when I hacked in."

Chapter 60

"After you said you wouldn't work for them? Why you done that?" JT said. "You crazy?"

Kyle shrugged. "I didn't mean to. I was playing around with the codes. I didn't think it would work. It's not my fault their security sucks."

"Fuck," JT said in a low voice. "What you done to their shit, boy?"

"I scrambled the uplink code."

"What?"

Kyle thought for a moment, then he said, "I broke the connection. They can't talk to HAARP."

"So? Why they can't just turn it back on?"

"They don't know how. At least not the way it was before."

Kyle stopped talking for a while. "I was scared as shit the night I cracked HAARP." He took JT's big hand in his cold trembling hands. "I can turn off the eye in the sky for a little while. I ran and hid in a basement. I tried like hell to bring HAARP back online, but I couldn't."

"And now they want you to fix what you broke?"

"Sort of. They want me to fix it and make it better than it was."

"You know how to do it?"

Kyle shrugged. "I don't know. I guess. I don't even know how I broke it."

"Don't they have people that fix shit?"

"Yeah," Kyle said, smiling a little. "But I locked them out. They'd have to reconfigure the whole memory array. They'd be off line for months. Maybe a year."

"And you can't get back in?"

"Of course I can." Kyle's voice was low and anguished. "If I sit in a room somewhere and work on it, I can bring it back up. But I'm not."

Kyle looked up at the stars, thinking of the way his father had straightened his back and fallen in step with the men who were marching him to his death.

"How come?" JT said.

Kyle pushed himself up and twisted around to face JT. "Would you fix it if you knew hundreds of thousands of people could die? Or if they'd killed your dad? I ain't playing their harp for them. Even if I have to be in here the rest of my life."

"Being in my cell was like, a real bad punishment for you, right?"

Kyle smiled a little at the note of wounded pride in JT's voice. "Yeah. They think if I'm miserable enough, I'll break down and do what they want."

Kyle fell silent, looking out at the moonlight on the restless waves. "Only they didn't count on me falling in love with you."

JT looked down at Kyle. "You did?" he said softly.

Kyle looked up at him. Before he'd said the words, he didn't know how true it was. He raised a hand to JT's dark, rough face and caressed his hard jaw line softly.

"Yeah, I did," Kyle said, and let out a sigh. "And now you're fucked too. I know about your chip."

JT looked at Kyle with hard suspicion. "How you know about that?"

"Same way I knew about Jessi. I hacked the system. That's where I saw his picture. Nobody showed it to me."

It was JT's turn to be quiet for a long time.

"JT?"

"What?"

"You mad at me?"

JT looked down at Kyle. "You ask weird questions sometimes, boy. How come you think I'm mad at you?"

Kyle shrugged. "'Cause I've lied to you since the moment you laid eyes on me."

JT caressed Kyle's face. "Ain't nobody perfect, boy."

"There's more," Kyle said, in a low reluctant voice.

"Fuck. After what you told me tonight, what else is there?"

Kyle took a deep breath and said, "They're giving you the Guardian Chip because of me."

Kyle held his breath, waiting for JT's answer.

"I know." JT told Kyle about the hologram in Matthew's office.

"Oh my God," Kyle said in a breathless whisper. "That's why you signed the consent form?"

"No," JT said, pulling Kyle close. "I did it 'cause I ain't never had nothing good happen to me." He looked down at Kyle. "'Til now."

"After they inject you, they'll make you a pirate, right?" Kyle went on without waiting for JT's answer. "And that fucking smoking creep's gonna come for me. They'll kill you the minute I say no to them."

"Don't worry, boy." JT's voice was low and calm. "They ain't giving me the chip 'til the day after the Maze. It won't matter no more after that."

"Why not?" Kyle said. Then he realized something. "Wait. Your delivery date is *before* the Maze. Two days before."

Kyle felt JT go stiff. "What do you mean?"

"I saw it today. You delivery date was moved up to two days before the Maze."

"Fuck," JT said in a low voice. "You sure, boy?"

"Positive," Kyle said. "I just saw it today."

"No," JT said in a low voice. "No, no. Fucking shit."

"What's going on, JT?"

"I ain't getting no fucking chip," JT said.

The low note of desperation in JT's voice scared Kyle. "You don't have to," he said.

"Stop talking shit, boy," JT said, irritated.

"Listen to me." Kyle rested his hand on JT's thick arm. "If you didn't bring me up here, I was gonna risk telling in the Clubhouse."

JT looked down at Kyle. "What?"

"I can hack the system. You don't have to get the Guardian Chip."

JT shook his head, looking more annoyed than ever. "You're crazy, boy. Ain't they gonna notice when I don't show up for my shot?"

Kyle had thought of that already. "It's all dispensed by computer. It has to be, to eliminate biohazards on the chip before it's injected. I can dispense a blank into your solution."

"How's that gonna help? They'd know as soon as they tried to track me."

"Not if you already had something on your body tuned to the same frequency."

"You ain't making no sense, boy."

"I know," Kyle said, "listen."

They talked long into the night. Kyle argued his point until JT finally admitted that he had nothing to lose.

Chapter 61

The library had become a kind of private battle ground for Kyle. Almost everyday he fought desperately to keep Tyrone alive.

"What you scared of, bitch?" Tyrone said. "I ain't doing nothing but saying hey."

Kyle backed into the shelf behind him, trying to get away from Tyrone.

"Why don't you do yourself a favor and leave me alone," Kyle said, looking up at him.

"You must like me bothering you, boy, 'cause you ain't said nothing to JT."

"I don't like it," Kyle said. "I just don't want you to die of being stupid."

"What you mean, boy?"

Kyle shook his head. "Forget it. Just leave me alone, alright?" He tried to push past him, but Tyrone blocked his way.

"No, bitch." Tyrone pressed close to Kyle. "It ain't alright."

"You got a death wish or you just stupid?"

Tyrone jumped back about three feet at the sound of Dante's voice.

"Hey man," Tyrone said in a voice shaken with panic. "I wasn't doing nothing. Can't a man say hey to a bitch?"

"Go find some other bitch and say it," Dante said, drawing closer.

Tyrone inched around Dante. "Alright man. I'm cool. I don't want no shit."

He backed away for a few steps, then left as fast as he could without looking like a scared dog.

Dante looked down at Kyle. "He done that before?"

Kyle dropped his eyes, shrugged his shoulders.

"What the fuck you mean you don't know?" Dante said in a tight, impatient voice. "He done it before? Yes or no?"

"I don't want someone to die just for talking to me." Kyle looked up into Dante's hard eyes. "Can we just leave it like that?"

Dante grabbed Kyle's arm and dragged the boy close. "No. We can't just fucking leave it like that. You can tell me or I can tell JT and he can beat it out of you."

Cold sweat broke out on Kyle's pale face. "He's been here before," he said in a low voice.

Dante let go. "How many times?"

"A few. After the Dark Game." Kyle shrugged. "I was scared JT would kill him. That's what he said he'd do if Tyrone came near me again. I couldn't live with knowing someone died just for talking to me."

Dante shook his head, looking at Kyle. "Let's go."

"You're telling JT, aren't you?"

"What the fuck you think, boy?"

Kyle trailed after him, trying not to think of what JT would do to him for not telling him about Tyrone.

———

Sitting on his top bunk, Kyle was just above JT's eye level. The high vantage point gave him the illusion of safety. Especially when JT was pissed off. Like now.

"Why the fuck you didn't tell me, boy?"

Kyle tried not to look down at his fidgeting hands. "I thought you'd kill him."

"He done anything to you?" JT said. "He fucked you?"

Kyle looked up, surprised. "No. Of course not. I would have told you. Just like I told you what he did before. He mostly just comes and talks shit."

JT looked from Kyle to Dante. "You knew about this?" he said to Dante.

"I didn't know nothing 'til I saw Tyrone and him in the library today," Dante said.

"Fucking shit, boy," JT said, in a low, amazed voice. "You *trying* to get me killed?"

"What?" Kyle's green eyes went wide with disbelief. "I don't understand."

"You don't understand nothing 'cause you're a fucking *idiot!*" JT yelled into Kyle's face.

He whirled around and swept the model plane and all the pieces off Kyle's work table. Pieces went flying all over the cell. The bottle of glue smashed against the wall. Shards of glass stuck out of the gooey mess, giving Death's horse a crown of strange thorns.

JT turned back to Kyle. "You think this is your fucking white bread world? This ain't nothing but a jungle, and you done painted a fucking target on my back."

Kyle hugged his legs, pushing himself against the wall, into the corner, as far from JT as he could get.

"JT, the boy didn't –"

"No," JT said, turning on Dante. "You know what this bitch done to me?"

Dante nodded. "I know. But he didn't mean it. He don't know how things are in here."

JT looked back at Kyle, who was staring at him with round green eyes filled with terror. He saw a tear slide down the boy's face.

"What the *fuck* you crying about?" JT said, descending on Kyle. "I'll fucking give you something to cry about."

"James."

Hearing Dante say his name soft and low like that stopped JT in his tracks. "What?"

"Don't. Not pissed off like that. You'll hurt him."

"I had it," JT said, turning back to Dante. "I fucking had it. I want that cock sucking punk gone."

Kyle panicked. "No," he said, "don't get rid of me. I don't care if you beat me. Don't sell me. Please. I'm sorry."

JT glanced back at Kyle over his shoulder, surprised at the boy's words. He laughed, a harsh sound with no humor at all. "I ain't talking about you bitch. I'll deal with you in a minute."

Kyle's eyes fell on the horses galloping out of the wall. He thought of a man trying to outrun them, and how the Horsemen would draw closer and closer, and how the cold breath of Death's horse would be the last thing the running man ever felt.

"I didn't want anyone to die just 'cause he talked to me," Kyle said.

JT looked at Dante. "I'll get with you later. I got to deal with this bitch."

Dante got up, looking at his friend. "You alright?"

"I ain't gonna hurt nobody," JT said. "Not tonight."

Chapter 62

Kyle heard Dante walk out and slide the cell door shut behind him. Then he watched with mounting fear as JT put up the curtain he usually put up after dinner. He heard JT lay back on his bunk.

"Come here, boy."

JT's voice froze Kyle in place. The memory of his beating came rushing back, filling Kyle with the urge to run. He glanced up at the Horsemen, and wondered how far he could run, and how fast?

"Kyle." JT's sharp voice broke into Kyle's dark thoughts of doom.

"Yeah?" Kyle said in a weak voice.

"You ain't heard me calling you, boy?"

Kyle slid down from his bed, feeling like he was sliding into a dark pit. He looked down at JT lying on his bunk. Without warning, JT sat up with the lithe motion of a trained warrior, and grabbed Kyle's wrist.

He moved much too fast for the boy to have any hope of escape. Kyle's feet left the floor as JT pulled him hard onto the bed and rolled Kyle onto his back.

Kyle squeezed his eyes shut, trembling, his face pale, his breathing heavy and labored.

"Why you didn't tell me?"

JT raised his big hand to Kyle's face. Kyle whimpered, his chest heaving. Cold sweat broke out on his face. "Please. I'm sorry," he said in a low, breathy whisper.

"Don't be scared, baby," JT said, stroking Kyle's face softly. "I ain't gonna beat you over this."

Kyle risked opening his eyes. "How come?"

JT sighed. "Cause if I beat you for all the dumb ass shit you did, I guess you wouldn't never sit down."

Kyle looked away, stung by JT's hard words.

"I didn't mean nothing, boy." JT turned Kyle's face towards him. "You're a good girl for me."

"I'm always fucking up," Kyle said. "You're probably sorry I'm in your cell."

One look into his boy's tormented eyes, and JT's anger passed with the swift fury of a summer storm. "Don't talk nonsense, boy."

Kyle tried to sit up, to escape JT's bulk hovering over him. But JT pushed the boy back easily. Kyle cringed from his touch, afraid.

173

"I told you I ain't gonna beat you," JT said. "What you still scared about?"

Kyle looked up at the bottom of his own bed, over at the black wall beside him, anywhere but at JT's hard face.

"I can't talk to you about it."

"You talk to me about anything," JT said. "I ain't gonna beat you just for talking. You know better."

Kyle shrugged, avoiding JT's eyes, clearly unconvinced.

"There ain't but one thing you scared to talk to me about, boy." JT took Kyle's face in his big hand made his boy look at him. "You scared I'm gonna fuck you hard and dry and make you scream?"

Kyle nodded, struggling to hold back the tears that filled his eyes.

JT wiped the side of Kyle's face. "Don't be crying. I ain't gonna hurt you. I ain't gonna do nothing, alright?"

Kyle nodded.

JT pulled Kyle into his arms, laid the boy's head on his thick chest, and ran his fingers through Kyle's hair. "Why you didn't tell me about Tyrone?"

Kyle was quiet for a while, listening to the steady rhythm of JT's strong heart beat.

"Because you said you'd kill him if he came near me again. I didn't want him to die just for talking to me. Then time went by. After you –"

The vivid memory of his beating stopped Kyle's words in his throat.

"After I belted your ass?" JT said in a low voice.

Kyle took a breath and went on. "Yes. After you got mad at me for saying no, I was too scared to tell you."

"You ain't a idiot." JT ran his dark fingers along Kyle's soft face. "I shouldn't of said that. And I shouldn't of done that to your toy plane. You just don't understand how it is in here. You got to tell me when shit happens to you. This ain't like the world on the outside. It's all fucked up in here. Understand?"

"No," Kyle said. "But I'll tell you next time."

"It's a different world in here, boy." JT pushed Kyle off him and lay on his side, looking down at Kyle. He ran his hand up and down his boy's smooth body, under Kyle's t shirt, caressing his soft chest. "Everybody knows me and Tyrone had a duel over you. And now, he's telling everybody he been to the library, talking to you behind my back, and I ain't done nothing about it."

Kyle gave JT a puzzled look. "I don't get it."

"You had a dog on the outside?"

Kyle nodded.

"In here, you're like my dog. You're my bitch, my property."

Kyle turned his face away, ashamed at JT's words.

"I ain't trying to make you feel bad, baby, that's just how it is," JT said. "And if men see I can't take care of my property, and I can't control who talks to my bitch, they ain't gonna do business with me."

Kyle looked at JT as if he were talking about life on Mars. "Not do business with you?"

"It don't end there. Nobody wants to do business with me. They'll do business with somebody else. That somebody else needs my territory to do business with my people. And they can't have my territory while I'm alive." JT paused, looking at Kyle. "Before you know it, somebody puts a hit out on me. And bang, one day the lights go out, and when they come back on, *I'm* the one laying on the floor."

Kyle felt his head spinning. "All that just because Tyrone was talking shit to me in the library?"

"Purgatory's a fucked up place, boy." JT looked at Kyle steadily. "That's why you got to tell me everything that happens to you. Even if you think it ain't no big deal. Alright?"

Kyle nodded. "I didn't know," he said quietly.

"I know. It ain't your fault. That's why you ain't getting a ass whipping over it. You're a real smart bitch. But there's a lot you don't know."

"I guess so," Kyle said.

JT got off the bunk and leaned against the wall, smoking, looking at the blanket over the bars, in deep thought.

"What is it?" Kyle said.

"You know how you said you wasn't gonna do what they wanted with that harp thing 'cause you would hurt a whole bunch of people?"

Kyle nodded.

"What if the only way to get rid of someone who was real bad was to do something bad to one person, but then a whole lot of other people would be ok. Would you do it?"

Kyle looked at JT, thoughtfully.

"I wouldn't kill anyone," Kyle said carefully, sensing this was more than a hypothetical question. "But if one person's suffering would save a whole lot of suffering down the line, then I guess I'd do it and say sorry later. Life sucks sometimes."

JT caressed Kyle's cheek. "You're real smart for a punk your age," he said quietly.

Kyle sensed something terrible behind JT's question. "What's wrong?"

"Forget it," JT said. "Just remember that sometimes a man's got to do things that he's real sorry for 'cause life don't leave him no other choice."

Kyle thought he understood. "Is Tyrone going to die?"

The change that came over JT frightened Kyle because it was swift and absolute. Quick as lightening filled a midnight sky, JT his lover became JT the avenging angel.

"When I get done with him, he's gonna fucking wish he was dead."

His harsh voice offered penance with no promise of redemption.

In the cold darkness of Purgatory's machine shop, metal gleamed with the stupid threat of heavy machinery that would grind a careless man's hand to red jelly in seconds. Two men stood just beyond the darkness, one a gladiator in flight, the other a former gladiator whose time in Purgatory was numbered not in years, but in life sentences.

JT's soldiers stood watch, far off, out of earshot. The eerie glow of a single light bulb bathed both men in worn out yellow light.

"What you gonna do about Tyrone?"

"I got to take care of him fast and hard," JT said.

"How?"

JT was quiet, thinking, then he told Dante his plan.

"Get the word out," JT finished. "Make sure Tyrone knows that I know and I ain't done nothing about it. We got to bait him so he makes his move in the next few days, before the Maze."

"You sure you wanna do that to your boy?" Dante said.

"If I don't do it that like that, I got to kill Tyrone. Time's too fucking short. If I kill him and I get caught, me and boy ain't never gonna get the fuck up out of this hole."

Dante nodded, knowing his friend was right.

"If I don't do nothing, I'm dead. And there'd be a gang war. A whole lot of good men would die for nothing."

"It's gonna be real hard on Kyle."

"You think I *wanna* do this to my boy?" JT said between clenched teeth.

"I know you don't."

JT threw his cigarette to the floor and ground it out on the grimy concrete. "Sometimes a man got no choice. "Get the word out," he said, heading into the darkness.

Chapter 63

Kyle looked down at his plate of ground beef sitting in congealed gravy that had turned to brown jelly.

"Kyle."

Kyle looked up at JT with alarm and stopped fidgeting with the food on his plate. His stomach curled into a knot.

"How come you ain't eating?"

"It looks like dog food."

"Eat it," JT said. "Don't be fucking with me."

Kyle didn't want JT to get pissed. He forced himself to take the smallest bite he could get away with.

"Look at this shit." Dante spooned up meat and gravy and hung his spoon upside down. The sticky mess plopped to his plate. "Looks like somebody come all over this shit. I got shit in my house he likes. Let me take him while you finish," Dante said.

Kyle could have reached across the table and kissed him.

JT gave Kyle a side long look. "You wanna go with Dante?"

Kyle hesitated. He was still learning how to be JT's wife in public. He didn't want it to look like he was defying JT.

Kyle looked down at his plate. "The food's really bad tonight," he said.

JT looked at three men coming toward the table. He used the cafeteria to do business and meet men on neutral ground. "I got business I still got to take care of," he said. "Yeah. Take him."

Kyle shot up from the table, anxious to escape the grey brick walls of the echoing dining hall. After the blackout, the high stone ceiling and the dark drafty corners gave him the creeps.

"Hey, bitch," JT said, when Kyle got up to leave. "Come here."

Kyle turned back to JT.

"I'll be home soon to fuck your tight little ass real hard," JT said loud enough for everyone at the table to hear.

Kyle blushed, feeling JT's hand rubbing his ass. The men at the table laughed.

"We ain't gonna keep you long," a man at the table said. "You'll be home to fuck your wife's tight pussy in no time."

"I'd be in a hurry too," one of the men who'd walked up said.

"Shit, if I had a pretty wife like that," someone else said, "I'd be fucking bitch pussy night and day, real hard."

The whole table laughed loudly at that. Kyle dropped his eyes and followed Dante out of the dining hall.

JT was the only one that saw the man who was hanging back near the door, watching, listening. When he left a few moments before Dante led Kyle out of the dining hall, JT thought of signaling to Dante, but held back. It would be better if it came as a surprise. They'd been waiting for Tyrone to strike. Tonight looked like the night.

It took every ounce of JT's considerable will to turn his mind to business, knowing what was about to happen to his boy.

———————

"I fucking hate it when he does that," Kyle said, once they were outside the cafeteria.

"He don't mean nothing by it, boy."

"You're always defending him," Kyle said, irritated.

"What you mean, defending him? There ain't nothing to defend. You ain't no new bitch no more. You know JT's good to you. He got to act like that in front of those men."

"Why?" Kyle said, even though he understood.

Dante looked at Kyle. "Cause you're his bitch. And he got to make sure everyone in here knows that he knows how to treat his bitch. It's part of how things get done in here. Ain't he good to you when nobody's around?"

Kyle thought of how JT had changed since he put the pink cage around his cock. At night, in the cell, JT flipped through magazines, laying on his bunk, telling stories that he never seemed to run out of.

"Yeah," Kyle said, "You're right. He talks that shit, but he doesn't really fuck me hard like he says he will." He looked up at Dante. "Don't tell him I got mad, okay?"

Dante shook his head. "You know I don't tell him nothing unless I got to, boy," he said. "You and me, we're tight like that." Dante looked thoughtful a moment.

"What?" Kyle said.

"I ain't never been friends with a bitch before," he said. "I fucked a lot of boys like you, but I never talked to them, like I talk to you."

"You probably had your dick too far down their –"

Kyle stopped talking because Dante had stopped walking.

"What is it?"

"It's too quiet for this time of night." Dante's killer instincts were setting off loud alarms in his head. "Something's wrong."

He grabbed Kyle's hand. "Let's go back."

Kyle turned with Dante, unresisting. They were making their way back to the cafeteria when a shadow detached itself from the dark wall.

"Hey Dante," the prisoner said. "What's going on?"

He talked to Dante, but he looked at Kyle.

"What's up Leroy?" Dante pushed Kyle subtly behind him.

Kyle saw Dante rest his hand near the knife he always carried.

"Where you taking the bitch?" a voice behind them said.

Kyle whirled and saw two other men who had melted out of the darkness. In seconds, they had been surrounded by three gladiators who all looked like hungry jackals.

"What the fuck's this about?" Dante said.

"JT's wife is real sweet," a soft voice said from the darkness.

Kyle would have known that voice anywhere. *I'm gonna have your ass, bitch. And you ain't gonna see it coming.*

Tyrone emerged from the dark end of the corridor, walking slowly between three men.

At a signal from Tyrone, the three men closest to Dante, jumped on him. Dante pushed Kyle hard, trying to getting him out of harm's way. He pulled the knife from his pocket and sliced at the man closest to him. The three men struggled with Dante for only a few minutes before they had him pinned to the stone wall, with a knife to his throat.

Kyle had fallen against the wall when Dante pushed him. Now he pushed himself to his feet, looking at Tyrone.

"You'll wish you was dead if you do it." Dante's voice was incredibly calm for a man with a knife pressed to his throat.

"JT sure got a fine bitch," Tyrone said.

He signaled another man, who pulled Kyle over to Tyrone and threw him at his feet. Tyrone picked up Kyle by the arm and pulled a knife from his belt. He ran the cold steel over Kyle's face.

"You're gonna be fucking sorry," Dante said, in that same eerily quiet voice.

Kyle's screams and cries echoed down the empty hall as Jerome rammed his cock into the boy again and again, grunting and groaning. He fucked Kyle hard, pounding his slender body into the wall, driving his thick cock into his squirming ass without mercy.

"Here I come, bitch," he said, groaning. He pumped hard into Kyle one more time and filled his ass with come.

As soon as he pulled out and the men holding Kyle let go, he crumpled to the ground, and curled into a fetal position, crying.

For a moment, Tyrone's eyes filled with fear as he looked from Kyle to Dante. Then it was gone. He signaled to his men, and they disappeared down the hall, melting slowly into the darkness, confident that Dante would stay behind to tend to Kyle.

The moment they left, Dante went to Kyle. The boy pulled away from him, curling himself into a tighter ball.

"I hate this place," Kyle said through his tears. "I wanna go home."

"I know, boy," Dante said, picking up Kyle gently. "Come on, put your pants back on."

"Why?" Kyle screamed at him. "Leave them off. Then they can fuck me all they want. I'm nothing but a *bitch!*"

Kyle's screaming voice cracked on the last word and he broke down into sobs, collapsing against Dante. JT's friend put on Kyle's jeans as best he could, then picked up the boy in his strong arms, the way a father would carry a child.

"Come on, boy," he said softly. "It's gonna be alright."

Dante's words to Kyle were gentle, but there was murder in his dark eyes. He would enjoy every second of what JT had planned for Tyrone.

Chapter 65

JT walked into his cell. Dante had unscrewed the single light bulb in the ceiling. Kyle lay on the bottom bunk in the semi-darkness, facing the wall.

"He alright?"

Dante nodded. "They ain't stupid. They didn't beat him up."

"He said anything?"

"Don't talk about me like I'm not here," Kyle said in a hoarse voice.

"I thought you was sleeping, baby," JT said, sitting on his bunk.

He stroked Kyle's back gently for a few moments.

"Come here, boy," JT said gently. "Let me see you."

"I don't want anyone looking at me," Kyle said, barely holding back more tears.

"It's just me, baby," JT said in a soft voice, coaxing. "Come on. Let me see you."

Kyle slowly turned over and looked up at JT. When JT had planned this, and set up Tyrone to fall into the trap of his own stupidity, he hadn't counted on this. It shattered his heart into a thousand pieces to see the anguished suffering on his boy's pale, tear streaked face.

It took every ounce of self control JT had to resist the urge to go find Tyrone and rip his fucking throat out. But if he did that, Kyle's suffering would be for nothing.

JT stroked Kyle's face softly. "You want anything, boy?"

"Yeah," Kyle said, with a faint smile. "A vacation to the Bahamas."

JT wrapped Kyle in a gentle embrace. He looked over at Dante while he held his trembling boy.

"I'm sorry, boy," JT said.

It didn't occur to Kyle to think about why JT would say he was sorry for something he hadn't done. Not yet.

"They hurt me real bad," Kyle said. His voice was muffled by JT's hard chest. "More than you ever did. Even when you're mad at me."

"I know, boy," JT said, running his fingers slowly through Kyle's hair.

"Don't kill him," Kyle said in a rush.

"You got it?" JT said to Dante.

Dante took a tiny box out of his pocket, got a glass of water and shook the pill out of the box into JT's waiting hand.

"Open your mouth," JT said to Kyle. He put the pill on Kyle's tongue, then gave him a few sips of water.

"I don't want him to die." Kyle raised his suffering eyes to JT. "Please. Promise me. Don't kill him."

"Lay down," JT said. "You'll sleep in a little bit."

All at once, Kyle felt unbelievably weary. He lay down again.

Both men sat in silence, watching. Within minutes, his breathing became deep and even. His body relaxed, and Kyle slipped into the last peaceful moments that he would know for a long time.

"Damn," Dante said. "That shit's a bomb."

JT looked at his boy in silence.

"You didn't have no choice," Dante said, reading the look on his friend's face.

"That don't make it right," JT said quietly, and walked out of the cell.

It was time to put the rest of his plan for Tyrone into action. He had to go see a jail house lawyer and get him to write a letter that would destroy Tyrone in Purgatory forever.

Chapter 66

Kyle woke up to the brightness of full day lighting on the tier. His head ached a little, and his throat was drier than the valleys of the moon.

"Hey, boy," Dante's voice said. "Here. I know you're thirsty." He handed Kyle a bottle of cold water.

"Jesus," Kyle said after he swallowed nearly half the bottle of water. "What did he give me?"

Dante smiled a little. "A sleep bomb."

"I guess." Kyle sat up slowly.

His ass hurt when he sat up. The memory of yesterday came crashing into his mind. Dante saw it in the boy's eyes.

"How you feel?" he said.

"Where's JT?" Kyle said, looking around the cell.

"Out doing business."

Kyle wondered if it was the dying kind of business. "My ass hurts and I'm pissed off," he said. "But I don't want Tyrone to die for what he did. Where's JT? How long did I sleep?"

"You slept like twelve hours," Dante said.

"Come on, Dante." Kyle looked up at him. "Where is he?"

"He ain't out killing Tyrone, alright? He should be, but he ain't. Tyrone's lucky. 'Cause if you was my bitch, he'd be a dead man."

Kyle still felt the heavy, draggy feeling of the drug he'd taken, slowing down his thoughts.

"Hey, boy," a voice said near the open cell door. "I heard about what happened. I'm real sorry."

He looked at Dante, who nodded it was okay, then walked into the cell. Kyle didn't want any men he didn't know near him. He pushed himself into the corner of JT's bunk when the man walked into the cell.

"It's alright, boy," Dante said.

"I brought you this," the man said, looking into Kyle's scared eyes. He laid a box wrapped in plain brown paper on Kyle's bunk.

Before Kyle could say anything, the man walked out. He stopped outside the cell and looked at Dante.

"Tell JT I was here, alright?"

With that, he left. Kyle got up and looked at the brown wrapped box.

"What is it?"

Dante shrugged. "I ain't got x-ray vision."

Kyle tore the wrapping and found a model airplane kit, with about two hundred pieces. What the hell?

"Dante, what's –"

Before Kyle could finish, another man paused at the door of the cell, looking at Dante the same way the other man had. When Dante nodded, he walked in and threw a package on Kyle's bed.

"Sorry, boy," he said, and walked out, barely looking at Kyle.

Dante looked at Kyle, an amused smile barely turning up the corners of his lips.

"What the hell?" Kyle said. Confused thoughts moved through his mind with all the speed of turtles swimming through peanut butter. "What's going on?"

"They're Tyrone's men. They all want JT to know they didn't have nothing to do with what happened. So they're bringing you gifts. That's how we do things in here. It's how we choose sides. They all know Tyrone's going down for what he done to you. They don't wanna be dragged down with him."

As Dante finished talking, another man paused at the open cell door and looked at Dante for permission to walk in. When Dante nodded, he did the same thing as the other men.

"Why don't you play one of your games, boy?" Dante said.

Kyle called up a 3D chess game, and lost every game as the afternoon wore on. An endless parade of men came and went.

"It's alright if I come in?"

Kyle looked up from the chess game he was losing. His eyes widened in terror, a low moan of fear escaped him. It was one of the men from last night.

Dante was on his feet in an instant. A long curved knife, like Death's scythe, suddenly appeared in his big hand.

"Get the fuck out unless you got a death wish," Dante said quietly.

The man swallowed. "It's from all of us who done it last night. We know we done wrong," he said. He held out a brown wrapped present in trembling hands. "We done it 'cause Tyrone said we had to or he was gonna fuck us up."

"Get out before I cut your fucking balls off," Dante said between clenched teeth. The only reason the man was still alive was because Dante had orders from JT.

The man looked past Dante to Kyle. "I know you don't know how things are in here, boy. But if you say it's alright, he got to let me leave you this." The man swallowed. "Please, boy. Take it. We don't wanna die for what we done to you."

Kyle took a couple of steps until he was behind Dante. "Alright," he said. "Leave it with the other stuff."

The man glanced at Dante, then sidled past him to Kyle's bunk and left his brown wrapped gift. His sweaty fingerprints were imprinted on the brown paper.

"Sorry for what we done to you, boy," the man said, pausing at the cell door.

"Get the fuck out before I forget my orders," Dante said, raising his knife.

The man walked down the hall at a fast clip that turned to a run.

After that, a steady stream of men – most of them Kyle had never seen before, or only in passing – came and did the same ritual. They all paused at the door and looked at Dante. When he nodded, they walked in, told Kyle how they were sorry for what happened, and threw something onto his bunk.

Pretty soon, Kyle's bunk was covered with hastily wrapped boxes that contained things that would have cost a fortune on the outside. In here, they had cost probably three times as much. The message was clear. Tyrone and the men who'd raped Kyle were alone in what they'd done.

In fact, Tyrone was *all* alone. Even the men who had helped do it were asking for mercy. No one in Purgatory was willing to go down with Tyrone.

Dante sat near the door of the cell, flipping through one of JT's magazines, keeping watch over the men who came and went.

"How can you remember all the men who came?" Kyle said.

"I ain't got to remember who came." Dante flipped through a magazine.

"What do you mean?"

Dante looked up at Kyle. "I only got to remember who didn't come." A hard flat shine came into his eyes that frightened Kyle badly.

"Dante, can I ask you something?"

He closed the magazine on his lap. "What?"

"JT's real smart. He figures things out. How come he didn't see last night coming?"

Kyle saw the way Dante grabbed the magazine from his lap and flipped through too many pages before he answered. If he didn't know any better, Kyle would have thought his question made Dante nervous.

"JT ain't no damn fortune teller."

"I guess not," Kyle said. "But I've been thinking all afternoon. If this didn't happen to me, I think maybe there would be a gang war and people would die. If he ever asks you, tell him I said sometimes when you play the harp, you have to say sorry later."

Dante looked at Kyle for a long moment. "What harp?"

"Just tell him. He'll know what I mean."

"You love him a lot don't you, boy?"

Kyle nodded. "He's not bad. Just different." He looked at all the brown wrapped packages on both bunk beds. "Now what happens? A White Sale?"

Dante looked up at Kyle. "We ain't selling you, boy."

For a moment, Kyle thought Dante was serious, then he saw the twinkle of humor in his dark eyes.

"I'm serious." Kyle pushed aside the pile that had overflowed to JT's bunk and sat down.

"A council meeting." Dante paged through his magazine.

"The council is like all the gangs together, right?"

"Kind of," Dante said.

"What happens at the meeting?"

Dante looked up at Kyle. "Can't you see I'm reading, boy?"

Kyle glanced at the magazine in Dante's hands. "There's no words in that, just pictures. JT's got tons of them. How come you don't wanna answer me?"

"I wanna see how many questions you can ask. You get to a hundred, you win a prize." This time, Dante grinned at him, showing his even white teeth.

"He's asking for permission to kill Tyrone, isn't he?"

Dante turned deadly serious. "There's things worse than dying, boy."

Yeah, Kyle thought. *Like back rooms with no windows.*

Chapter 67

JT was impatiently waiting his turn to speak. He watched while men went before the Council, asking for favors, explaining fuck ups, demanding payment for wrongs. JT wasn't going to demand anything. All he wanted was what rightfully his.

Finally his turn came. JT got up from his place on the couch and sat in the chair in front of the council tables. The seven most powerful men in Purgatory faced him. Together, the seven men and JT represented all the gangs in Purgatory.

"We all heard what happened," LaRoy, leader of the Khofir gang, said.

"We're real sorry man," Jamal said. He was the leader of the Axemen.

JT said nothing, waiting for them to stop talking so he could say what he wanted. He wouldn't take long.

"We didn't have nothing to do with it," Lavonne said. He was the leader of the Golds, Tyrone's gang.

"He done wrong against all of us," Marcus said. His gang, the Vegas Men, ran whores and gambling. "What he done wasn't right. Not to your boy."

"Tyrone broke our laws," LaVonne said. "If you take him out, ain't nobody gonna stop you."

"I don't wanna kill nobody," JT said quietly.

"What then?"

They listened to JT outline his plan for Tyrone. All the men on the council were brutal, hardened killers, imprisoned in Purgatory for committing unspeakable crimes. But as they listened, their faces looked like frightened children who glimpse the glaring red eyes of the monster in the closet; or worse, under the bed.

"That's how you want it?" Marcus said when JT was finished.

"He hurt my boy," JT said. "That's how I want it."

The men on the council looked at each other for a long, silent moment.

"No one's gonna get in your way," LaRoy said, looking at the other council members. All the men nodded. A couple of them shuddered.

"He's yours," someone murmured.

Chapter 68

The word was out on Tyrone. The word was that Tyrone had punked JT by fucking his bitch. Now, JT was out for revenge. Rumors of vengeance ran rampant all over Purgatory. JT was gonna cut up Tyrone real bad. JT was gonna slit Tyrone's throat next time he saw him. JT was gonna beat Tyrone so bad, he'd crawl out of Purgatory. JT was gonna make Tyrone wish he'd never been born.

Only the last rumor was true.

The rumors chased Tyrone from one end of Purgatory to the other. Men he did business with started backing off, waiting to see what was coming. No one was sure what JT would do. They knew only one thing. JT was going to make Tyrone pay for what he did to Kyle.

Tyrone lived the way he fought. He went for the quick, painful blow, without any strategy, just striking out to hurt his opponent. He'd done what he did to Kyle without looking ahead to what it might cost him. He'd been waiting since the Dark Game to make JT pay for carving his initials into his back. Taking it out on Kyle had seemed like a good way to do it. Now, days later, Tyrone was begging for his life.

He stood in the Clubhouse, deep in JT's territory, trying to look at ease when the pit of his belly was nearly down to his knees. Sweat beaded his upper lip. JT sat in a big leather chair in the shadowy darkness of candlelight. Gladiators lounged around, watching Tyrone from the shadows.

Dante stood just behind JT. Kyle was on the floor, sitting between JT's legs. Tyrone was here under a truce. JT couldn't try anything. He'd lose his reputation if he did that.

"What do you want?" JT said, running his fingers through Kyle's hair.

"I just wanna talk," Tyrone said.

The way the boy looked up at him unnerved Tyrone. Kyle looked at him with unblinking attention, with dark eyes that held no anger, no passion, no forgiveness. If JT's bitch was mad, Tyrone was sure he was a dead man.

"What you wanna talk about what?" JT looked down at Kyle. "Turn around, boy. Unzip my pants."

Kyle turned and faced JT. He unzipped JT's jeans and opened his fly. He started kissing JT's hard cock, pressing his lips to the hardness bulging out of his jeans.

For some reason, seeing the boy like that made Tyrone even more nervous.

"I'm waiting," JT said.

Tyrone looked at Dante's bored face. He knew it was a trick. He used to wear the same bored look when he met gladiators in the ring, His face never changed, even after he sliced into them and blood dripped from his knife.

"I wanna talk about what I can do," Tyrone said.

JT gave Tyrone a penetrating look, then shrugged.

"I don't know," he said. "What can you do?"

A wave of low laughter echoed off the stone walls, like far off church bells in Hell.

Tyrone swallowed past the lump in his throat. "I mean, about your boy," he said.

"My bitch?" JT stroked Kyle's face while the boy kissed his crotch. He spread his legs wider, letting Kyle bury his face deeper between his legs.

Tyrone swallowed and said, "About what I done to your bitch."

JT shrugged. "What you think I should let you do about it?"

"Whatever you want, man."

Tyrone knew that by nightfall, every man in Purgatory would know that he'd been in JT's territory, begging. But begging was better than dying.

JT tilted Kyle's face up so he could look at him. "You want Tyrone to do something about what he done to you, boy?"

Kyle looked at Tyrone over his shoulder. The boy's eyes went dark with fury. "I want the same thing to happen to him," he said quietly.

JT pressed Kyle's face back into his crotch, moving his hips slightly as the boy's attention made his hard cock throb.

"You hear that?" JT said, looking up at Tyrone. "My bitch thinks you should get what he got."

For a long, tense moment Tyrone was silent. He was painfully aware of the dozen or so gladiators in the darkness. If they jumped him, he wouldn't have a chance.

JT burst into laughter. All the men in the room laughed with him.

"He thinks you should get fucked like a bitch, ain't that funny?" JT said, through his laughter.

Tyrone noticed that the laughter on JT's face didn't reach his cold, hard eyes. He forced a laugh and said, "Sometimes a bitch can say some stupid shit."

JT turned serious, the laughter fleeing from his dark face. "You calling my bitch stupid?"

"No," Tyrone said. "I ain't gonna dis you like that, man."

Tyrone's hands hung at his sides. He hoped no one saw how they trembled.

JT shrugged again. "Don't matter," he said. "Ain't nothing you can do. You fucked my bitch."

He looked Tyrone in the eye for a long, silent moment.

"I got to ask you something." JT's voice was so quiet Tyrone had to strain to hear him.

"What?" Tyrone thought he was ready for anything. He was wrong.

"Was it good?"

Tyrone's face went blank. It was the last thing he'd expected JT to ask.

"Was my bitch a hot fuck?"

JT held Tyrone's eyes, running his fingers slowly through Kyle's soft hair, while the boy's tongue pressed against his hard cock through his thin underpants.

Tyrone saw the rising tide of murderous violence in JT's dark eyes.

"Did you come real good up my boy's ass?" JT said in an even quieter voice.

There was dead silence in the room. Tyrone wished he was anywhere but here. Even the deepest shit pit of Hell would be alright.

"I'm sorry." Tyrone's broad shoulders sagged. "I don't wanna die, man," he whispered.

"You shouldn't of hurt my boy," JT said. "If you'd come after me, I wouldn't of done nothing but beat the shit out of you." JT narrowed his eyes to tiny pinpoints of rage. "But you hurt my *boy*," he said through clenched teeth.

JT leaned back, stroking Kyle's hair, looking hard at Tyrone.

"Get this walking garbage out my sight," JT said to Dante.

"JT –" Tyrone started to say something. But Dante didn't let him finish.

"You heard the man. Get the fuck out. Move." Dante gave Tyrone a hard shove toward the archway that led out of the Clubhouse.

"Dante," JT said in a sharp voice.

Dante looked at JT over his shoulder. "What?"

"Don't let nothing happen to him. Safe walking. You got me?"

Dante gave Tyrone a side long look filled with murderous fury.

"Whatever you say," the ex-gladiator said.

JT watched both men leave, running his fingers through Kyle's silky hair.

"Did I do it right?" Kyle said, looking up at JT.

"You did it just right, boy."

"What's going to happen to him?"

"That ain't nothing for you to worry about, boy," JT said quietly. His eyes were filled with stormy rage.

Chapter 69

JT and Kyle lay on JT's bunk. He'd come in Kyle's mouth after they came back from the Clubhouse.

"You sucked me real good, boy," JT kissed Kyle's lips.

"I came real good." Kyle looked into JT's dark eyes, fear darkening his green eyes.

"What is it?"

Kyle looked even more scared.

"I ain't gonna hit you. Tell me."

"I know I'm not supposed to ask you about business, but –"

"But what?" JT's voice had turned hard and cold.

Kyle took a deep breath and said, "You looked so mad at Tyrone in the Clubhouse. You're not gonna kill him, right?"

JT looked at Kyle for a long time before he got up and sat on the edge of the bed. He lit a cigarette and smoked in silence. On the wall opposite the bunk bed, the Horsemen galloped like mad men, bringing Hell with them.

"Get dressed. If we're doing it tonight, we go now."

Kyle didn't press JT for an answer. He was too afraid of what he might hear.

"Yeah." Kyle got up and slipped into his clothes. "I'm ready."

"You sure this will work, boy?" JT said, as he let them out of the cell.

"If I can crack HAARP, I can crack their sorry ass security code for the Guardian Chip. No sweat."

They walked through the darkness of the tier. Without asking, Kyle knew that JT had somehow arranged for the guards on the tier to be somewhere else for a few minutes. No guards saw them leave. Any prisoners who saw them would keep their mouth shut if they wanted to stay alive.

They made their way to the library, taking a short cut underneath the library, down through the basement, then up uneven steps carved out of ancient stone. At the top of the steps, Kyle recognized the doorway that Ryan had used to get into the basement.

JT let them into the library, warning Kyle to silence with a finger pressed to his lips. Once they were inside, Kyle found a card catalog terminal, sat down, and started typing. JT watched over Kyle's shoulder as symbols and numbers flowed across the screen in bewildering patterns that made his eyes cross.

"You sure you know what you're doing, boy? Looks like nothing but a whole of bunch of shit to me."

"I'm sure," Kyle said, looking at the screen, paying JT almost no attention. "Quiet. Let me concentrate."

Kyle navigated his way through encrypted pages until he found his way into the National Watch Over Me database.

"I need your prisoner id number." Kyle's voice was sharp, to the point.

JT gave it to him and watched as Kyle input the number then tapped out a flurry of instructions that went across the screen in coded nonsense.

They both looked up and held their breath as footsteps sounded outside the library. It was a guard doing rounds. Kyle turned off the monitor. They both sat perfectly still in the pitch black darkness that descended.

The footsteps stopped in front of the library door. They ducked just in time to avoid a sweeping flashlight beam. The footsteps hesitated a moment, then moved on. Kyle and JT waited until they heard the footsteps disappear down the hallway.

"You almost done, boy?" JT said, as Kyle turned the monitor back on.

"Almost."

Long minutes went by as Kyle ran his fingers over the keyboard, pausing occasionally to read the screen.

"Okay," Kyle whispered in the dark. "Your thumbprint."

JT put his thumb to the reader beside the computer and waited for the digital scan to come up on the screen. "One hundred percent match," the screen said. "Operation successful."

"What operation?" JT said.

Kyle waved JT back and typed furiously, paying no mind to the tiny beeps that came from the computer.

"What the fuck you doing, boy?"

Kyle was deep in the zone, walking to nowhere. "Nothing if you don't shut up and let me work," he said quietly.

JT paced restlessly to the door, listened, heard nothing.

At the computer Kyle typed one last line of code. He hesitated for the first time all night, his finger hovering over the "Enter" key. Once he sent the code, there would be no turning back. He looked up at JT's broad back, waiting for him by the door.

"Whatever you're doing boy, hurry it up. We ain't got all night in here," JT called in a soft whisper.

Kyle pressed the "Enter" key. "I'm done."

When JT walked back to the monitor, the screen was blinking, and a line across the bottom read, "More books?"

"No more fucking books," JT said. "Turn that shit off."

Kyle turned it off, and they left the library, locking the door behind them. They hurried down the dark corridor, heading for the machine shop.

"Take off your earring," Kyle said, once they were inside.

JT took off the diamond stud that marked him as a gladiator and gave it to Kyle.

"How you gonna fit anything in there, boy?"

"A diamond can be imprinted and carry a frequency," Kyle said. "I'm going to imprint it with the same frequency they were going to use for the real chip."

"How the hell –"

"Trust me."

Kyle took the earring, put it onto a flat glass slide, then slid the slide under a strange looking machine that looked like a giant microscope.

"What's that?" JT said, watching carefully. "We never use it."

"A coder," Kyle said, calibrating the instruments to a piece of paper he'd written down carefully in the library.

"They keep something for the chips in here with us cons?"

Kyle shrugged. "Why not?" He typed a few lines into the terminal next to the coder. "How many of you know how to hack the system?"

Kyle typed fast. Dawn was coming. They had to be back in their cells for head count. He finally got into the system. He found JT again and sent the code to the diamond. A red line of text blinked at Kyle.

"Shit," he said.

"What?

"Cut your finger."

"What?"

"Do it. Hurry up. The system's gonna lock me out. It'll change the codes. I won't be able to get back in tonight."

JT slid a knife from his boot and cut a tiny slit in his finger. Kyle grabbed his hand, slid the slide out and squeezed a tiny drop of blood onto the diamond stud.

After that, Kyle worked fast, sliding the earring back under the coder. He hurried back to the terminal. A countdown had begun. "Thirty seconds to lock out," the screen read. "Please verify DNA sequence."

Kyle typed fast and furious. His fingers were barely visible blurs on the keyboard. JT watched in silence, holding his breath.

"Coding sequence accepted," the screen said in green letters.

JT didn't know what that meant. But green had to be better than red, right?

A tiny flash of blue light came from the coder, then the slide slid out by itself.

Kyle grabbed the earring and gave it to JT. "That's worth your life. Don't lose it."

Kyle hurried back to the terminal, typed in more codes, and then finally, turned off the system.

"Let's go," Kyle said.

"Now what happens?"

"You'll go for your shot today, like normal. The DNA coding sequence will hold up for two, maybe three days." Kyle looked up at JT. "It won't matter after that, right?"

"No. That's my business. Don't be worrying about it," JT said. "I won't get no chip in the shot, right?"

Kyle shook his head. "No. In the library, I dispensed a blank into your solution. It's like they'll inject a computer in you, but with no program. It'll be useless. When they check the Eye in the Sky, your earring will be generating the right frequency. Maybe a little low. But Nanos aren't that stable. They won't suspect anything. But in forty eight to seventy two hours, the solution on the earring starts breaking down. After that, it's over."

"That's after the Maze. Nothing won't matter after that."

Chapter 70

JT walked into the infirmary. They'd put him in shackles, because they expected a fight. Matthew was there, waiting for him.

"Good Morning James," Matthew said with a broad smile. "It's a beautiful day, isn't it?"

"This is the day the Lord hath made. Let us rejoice and be glad in it," JT said, smiling right back at Matthew. Preacher used to quote the Bible all the time.

Matthew's smile faltered a little. "Happy are those who find their way to the blessings of our most Merciful Lady and her blessed Son."

Looking straight into Matthew's dark brown eyes, JT said, "Fuck you."

"May the Lord have mercy on you my son," Matthew said. His voice was soft and kind. His eyes were cold and inhuman.

"If you got any religion in you, you best pray there ain't really no Hell. 'Cause you'll be the first motherfucker burning up in there."

Matthew stepped close until he was only inches away. He embraced JT, the way a dedicated minister would lay hands on an anguished, suffering soul. He put his lips to JT's ear, pitched his voice low, so only JT heard him and said, "One fuck up after they inject you and I'll see to it that your little bitch gets fucked by every gladiator in Purgatory. I'll chain you in front of a holo and make you watch while he screams."

Stepping back, Matthew said, "I understand this is a very trying time for you, my son. May the Lord give you strength." Matthew made the sign of the cross. "I leave you with the peace of our Lord."

He left the room amidst a graceful swirl of his black robes. JT stared after him with such dark fury in his black eyes, that the doctor, who'd been about to ask the guard to undo JT's shackles, said nothing.

JT turned his dark, furious eyes on the doctor, standing a few steps away. The man in the white coat swallowed. At five foot ten, with a slight build, he looked short and skinny standing next to JT.

"I'm nobody." The doctor fell back a couple more steps. "They just pay me to come here and do this. It's nothing personal."

JT held up his shackled hands. "Take this shit off and do what you got to do. I ain't gonna do nothing to you."

The doctor signaled nervously for the guard to remove the shackles. While the guard did that, the doctor got the injection ready. He took a vial full of clear liquid and filled a syringe.

"If you don't mind, could you sit down please?" The doctor held up the syringe.

"Sure doc, but you got to answer a question for me first," JT said, with a cold smile.

The doctor nodded. "Of course. But you needn't be concerned. The chip won't have any effect on you at all. Some people report mild dizziness within the first couple of hours. But nothing more serious than that."

JT shook his head. "It ain't that. I just wanted to know. Am I getting shot up by a bitch?"

The doctor's face went blank. "I beg your pardon?"

JT looked into the doctor's scared eyes. "I just wanna know if you ever got it up the ass before. Was it a big black guy, with a fat cock that made you scream and beg for more?"

The doctor's round white face turned beet red. The syringe in his hand shook. He looked at the guard, but he seemed to have found urgent business looking out the window, and hearing nothing at all that JT said.

JT burst into merry laughter, and sat down. "Come on over here and do me. They ain't paying you to stand around all day long looking at my black ass."

The doctor calmed his shaking hands, took JT's bicep in his sweaty hand and injected him with a blank chip.

Chapter 71

At midnight of that long day, Kyle was sitting on the leather couch in the Clubhouse. The hard, unyielding walls, roughly carved in some volcano centuries or millennia ago, surrounded the men in darkness. Dark blue candles burned all around the underground stone cave.

JT and Tyrone stood facing each other. Both men were shirtless. Their muscled bodies were tightly tense. Two men held Tyrone's hands behind him. There was no truce tonight. There would be no more talk, like two nights ago. Tonight was a night for vengeance.

"Let him go," JT said.

"You sure?" Derrick said. He was holding Tyrone's right arm in a tight grip.

JT nodded. The men let go of Tyrone. JT waved them back.

"What you gonna do?" JT said, looking at Tyrone.

"Nothing." Tyrone sounded like a sulky child. "You probably got a knife. What I got?" He held up his empty hands.

"I ain't got no knife," JT said.

Tyrone looked at the half dozen gladiators all around them. "You got your men watching your back."

JT waved them back. "Nobody come near us," JT said, looking into Tyrone's eyes.

"Whatever you say, JT," Derrick said, backing off. The other men backed up, leaving JT and Tyrone in the middle of a wide arc of men.

"You fight your way past me," JT said, "I'll let you go. Won't nothing happen to you."

"What about your men?" Tyrone said, looking around.

JT shook his head. "They do what I tell them. I say we fight, you win, you walk." JT raised his voice, talking to the gladiators. "You men heard me?"

"He wins, he walks," Dante said. "Ain't nobody gonna touch him."

Tyrone saw the eager gleam in JT's hard eyes. "I fight you tonight, you'll kill me after what I done to your boy."

JT shrugged. "Maybe. Depends on how long you think you can live with my fingers wrapped around your neck."

Tyrone had killed a man before he came to prison. Only one. He didn't see the man die. He'd shot him and left him for dead. But here in Purgatory, he'd seen plenty of men die. Death was ugly and terrifying.

"I don't wanna die man," Tyrone said in a tight voice. "I'm begging you. I'll do what you want. Don't kill me."

Kyle, who'd been watching this mini drama unfold from his place on the couch, burst out laughing. It had been over twenty four hours since he slept, and suddenly, the whole thing struck him as absurd.

Tyrone had to be crazy to think JT was going to let him go after what he did. It was the cruelest thing Kyle had ever done, but he couldn't help himself. For some unexplainable reason, the extremity of Tyrone's fear tickled him. He covered his mouth, trying to hold back his bizarre laughter.

The gladiators picked up Kyle's infectious laughter. Tyrone and JT looked at each in deathly silence, surrounded by the sharp laughter of men enjoying a cruel, but hilarious joke.

"Anything I want?" JT stepped closer to Tyrone.

"Whatever you say," Tyrone said in a low, breathy whisper.

JT stepped closer until he and Tyrone were inches apart. "Get on your knees and suck my dick like a bitch."

Silence filled every space in the stony cave. Even the sound of men breathing was gone, sucked away in the enormous quiet.

"Fuck you," Tyrone said. "I'll die first."

JT shrugged, unconcerned. "Alright." He looked at the men behind Tyrone. "Grab him."

Tyrone tried to fight, but he was far too outnumbered. The gladiators grabbed him and dragged him to a table JT had built especially for tonight. It was a heavy metal table with thick manacles built into the black metal.

"Get the bitch up there," JT said.

Seeing the cart, Tyrone understood what was going to happen to him. He struggled wildly, bucking and jumping like a wild stallion.

"No," he screamed. "Kill me. Just do me. No!" he cried over and over.

Kyle watched Tyrone from his place on the couch. He didn't move from the couch because JT had told him not get up, no matter what happened. That was fine by him. It wasn't funny anymore. Tyrone's screams had dried up Kyle's humor.

It took six gladiators to do it, but finally Tyrone was dragged to the table. The men ripped his clothes off, clawing at Tyrone until he was naked. When the six gladiators were done, Tyrone was manacled to the table, on all fours, naked, his ass up.

"Don't do it JT," Tyrone begged. "I'm sorry. Just kill me."

"Get them," JT said to Dante.

The gladiator left, taking two other men with him.

"You punked me when you fucked my bitch," JT said, standing in front of Tyrone. "I can't let it stay like that."

"You ain't got to do this." Tyrone's' voice trembled on the edge of hysterical fear.

"I'm gonna make you into a bitch tonight," JT said.

He slapped Tyrone's face hard. Blood dripped from his lips.

"I can't," Tyrone said. "I ain't never had it like that."

"They're here," Dante said from the archway.

"Bring them over here," JT said.

Dante signaled into the darkness, and the three men who'd fucked Kyle along with Tyrone walked in. They all stared at Tyrone in disbelief.

"Don't be fucking looking at me!" Tyrone screamed at them, completely unhinged at the sight of his men. "Don't look at me like this." Tyrone's screaming voice cracked.

JT turned to Tyrone's men.

"You all made me a punk when you fucked my bitch." JT looked at the man in the middle. "But when you brought my bitch a gift Terrell, you done the right thing. It's over between the three of you and me."

The three men standing at the entrance to the Clubhouse thought they had come here to die. The relief that spread over their terrified faces was clear, even in the shadowy candlelight.

JT walked over to Tyrone. "But this pathetic shit bag was your Lieutenant. He's the one who's gonna pay for what happened to my bitch. Tonight I'm gonna make Tyrone into a punk," he said. "And you're gonna be witnesses."

JT signaled to one of his men. Derrick stepped out of the darkness and handed JT a letter.

"Before I make you a bitch, I'm gonna read you a letter I got that real nice lawyer over in D Block to write."

Tyrone looked up at JT uncertainly. He couldn't imagine what a letter had to do with anything.

"You listening bitch?" JT said, looking at Tyrone. He raised his big hand to slap Tyrone again.

"Yeah," Tyrone yelled. "I'm fucking listening."

JT unfolded the letter that would give Tyrone nightmares for the rest of his life.

Chapter 72

JT read in the low quiet voice of a preacher reading Revelations. Tyrone listened as JT revealed what plagues would be poured down into his life.

Dear Father Matthew:

I am a very sinful man. I have done a lot of things that I am real sorry for. I have lied and cheated and stolen and I even killed. I have confessed my sins at the Chapel, but that is not enough. I need more help so that my sins will not be so much when I go to heaven. I know that you need men for Redemption. I am volunteering for Redemption.

Sincerely

Tyrone Rogers

By the time JT got to the word 'Redemption' the first time, Tyrone was already screaming and pleading with JT for mercy. JT signaled to Derrick, who took the letter from him and slipped it into an envelope while Tyrone watched. The envelope was clearly addressed to Father Matthew.

"Take it to his office," JT said, when Derrick had sealed the envelope with the letter inside. "Slide it under his door."

"No!" Tyrone screamed. He looked up wildly at JT. "Don't, JT. I can't get whipped like that. I ain't no bitch."

JT grabbed Tyrone's face and bent close.

"After tonight, you'll be everybody's bitch," he said, loud enough for Tyrone's watching men to hear. JT looked at Tyrone's men. "Tell everybody what you seen here tonight. Tell everybody how you seen Tyrone get it up the ass like a bitch. Tell them how he was loving every minute of it. You got it?"

The men all nodded. They would have said anything JT told them, in exchange for walking out of the Clubhouse alive.

JT unzipped his jeans, standing in front of Tyrone.

"Get over here, boy," JT said, without turning to Kyle.

Kyle hesitated a moment, unsure if he should go or not.

"It's alright, bitch," JT said, sensing the boy's hesitation. "I want you over here."

Kyle hurried to JT's side. From up close, the terror in Tyrone's eyes was electric. He looked like a man about to jump from the twentieth floor of a burning building.

JT pushed Kyle to his knees. "Get me hard so I can make him a punk," JT said.

Kyle slipped to his knees and took out JT's semi-hard cock. He licked and sucked JT, while Tyrone watched.

"I should make you suck my dick," JT said, as he slid in and out of Kyle's hot mouth. "But you might try something stupid, then I'd have to kill you and I couldn't make you a bitch."

Tyrone watched in horror as JT's thick cock slid between Kyle's lips. JT fucked Kyle's mouth, looking into Tyrone's eyes.

"You almost ready for my hard cock up your ass, punk?"

Tyrone went crazy. He struggled with the reinforced, heavy duty manacles. JT watched his useless struggles, while he fucked Kyle's mouth.

"Don't send the letter," Tyrone begged. He was openly crying. "Don't let them whip me like that. They beat you like a animal, man. Don't do it. I'm sorry I fucked your bitch. I'm sorry."

"You ain't sorry yet," JT said, sliding his dick in and out of Kyle's mouth.

"Go on and fuck me," Tyrone said. "As hard as you want. I don't care. But don't let them whip like I ain't nothing but a animal, man. Come on, I'm begging you."

He looked up at JT with big ugly tears rolling down his terrified face.

"It's gonna hurt a lot when they whip your punk ass. The whole fucking country's gonna see you scream and beg like the bitch you are." JT pulled his hard cock out of Kyle's mouth. "I'm ready for your punk ass."

JT pulled Kyle to his feet and shoved him hard. "Back to the couch."

JT got behind Tyrone and looked up at Tyrone's men, watching their leader about to fall as low as a man like Tyrone could fall in Purgatory. It would have been kinder if JT had killed Tyrone.

"Tell everybody what you seen tonight," JT said, putting the head of his cock against Tyrone's ass.

"I ain't no bitch," Tyrone screamed.

"Tonight, you're my bitch," JT said, opening Tyrone's ass. "You're my fucking punk tonight."

JT pressed the head of his cock to Tyrone's ass, then plunged deep into him, with no mercy. He raped Tyrone savagely. JT clenched his teeth, driving hard into Tyrone, forcing his thick cock deep into the screaming man's ass. Tyrone cried out, struggling desperately with the manacles. Every muscle in his body stood out. He was bathed in sweat. His eyes were squeezed tightly shut, while JT plowed into him with a furious rage that spoke of vengeance, not desire.

Kyle watched in horror, hearing Tyrone's screams wash over him in waves of despair and anguish. Tyrone's torment came from him in a screaming rapture of animal fear, until finally his head hung limply between his muscular arms, waiting for JT to be done.

"Fucking punk," JT said through clenched teeth, driving so hard into Tyrone, the metal table shook.

Tyrone cried out, throwing his head back, howling at the ceiling when he felt JT's hot come shoot into him. His life in Purgatory was over.

The moment the watching men got the word out, Tyrone would be ruined forever. JT had made him into a punk, a bitch. The only thing Tyrone could hope for now was that the man who bought him wouldn't beat him too often or fuck him too hard.

JT pulled out of Tyrone, and walked to the other end of the table.

"Take off the brakes," JT said, pulling his jeans back on.

Dante bent and made some adjustment to the wheeled table.

"Let's take the bitch home," JT said, rolling the table toward Tyrone's men.

Tyrone's men followed after JT and Dante, rolling Tyrone on the table. They went through long, twisting tunnels that rose upward gently, avoiding the stairs. Tyrone was quiet until he recognized where they were taking him.

"No," he started screaming. "Don't, JT. Not there."

"You best be quiet bitch, unless you wanna wake up the whole tier," JT said quietly.

They rolled Tyrone around twisting turns and narrow stone halls until they emerged in the main prison.

"Here?" Dante said, looking at JT.

They were on the bottom of Tyrone's tier. Row upon row of cells rose above them. Any man who looked through his bars would be able to look down and see Tyrone on the table.

"Yeah," JT said. "Let's turn on some lights."

They locked the table in place and went to the empty guard house. JT had arranged for the guard not to be there for the next fifteen minutes. That's all it would take to destroy Tyrone completely in Purgatory.

While JT found the main light switch for the tier, Dante was busy with Tyrone.

"You look so nice like that bitch, with JT's come dripping out your asshole, maybe I'll try out that ass," Dante said, reaching for his zipper.

Tyrone screamed for help, forgetting where he was, just like JT said he would. Men on the tier started waking up. JT waited one more minute, then he flipped the main light switch. The tier was flooded with full light. Men came to their cell bars, puzzled.

"Hey," Dante said loudly. "JT made Tyrone into a punk. Anybody who wants this bitch, come and get her."

Dante laid a metal key on the table between Tyrone's legs, where he couldn't possibly reach it.

JT's cum dripped from Tyrone's ass.

"Get me off this," Tyrone yelled at his men.

But they looked at him in disgust and melted away. The tier was filled with cat calls from the men in their cells, telling Tyrone what a pretty bitch he was gonna make. Tyrone hung his head and cried. Kyle was the most expensive piece of ass he'd ever had. And his last.

Chapter 73

"Guess this is it," JT said, not looking at Dante.

"Yeah," Dante said.

"Everything's ready?"

"Kyle's at the infirmary with the doc. Matthew can't do nothing about it 'til tomorrow. And the doc says they're gonna be waiting for you and your boy."

"All I gotta do is win The Maze," JT said.

"There's something I got to tell you."

"What?" JT said.

"Kyle gave me a weird message for you. With everything that's been going on, I forgot."

JT nearly stopped breathing. "What?"

Dante told him about playing the harp. "That make sense to you?" he said.

JT remembered Kyle telling him on the roof that he wouldn't fix their harp, even if it meant he suffered in Purgatory the rest of his life. Kyle's words went through his mind, *sometimes life sucks*. JT leaned his head back against the brick wall and closed his eyes.

"That's all he said?"

"Yeah," Dante said. "He figured it out, didn't he?"

"Yeah," JT said.

"He's a real good bitch. Take care of him. Or I'll find my way out and hunt you down," Dante said.

"I got something for you." JT looked past Dante into the darkness. "Come out here, boy."

Taylor emerged from the shadows, looking at both men.

"You mad at me, Sir? That's how come you brought me down here?"

JT's dark eyes fell on Taylor. "I keep my promises boy. Best I can do is give you to Dante. Or you can take your chances in a auction. Derrick can afford to buy you."

Taylor looked up at Dante, and stepped closer. "I'll be with you, if you want me."

Dante's dark face broke into a small smile. He ran his rough fingers across Taylor's soft cheek. "Yeah, boy. I'll make you my bitch."

Taylor looked up at JT. "Thank you." He leaned close and solemnly kissed JT's rough cheek.

JT couldn't bring a smile to his face. Not tonight. "Go wait for us where I told you."

Taylor faded into the darkness again. Dante watched him go. "He's a sweet bitch."

JT looked at Dante. "How long we been running together, man?"

"Long time," Dante said, in a quiet whisper.

"Now you got what you always wanted." JT looked down at the filthy concrete. "Your own territory. You always knew it was gonna be yours. They'll let you have a bitch. With me gone, Matthew ain't gonna pull no shit with you, unless he wants a gang war on his hands."

"Won't be the same without you."

"Why it got to be like this Dante? Why we always got to give up something to get something else we really want?"

Dante was quiet for a long time. "You and your boy gonna be real happy when you wake up tomorrow and you ain't in this fucking hole," he finally said. "Take it for what it is, JT. Some men never get nothing that makes them happy."

Both men fell into silence, then Dante said, "Fucking Father's gonna be pissed as all shit when he don't find you nowhere tomorrow."

That made both men smile for a moment.

JT's low voice had a note of desperation. "There's gotta be a way –"

Dante shook his head slowly, making his dreads wave. "Ain't no way for nothing man. I got a chip. Take me with you and you're dead in the water."

"But –" JT was nearly pleading.

"I'm gonna miss you man."

Dante walked away, swallowing painfully past the lump in his throat.

"Dante –" JT started to go after his best friend who'd risked his life for him, shared everything with him since they were ten years old.

But Dante shook his head slowly without turning around and raised his hand to his friend. "Peace," he said.

Taylor came out of the darkness and walked beside Dante. The last time JT saw his friend, he was taking Taylor by the hand and talking to him in a soft low voice that JT knew he would never hear again.

Chapter 74

JT looked down at the Four Horsemen of the Apocalypse that guarded the entrance to the Maze. They were all that stood between him and freedom.

Death, War, Famine and Victory galloped straight out of the black stone wall, six feet above the Maze. The incredible sculpture seemed to float on air. The horses rushed out of eternity to wreak havoc on the four corners of the world.

The angels of destruction were shirtless men sculpted in brutal strength. Their naked muscled legs gripped their mounts with brute strength. War bent over his mount, the ultimate warrior, his great sword high, his handsome face twisted into a wicked grin.

Famine rode hard on the heels of War. Desperate hunger and cunning twisted his lean face into a leering mask of pain and madness. Death led the galloping pack of dark angels, eager to gather luckless souls to his realm of shadows. Victory flanked Death, his bow and arrow riding high on his muscular back.

JT heard the murmuring crowd. Only the very rich could afford to be here and watch the Maze in person. All over the country and in all the occupied lands, giant holograms of the Maze stood in theaters, surrounded by eager audiences, hungry for the sight of blood and mayhem. The holograms would be nearly as real as sitting here in Purgatory. The only thing missing would be the scent of sweat and blood from the gladiators.

A soft bell sounded. JT closed his eyes. Five minutes to game time. He felt the other gladiators nearby. Four cages hung above the Maze, in darkness, just beyond the sight of the crowd. They would be lowered to four different quadrants inside the Maze. Only when they were on the ground in the Maze and the cages opened, would the dim lights of the labyrinth come to life.

JT waited, fighting the urge to grow restless. He pushed back the doctor's words – *win the Maze, JT. Or it's all over.* Those thoughts were nothing but distractions. Kyle's face tried to surface in his mind, but JT pushed it away. This wasn't the time.

He thought instead of the three men in the other cages. They were men from other prisons across the country, Regional Champions, just like him. He'd seen all of them fight. This would be a brutal game. There was only one rule in the Maze – aim to maim, not to kill. It was blood sport taken to the extreme.

A knife was the only weapon allowed. JT clutched his knife tightly in his fist. The curved weapon had a smooth inner edge. The outer edge was lined with teeth, designed to rip and tear flesh right down to the bone. JT had designed it himself in the machine shop. He'd practiced with it for weeks.

He looked down at the dark angels riding out from the wall and closed his eyes, calling up the darkness within him. The red tide of fury that lived inside him would be his salvation tonight. He let it flow through him like molten lava, igniting his blood. He saw himself on a black horse, his sword raised high, like a demon fresh from Hell, eager to harvest the Devil's fields. Tonight, JT was War, the ultimate warrior.

A slight jerk told JT the cage was being slowly lowered into the Maze. The cage slid lower and lower until it finally settled on the floor with a gentle thump. JT stood back, his knife gripped in his hand, his whole body relaxed, his mind focused on the dark work ahead.

"Ladies and Gentlemen," the announcer's voice boomed in the arena. "Let the battle begin!"

The door on JT's cage rose slowly. The crowd roared as the lights in the Maze came up. A dull yellow glow filled the Maze with dim shadows.

JT stepped out of his cage, and crouched low, listening. He heard the soft murmur of the audience. His lithe body gleamed in the low light, outlined in dark muscle, a shadow among shadows. He had no idea where the other men were. A panel beside him, flush with the stone wall, had a green arrow pointing right. There would be four arrows all together. The next three would light up when JT conquered the gladiator in each corner of the Maze.

JT slowly rounded the corner, going the way the arrow pointed. He stopped and listened, heard nothing, and kept going, one slow step at a time. A collective gasp from the audience made JT draw back an instant before a shadow leapt up in front of him.

The other gladiator was Striker, Southern Regional Champion. He stood an inch taller than JT, heavily muscled, deeply tanned bronze skin. His teeth were bared and his knife slashed down at JT, barely missing him in the dark shadows.

JT jumped back, avoiding the knife that slashed an inch away from his eyes. He fell back a step, drawing his enemy closer. A platform was one, maybe two steps behind him. His enemy came at him again, this time swiping low and fast, going for his knees. JT took a gamble and jumped back and up. He landed on hard stone, gaining a sudden three inch advantage on Striker.

The crowd roared as JT's knife came down across Striker's forehead, gouging deep through flesh, all the way to the bone. The gladiator fell back screaming. A screen of blood covered his eyes.

"Back down," JT whispered when the man got up. "Don't make me hurt you bad."

"Fuck you," the man said, struggling to his feet. Striker wiped blood from his eyes. But it was useless, more dripped from the cut in his forehead, blinding him with stinging pain.

When he swiped clumsily, JT rammed his knee hard into Striker's balls. Striker doubled over, screaming again, both hands pressed to his crotch. JT knocked Striker's knife out of his hand and kicked it away. It went skittering into the darkness.

As JT watched Striker writhing on the floor in pain, he felt the power of the darkness rising within him. Tonight was a night of extremes. The monsters of rage within him were like tigers straining against thick chains. JT let slip the dogs of war within him. The arena was their turf. The Maze was their game; and they hungered.

He rode the wave of wild ecstasy that came with the thrill of the hunt. JT's dark muscled body seemed to swell even bigger. He raised both hands over his head and let out a battle cry. The audience roared back at him, demanding more blood. Any man who stood in JT's way tonight would regret it.

Chapter 75

In the infirmary, Kyle watched the game nervously on holo. The doctor came in occasionally to check on him. But the truth was, every time the doctor gave him a shot, Kyle felt worse. He'd been feeling good today, until JT gave him a pill that made him sick as a dog.

He sent Kyle to the infirmary, where Dr. Maxell had been keeping a close watch on him all day. Something was wrong. Kyle felt it in the way the doctor took his pulse, the way he kept looking at him. Doctors were supposed to make you feel better. Everything Dr. Maxell did made Kyle feel worse.

Dr. Maxell stood beside him, watching the game with tight concentration. Nothing was happening yet. The gladiators were still suspended in the dark somewhere above the Maze. Kyle knew that JT hung somewhere in the darkness. Somehow he knew that JT *had* to win tonight's game.

"I didn't think a doctor would like the games so much," Kyle said carefully. His head ached and pounded. It hurt just to talk.

"They're barbaric bloodletting that will be remembered forever as a stain on our history in this shameful period we're living through," the doctor said with undisguised disgust.

That took Kyle by surprise. It was the last thing he'd expected the doctor to say. Especially since Dr. Maxell was watching the game with nearly unblinking attention.

The door to this area of the infirmary swung open. Kyle didn't have a private room, but his bed was the only occupied bed on the floor. Father Matthew swept in. Kyle noticed that the doctor immediately became a different man. His face turned cold and harsh, his eyes glazed over with cool frost. Everything about him said how much he hated Matthew and all men like him.

"Good evening doctor," Matthew said, looking into Dr. Maxell's cold eyes. "I trust your patient is well?"

"If he was, he wouldn't be here," Dr. Maxell said, checking Kyle's pupils with a tiny light, even though he'd just done it not five minutes before.

"What's wrong with the poor boy?" Matthew said, looking at Kyle.

Kyle looked away quickly. Something about Matthew made his skin crawl. He couldn't stand for the Father Confessor to even get near him.

"Fever, vomiting, diarrhea," Dr. Maxell said.

Matthew stepped closer to Kyle. "What's the cause?"

Dr. Maxell shrugged. "Maybe the shitty food you serve here. Maybe if you acted like the prisoners were men instead of cattle, they wouldn't get sick in this hell hole you call a prison."

Kyle's green eyes grew wide. He couldn't believe Dr. Maxell had talked to Father Matthew like that. He looked at the holo, pretending he didn't hear the doctor's answer.

"Such a Good Samaritan you are doctor." Matthew stood beside the bed and looked closely at Kyle. "You feel unwell, boy?"

"His name's Kyle," Dr. Maxell said.

Father Matthew didn't turn around. He looked down at Kyle with an unblinking, unnerving stare, waiting for an answer.

"I feel really bad, Sir," Kyle said, telling the truth.

"I'm sorry to hear that, boy." Matthew put a delicate emphasis on the last word. "I hope you'll be feeling better soon."

"Me too, Sir," Kyle mumbled. He wanted to look Matthew in the face, but he couldn't stand the thought of those dark, cold eyes boring into him.

"You have an excellent doctor," Matthew said. "But you know what the problem is with doctors?"

"No, Sir." Kyle looked down at his fidgeting fingers.

"Sometimes, they lose perspective and help those who've been deemed sinners by those who know better than they do. They like to help the sewage of society. Your doctor is a collector of human garbage. That's why he's here in a garbage dump for men. He thinks he can do some good."

Matthew said all of this in the kind tones a man would use when talking to the very sick, and commending those giving him good care.

Dr. Maxell's eyes filled with dark hatred. Kyle was sure that if the doctor had a knife, Father Matthew would be telling God his prayers in person.

"He's tired," Dr. Maxell said. His face had turned bright red with the effort to control his temper. "Leave him alone. He needs to rest."

"Of course." Matthew turned and looked at the doctor. "Your work is very important to someone, I'm sure."

Dr. Maxell glared at Matthew in silence, clearly waiting for him to get out.

"Enjoy the game, boy," Matthew said, turning to go.

He left, closing the door softly behind him.

"What was he doing here?" Kyle said.

"He smells something rotten in the cotton."

"What?"

"He suspects something's up, but he doesn't know what it is."

When Kyle looked up at Dr. Maxell, he was filling a syringe.

"Oh no," Kyle said, dismayed. "Not another shot. They make me feel bad."

"I know." Dr. Maxell tapped the syringe. "I can't risk you feeling any better. Not yet. You're about to feel worse. I'm sorry."

He took Kyle's arm and slid the needle into his vein.

Chapter 76

JT slowly crept along dark stone walls, every sense alert, his eyes finely tuned to the shadows all around. Up ahead, a corner loomed, as dangerous as a cliff hanging over an acid sea.

The Maze was color coded. He was entering the blue quadrant. That meant another gladiator could be waiting for him, unless the gladiator was somewhere else in the Maze. He saw a shadow move among the shadows and knew that the next gladiator waited for him. He didn't want the audience to warn the other man as they'd warned him.

He sped up, running heedlessly to the corner, as though he were about to run recklessly around the corner. Just as he knew they would, the audience roared, anticipating the coming fight. At the last moment, JT stopped short and backed away two steps. He pressed against the wall, and became still, slowing his breathing, melting into the dark shadows. The audience fell into near silence, waiting for the next thrill.

JT saw the other gladiator creep slowly around the corner. Bad mistake. JT was on him in an instant, before the crowd could react and destroy the element of surprise. He grabbed the man around the waist and slammed him into the opposite wall, knocking the breath from him. The audience went wild, chanting JT's name.

JT recognized the other man's blonde hair. He was Razor Edge, Western Regional Champion. Before Edge had a chance to recover, JT kicked hard at his ankle, feeling bone crunch. As the man fell to his knees, JT brought his elbow down in a savage arc in the middle of the man's back. The other gladiator fell to the floor in a heap, his ankle broken. He was out of the fight. Two down, one to go. *The fun ain't even half started yet*, JT thought.

JT walked by the blue arrow, going the way the arrow pointed. He crept around corners, until he got to a narrow lane that he thought must cross the Maze from East to West. He was on his way to the other side of the Maze, where the last gladiator waited for him.

Instinct told JT that the hardest fight lay just ahead. Three loud bells sounded. A platform emerged from the floor in front of JT. He hopped up, like they'd taught him in Maze training. JT watched the walls of the Maze start moving and shifting around him. This was part of the game. The Maze could change at any time.

Walls slipped into the ground, while other walls slid into place, changing the configuration of the Maze. The trick was to keep going in the same direction, even when the walls moved. After a minute or two, the new walls settled in place. Three bells sounded again, and JT hopped down off the platform.

JT stood still, getting a sense of the new walls around him. He felt the air on his naked back coming from different directions. The shift of air on his back told him that a new path had opened in that direction. Before him, no subtle breeze of air came, telling him it was a dead end up ahead.

In the grip of the powerful dark tide, his senses were heightened. The air currents made a map in his mind that he followed with unerring steps, rounding corners slowly, creeping with catlike grace along walls in the low, yellow light.

JT stopped, sniffing the air. The subtle scent of sweat and the stink of fear was just up ahead. His last opponent in the Maze was feet away. JT moved with light steps, turning every few steps to make sure that no one moved in behind him.

The last place that JT expected a threat to come from was the dark ground at his feet. He was utterly surprised when a strong hand grabbed his ankle and twisted hard.

Chapter 77

Kyle woke up to the voices of arguing men. His head ached horribly and sweat coated his whole body.

"The whole place is on lock down 'til after the game. Sorry, doc. No exceptions. Only injured gladiators get out before the game's over. The kid's got to wait."

"That's impossible," Dr. Maxell said, asserting his authority as Kyle's doctor. "He's running Van Dam's fever. His temperature rises to dangerous levels."

There was no such thing as 'Van Dam's fever', but Dr. Maxell counted on the guard's sixth grade education not covering medical school jargon.

"I never heard of Van Dam's fever," the guard said.

"Is that right?" Dr. Maxell said, looking at the guard with cold eyes. "What medical school did you attend?"

Kyle realized he wasn't in the infirmary anymore. He was somewhere near the main gate. The doctor was trying to get him out of Purgatory. He tried to get up and see where he was exactly but his head nearly exploded with pain. He groaned and let his head fall back to the soft, inviting pillow, and listened.

"He can't stay here," Dr. Maxell was saying. "His fever goes too high. He needs to be monitored on equipment that I don't have here or his brain will cook in his head."

Dr. Maxell showed the guard a red slip of paper. "I have authorization," he said. "Do you want to be the one to explain how a nineteen year old kid died on your shift because you wouldn't let him go out in an ambulance?"

The guard grabbed the paper and looked it over.

"Time's wasting," Dr. Maxell said, sounding unconcerned. "But it'll be on your conscience, not mine."

"Says here, he got a chip. Is that right?"

Dr. Maxell nodded. "Yes."

"Shit," the guard said, stepping back. "Why didn't you say so? Go on. Take him."

He stepped back into his little booth and pressed a button. The main gates of Purgatory Prison opened and Dr. Maxell wheeled Kyle to freedom.

"It's almost over for you kid," Dr. Maxell said to Kyle softly.

Chapter 78

Only JT's cat like reflexes saved him from a broken ankle. He moved with the twist, letting himself fall, taking his weight on his hands. His knife went skittering across the stone floor, out of his reach.

The crowd was on it's feet, cheering, applauding. The other gladiator rolled on top of JT the moment he hit the floor. JT felt the swish of air as the gladiator raised his knife to carve into his back and shoulder. JT knew he couldn't avoid the blade completely. He waited until the last second, then rocked back hard, throwing the man off balance, so that only the tip of his knife raked a shallow cut across his back.

JT got his hands under him and pushed hard, toppling the man on his back. He jumped to his feet and slammed his foot into the man's ribs. But the gladiator was too fast for him. He rolled away and only the tip of JT's booth grazed his ribs. The powerful blow hitting nothing but air nearly sent JT flying backward, but he caught himself and smiled. This was going to be fun.

The gladiator came at JT, overly confident because JT's knife was gone. He didn't know that JT could do more damage with his bare hands than most men could do armed to the teeth. JT back pedaled, letting his enemy think he had him on the run. The gladiator, Wicked Kane, was no fool. His jet black hair hung around his face, his hulking body was a match for JT. Kane pulled up short, not fooled by JT's backward steps.

"Come on," JT said, taunting him. "What you scared of? I ain't got no knife."

He made little 'come on' gestures with his hands.

The other man fell back "I seen you fight, JT. You're a animal. I ain't going out like that."

"Then drop the knife and make it easy on yourself. I won't hurt you too bad."

"Fuck you," the other man said.

JT shrugged, and went into a low couch. "I knew you was gonna say that."

The two men circled each other, but only one of them was waiting for an opening. JT could have taken Kane any time, but he wanted a sure strike. He wanted this over. No more fucking around.

The other man didn't have JT's patience. He came in hard and low. JT jumped back, taking a shallow cut on his hard belly.

"That all you got, punk?"

Kane fell back. JT saw the anger in his eyes. Anger in an enemy was good. It made men do dumb things.

They circled each other again. JT's big body looked relaxed. But his mind was flying a mile a second. He saw everything with that primitive ease that came to him in every fight. Kane was going to lose for one reason: he was afraid to get hurt. JT had no fear. He could deal with getting hurt. He just didn't want to get dead. Not tonight.

JT kicked out, aiming for his opponent's right knee. Kane jumped back, avoiding JT's decoy kick. The moment his enemy jumped to the left to avoid his kick, JT was there with a hard kick to his ribs. Before the other man could bring his knife up, JT kicked out again, aiming for his knife hand. JT connected and felt bone shatter in Kane's fingers. Kane screamed. The knife slipped from his injured hand.

JT's next two devastating kicks landed on the man's right knee, then found the center of his belly. When his enemy doubled over, JT came at him with vicious force and drove his fist hard into Kane's face, crushing his nose. Wicked Kane fell back in a spray of blood. JT jumped on top him, straddling him.

The crowd was on it's feet, roaring, jumping up and down, crying out JT's name in a thunderous wave of sound that rocked the stone arena.

JT bent low and whispered in the man's ear. "You had enough, or you gonna get up?"

The man turned his head to one side and said in a voice distorted by his broken nose, "Enough."

JT jumped up, assured of his victory and headed for the yellow path. A path of yellow light that led out of the Maze had lit up, when JT's opponent showed no signs of going after him. He was the winner. He trotted along the road, smiling to the audience, wondering how the fuck the doctor was gonna get him out of Purgatory tonight.

JT reached the gate that would let him back into the main arena. It slid up slowly. JT ducked under it. The moment he ducked under the iron gate, pitch blackness fell in the arena. A voice was beside him in the darkness.

"Don't move JT. We're getting you out."

JT nearly knocked the man behind the voice to the ground before he could stop himself. But he relaxed and let himself be led through the dark confusion. People were running back and forth, alarms sounded, the audience was in a hysterical panic.

Some idiot jumped down into the arena. JT heard bone crunch as he landed on the stone floor. Two men guided JT through the chaos and confusion, one on each side of him. They moved quickly and silently. They had to have night vision contacts in. They could obviously see in the dark. They came to a sudden stop.

"There's a gurney behind you. Take two steps back and lay down."

JT did as he was told. The second he lay down, he felt tight straps fitted in place across his body.

"Say goodnight, JT," a voice to his left said.

He felt a cold needle slide into his arm and within moments, darkness fell. The men set to work with professional precision, in silence, carefully 'painting' the white sheet they laid over JT's sleeping body.

Chapter 79

Rob Tomiko loved his job at Purgatory Prison. He was outside guard. He sat in his little booth, let people with the right papers in and out, then went home at night to the mainland. Purgatory even ferried him back and forth. He lived real close to the ferry. He walked there. He didn't have to spend a couple hundred bucks a week in gas like most people.

Most nights, he sat here in his little booth, reading comic strips, and snacking on black market stuff the Father gave him. Sometimes he helped the Father out and didn't see certain people come and go. The Father helped him out with all the black market stuff Rob's considerable gut could stand. But tonight, Rob's peace was being ruined. First the kid and the doc. Now a Class One, Red – a hurt gladiator who had to get out.

"Are you deaf?" the medic was yelling at him. "Can't you see this guy's dying?"

Rob looked out his window at the gurney. A huge red splotch covered the front of the guy. Roses of blood were on his legs.

"I got eyes," Rob said, putting down his comic book. "Why can't he go to the damn infirmary?"

"Too serious," the other medic said. He was fiddling with some fancy medical equipment. "Shit," he muttered. "He's about to go flat line. If that idiot doesn't let us out, JT's a dead man."

"JT?" Rob said. He followed the games like religion. The only thing his damn booth didn't have was a holo player. "He's hurt?"

"He's almost *dead*," the medic snapped back at him, pressing buttons on a pack snapped on the side of JT's cart.

"How long?" the other medic said.

"I make it –" the guy checked some read outs, "ten minutes to total failure."

"Total failure?" Rob said from the depths of his sixth grade education.

"He's going fast," the other medic said, not looking up from his screens.

"It's a Class One, Red. He's got a chip. What else do you want?"

Rob looked at his authorization list for the second time. JT's chip showed on his reader. The frequency was a little low, but no big deal. Class One Red was the only clearance he had. He needed final clearance from Father Matthew, but the interior of Purgatory was on a fucking rolling black out. All communications were down. Damn.

"Whatever the fuck you're doing, do it fast," the medic at JT's side yelled. A loud buzzing sounded. "Goddamn it!" the medic said, and pulled something from his pack.

The other medic looked at Rob. "Are you gonna let a man die on your shift because there's a blackout?"

Rob bit his lip. He couldn't let JT die. He'd explain to the Father. Matthew was a good guy. He'd understand.

Rob's hand wavered over the button, then with a final decision, he let his hand fall. The gates of Purgatory swung open.

Chapter 80

JT woke up to cold, wet wind blowing in his face. A hard hand was slapping his face. He reached up and took hold of the offending hand, bending it back.

"Hey!" the hand's owner said, "what the fuck? You're gonna break my wrist."

JT remembered the Maze, the gurney, the needle in his arm and let go, before the man's wrist broke.

He sat up. He was on the bottom of a boat. He reached up for the earring.

"It's gone," Dr. Maxell said. "We threw it overboard."

Kyle came running through the men, pushing them aside.

"What's happening, JT?" Kyle said, kneeling beside him. "They won't tell me anything."

JT looked up at the doctor and the men standing around. "Give me a minute with my boy."

"Two minutes," Dr. Maxell said. "The clock's ticking."

JT got to his feet, and pulled Kyle up beside him. A cold wind whipped across the boat. Icy waters lapped at the sides. Two men in scuba suits waited in the water, looking up at Kyle and JT.

"What's going on?" Kyle said. "You can't do this. Take me with you, and they'll find you. I told you about my chip."

"You trust me, boy?" JT said quietly, looking into Kyle's green eyes in the light of the full moon.

"Yeah," Kyle said in a low, scared voice. The wind whipped his red hair all about his beautiful face. "I trust you with my life."

"It don't matter what happens tonight, boy. I love you. I always loved you the best of all the boys I ever been with."

"We're running out of time, JT," Dr. Maxell's voice said behind them.

A short man in glasses came up beside JT and Kyle. "You have to be the one who does it, JT. Everyone does his own."

"Do what?" Kyle said, looking from the man in glasses to JT. "What's happening?" He backed away from JT, suddenly very afraid.

JT shut his eyes a moment and prayed to whatever God there was, begging forgiveness for what he was about to do. He grabbed Kyle hard and hurled the boy into the roiling waters. Two men in scuba suits caught Kyle and pushed the screaming, struggling boy beneath the waves.

"Don't watch," the man behind JT said. "It's too hard." He tried to pull JT back from the edge of the boat, but JT pushed him away, sending the man back pedaling nearly to the other side of the boat.

JT watched as the men in the water held Kyle down under the frigid water. The boy came up a few times, but he had no chance with the two men forcing him down into the icy waters. Finally, after an eternity that JT spent in Hell, Kyle's lifeless body floated between them.

"Move," a harsh voice behind JT said.

The men in scuba suits handed Kyle up out of the water. Men swarmed around him. Tiny metal sensors attached to cups were pressed to Kyle's chest. A machine beeped a flat monotonous tone.

"Flat line. Start the count," a voice said.

"Five seconds," someone else said.

They moved around Kyle too fast for JT to follow everything that was happening to his boy.

"Charged," the man in glasses who'd talked to JT said. "I'm on a five second count. Time," he said, looking up at a man with a stop watch.

"Thirty seconds," the man said.

"Fuck it," JT said, fighting the urge to charge into the midst of the men. "Bring him back. Now!"

"Can't, JT. Too soon. You're not helping. Let us do what we know how to do."

"Time!" someone shouted.

The answer came back fast. "Forty five seconds."

The men went into high gear. Machines came to life, tiny screens showed flat lines. JT was no doctor, but he knew what a fucking flat line meant.

"Charging," someone shouted.

"Fifty five seconds," came the response.

"Five, four, three, two, one – clear!"

The man pressed paddles to Kyle. The boy's lifeless body jumped once. All the men were silent, watching the computer screens.

"Flat line."

"Shit."

"Charging. Five seconds," the man with the paddles shouted.

JT watched in an agony of fear. They were the longest five seconds of his life. His eyes focused over and over on Kyle's soft lips, now an ugly shade of blue.

"Do something!" JT shouted.

"Clear!"

The paddles came again. Kyle jumped again.

"Talk to me," the man with the paddles said.

"Flat line."

"Fucking shit," a low, frustrated voice said.

"Bring my boy back!" JT shouted.

"Five seconds!"

JT had fallen into Hell. He was sure of it. They'd go on all night shouting at each other, and shocking his boy until nothing but a charred black husk was left. He was about to charge into the middle of them and grab Kyle and start killing them all. After all, he had nothing to live for now. His freedom meant nothing without Kyle.

"Clear!"

The horrible sound of Kyle's body arching and falling to the deck came again.

"I got a pulse," someone shouted.

"Get him juiced. Fast."

Again, the men worked as an incredibly fast, well trained team. They all did something different to Kyle.

The air was filled with the men shouting at each other.

"Pressure's rising."

Needles glided into both arms.

"Pulse rising."

The monitors started flashing cryptic messages.

"Respiration weak, but steady."

"He alright?" JT said, nearly too weak to talk. His heart was doing a little jig of it's own in his chest.

"Don't know yet," someone said without turning around.

They worked on Kyle for long minutes. Then Kyle's eyes flew open. His hands came up in weak flailing gestures, as if he thought the men were trying to drown him all over again.

He coughed weakly onto the deck. They turned him onto his side and JT saw a thin stream of liquid come from his lips.

"Clear his lungs," someone shouted.

"Got it," another voice answered.

They turned Kyle onto his back roughly and ran a thin tube down his throat. One man fended off the boy's weak struggles while another man held the tube firmly in place. He flicked something behind him and in seconds the clear tube was filled with liquid coming out of Kyle. That lasted only a minute. They pulled out the tube and shined lights into Kyle's eyes.

"What's your name?"

"Kyle," he said hoarsely. "Who the hell are you? Dr. Electro?"

"You're back from the land of the dead, kid," the man said. "How's the other side?"

"Cold and wet," Kyle croaked.

"Scan him," someone said.

All the men fell silent. Cold wind whipped across the roiling waters. This was the moment of truth. This was the reason JT had thrown Kyle into the dark cold depths and risked losing the only thing he had ever cared about. JT held his breath, watching the monitor as the man ran the Chip Scan up and down Kyle's body.

He did it once, twice, three times. The monitor behind him stayed dead and unresponsive.

"He's off the radar," the man said quietly, and looked up at JT. "You and the kid are free."

221

Kyle suddenly understood everything. He knew now why JT had thrown him into the water.

After they ran a few more tests, they dried off Kyle and wrapped him in a thermo blanket. Someone picked him up and handed him into JT's strong arms.

"If this is hell, then that's alright," Kyle said in his scratchy voice, looking up at JT.

"It ain't hell boy, else you wouldn't be here. Me, yeah. But not you," JT said. He kissed Kyle's forehead tenderly. "How you feel?"

"A little like Frankenstein's monster, I guess."

"You talk some weird shit, boy." JT carried Kyle to a far side of the boat.

"Why didn't you tell me?" It hurt Kyle's sore throat badly to talk.

"I didn't want you to be scared," JT said quietly. "You mad at me?"

Kyle shook his head. "I always heard the chip could be deactivated like this, but I never knew anyone who tried it."

"The doc said, lots of adrenaline stuff in your blood, no heartbeat for sixty seconds, the water turned you ice cold. That's all it took. The chip thought you was dead and turned itself off. They can't turn it back on, right?"

"No. They'd have to send a pulse to every chip in the country. Some people would have heart attacks, other people would die outright. They can't."

"Then we're free," JT said.

Kyle back looked over JT's broad shoulders. "How come they're not chasing us down?"

"Can't," JT said, smiling a little. "These people are good. Rolling blackout. A bad one. Even their radios don't work. By the time they're back up, we're long gone."

"We're free." Kyle looked over JT's big shoulders, back at Purgatory.

The dark mountain of Purgatory Prison rose up from the roiling waters, like a monument to unforgiven souls, risen from the depths of hell.

Kyle looked up at JT. "I love you."

"You're mine, boy," JT said.

He pulled Kyle close, settled back in the boat. They looked at the skyline of the city a few miles away. A new life, filled with new dangers waited for them there.

The moon beat a path across the waves, and Kyle knew it was the bridge into forever.